CRIMSON

CRIMSON

A NOVEL

ARTHUR SLADE

HarperCollins*Publishers*Ltd

For Tanaya

CRIMSON

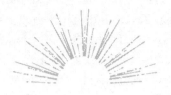

PROLOGUE

Fᴇɴ ᴅɪᴅ ɴᴏᴛ sᴛʀᴜɢɢʟᴇ ᴀs sʜᴇ ᴡᴀᴛᴄʜᴇᴅ ᴛʜᴇ Qᴜᴇᴇɴ's guard dismount from his charger and draw the blade that would soon sever her hand. She was in the middle of the village square, in the middle of her eleventh summer, and despite the fear in her heart, she decided the guard was the most beautiful and perfect man she had ever seen: he was slim, ivory-skinned and wide-shouldered. He towered over the villagers as they parted to let him through.

His golden eagle diadem, a symbol that he was an extension of the Queen, held his shoulder-length hair out of his eyes. That hair was a bright red, as were the locks of all Queen Servilia's elite guardsmen. The colour was a sign of the magic that had shaped him.

His armour shone, detailing every chest muscle. There were tales the metal was poured directly onto the guards' flesh—an impenetrable skin. The Royal Red Artificers, the only crafters allowed to shape magic, had designed the armour. Even if the suit was penetrated, the wounds of the Queen's guards were said to heal in moments, due to the Queen's blood in their veins.

Fen just wanted to touch the armour. Once. And the hair too.

Her own hair was dark and long, her skin a yellowish brown. Much the same colour as every other villagers'. They were the people of Village Twenty-One, the workers of the red earth mines and the rice fields. The Queen's guard looked as if he had stepped down from the heavens.

"Keep very still," Fen's mother whispered. She pressed her daughter's right arm against the execution block. Lin was a wiry woman; a lifetime of working in the mines had tightened every muscle. But the wrinkles around her eyes didn't hide her tears. She'd chosen to be at her daughter's side instead of letting another villager do this duty. "I won't see you as a thief. You'll always be my child, whether you have one hand or two. But don't steal again. We don't need pretty things."

"I know, Mama," Fen breathed. "It was stupid. Stupid."

Moments earlier, Lin had slipped Fen a ginger stone. It burned sweetly on Fen's tongue.

"Swallow that candy, my dear." Lin's voice was gentle. "You don't want to choke on it." Fen bit into the soft centre, all the while staring at the approaching Queen's guard. He moved with such magnificence. No wonder the Queen's enemies broke at the sight of a charging column of these red-haired sentries. Fen swallowed the remains of the ginger stone in one gulp.

"Be as strong as a horse," her mother intoned. "Be as brave as a tiger." It was an old saying.

Fen didn't feel brave. She'd nearly wet her trousers when the cries of "A rider! A rider from the Queen!" had echoed through the village. First, a mud-speckled herald on a grey gelding had galloped down the River Road and past the huts, his purple cloak—the Queen's colour—flapping.

"The Queen's justice shall be done," the herald had shouted to the gathering crowd. He was a short, pale man with a scar that slithered from his chin to his cheek, splitting both lips. Despite his spattered clothes, he smelled sweet. Those from Regentium often wore perfume. They lived in houses stuffed with cushions and carpets. Most were as light-skinned as this man. "Bring the offender to me."

Lin had taken Fen's hand. "We cannot change this," she'd whispered. "We can only face it." She led Fen to the herald. "This is my elder daughter. This is Fen."

"Place her arm on the executioner's block. Be quick! We have three more sentences today."

On the previous morning Fen had been at the market, staring at a glass butterfly that glittered with such delicacy it looked real. The Regentium merchant was a portly, fair-skinned man with a big leather hat and a high-pitched, haughty voice. He wasn't the greatest of merchants or he wouldn't have been trading at such a small village. His voice dripped with disdain for the villagers, but he was plenty happy to take their copper coins.

He'd been distracted by a fisherman who was haggling over a jade pendant, so Fen had slipped the butterfly into her muddy cloak. When she was twenty steps from the stall, the ornament began to whistle so loudly she covered her ears. The villagers and other merchants stopped their trading and stared. She ripped the butterfly out of her cloak and threw it, expecting the fragile creation to smash on the ground, but instead it had flapped its glass wings, flown back to the merchant and landed on his hand.

He had pointed at Fen. "Thief! Dirty thief!" His accusation had frozen her. She hadn't known whether that was a spell or her own fear. Then two of his guards had grabbed her. "I demand justice!" the merchant shouted. "Queen's justice!"

A messenger raven had been sent to Regentium. By that evening the merchant was safe again behind the red walls of the capital city, sitting in his soft-cushioned bed drinking ice wine. The next morning, justice arrived at Village Twenty-One on horseback.

Fen had never stolen anything before. She had wanted a gift for her sister, who would soon be turning five summers old. Not just a couple of buttons pasted on a stick but something real. Something amazing.

"Hold the thief's arm straight," the herald commanded. "We want a clean cut." Lin's mother tightened her grip.

The Queen's guard stopped before Fen. This man had likely fought for a hundred years, or even a thousand, perhaps had been in the War of the Ten Cities itself, and yet he looked no older than eighteen. "Is this the transgressor?" His jaw was hairless and smooth. He'd been forged in the same way a sword has been forged.

"Yes, she is," Lin said. "Though she's just a child."

"Silence!" the herald shouted. "Every citizen, no matter the age, must obey the Queen's law. That is what keeps the peace."

The Queen's guard looked directly at Fen. His eyes were blue and cold and perfect—the same as the Queen's. Each guard was designed to reflect her likeness. Everything about him was so unbelievably immaculate. Not a hair out of order, not even a scar on his face. She wondered if the awe she felt was forced on her by the Queen's magic.

"No!" it was a small voice, but shrill. "Not her hand!"

May, Fen's sister, pushed her tiny body between the guard and Fen. "You can't have her hand!" Somehow May had escaped their neighbour's clutches. May put her own hand over Fen's.

"Get out of here," Fen whispered. "Go!"

"Yes, go!" The herald grabbed May. "Or we'll cut off your hand too!" He tossed her toward the crowd. Fen didn't see who caught May. Only that she was being held. And she was safe.

"Now," the herald said. "Down to business." He unrolled a muddy scroll. "Queen Servilia, she who freed you from the tyranny of Mansren, she who has brought you a millennium of peace, she who is the mother of our land, she who is the law incarnate, has declared Fen of Village Twenty-One a thief. On this the twenty-fifth day of the month of Maia, in the one thousand and seventh year of Her Majesty's reign, Fen has been sentenced to have her right hand removed. The Queen, in her mercy, will not take her subject's life." He closed the scroll. "Prepare for the Queen's justice."

The Queen's guard lifted his sword, and the sun caught the blade. The villagers made a small sound of expectation. Somewhere in the crowd May began to squeal.

"Don't let your tongue slip between your teeth," Lin whispered. Then, even quieter, "I love you."

The Queen's guard was the arm of the Queen reaching all the way from Regentium. Fen had dreamed of meeting her someday. Of standing in her presence and being raised up to the royal court. Fen's mother and sister would be so proud.

But today, she would meet the Queen in another way. For Fen had heard that at the moment of punishment, the Queen herself would look through her guard's eyes to be certain justice was done.

The guard swung the sword. Fen, despite her best intentions, tried to jerk away, but her mother held tight. There was a *thunk* and her forearm became a circle of pain.

"The Queen's justice has been served," the herald said.

Fen's ears felt as if they were floating above her—the words rose up to them. At any moment she would fly to the heavens, perhaps to join her father and all the other ancestors . . . but her burning arm held her to the ground. "All hail Queen Servilia," the herald commanded.

The villagers gave a muffled shout in reply. Within the hour they would be back in the red mines, out in the rice fields or plying the river for fish and eels. Her mother was murmuring, "*Fen Fen Fen oh Fen.*"

The herald dashed to his horse and was galloping along the road in the space of a few heartbeats. The Queen's guard turned away from Fen. His cloak shifted in the breeze, revealing the smooth metal that ran along his back and outlined his spine.

Fen did not look at her arm. She swore she wouldn't allow her thoughts to go dark.

The smithy said, "Keep a tight grip on her."

"Grit your teeth hard, Fen," Lin said. "You are brave and you are strong. Your father would have been proud of you."

The last sight Fen saw that day was the Queen's guard trotting on his charger, not looking back at the justice he had left behind. Then a white-hot iron bar was pressed against her stump and her vision went black and, mercifully, the pain went with it.

CHAPTER ONE

A BROKEN FALL

THREE YEARS HAD PASSED.

The sun began to rise on Village Twenty-One and at that same moment, Fen's sleep was broken by Queen Servilia's voice: *"Arise, your Queen commands it. Be fruitful and obey my laws."* The regent's flawless image shimmered in Fen's mind. Her royal red hair—a symbol and symptom of her magic—was held back by a golden crown. Her red diamond necklace, invested with the power both of her office and of her magic, glittered at her pale throat. Her darkly painted lips moved a few moments after the words were spoken, as if the image were coming from a very distant place.

Fen sat up, knowing her mother and sister in the room next door were also awaking on their sleeping mats, for they, too, would have seen the same royal face and heard the same royal commands, along with every slumbering member of the five hundred villages and the city of Regentium—each citizen throughout the whole queendom of Illium.

Queen Servilia had awakened her people this way for the last one thousand and ten years. Ever since the day she'd defeated Mansren, a demon of pure magic. He had started the War of the Ten Cities, fighting against kings, czars, khans and emperors, each of whom controlled their own city and lands. Mansren sacked and obliterated nine of the cities with his army of shirkers—terrifying creatures he'd formed from magic dust and blood. Servilia, Queen of Regentium, the last remaining city, had sent her elite guards and soldiers to fight against the demon, and while he was distracted, she'd descended from the sky on an equusa—a flying horse—and turned Mansren to stone with a spell from her red diamond necklace. He had then been shattered into pieces by Marcellus, the first Queen's guard. The shirker army was scattered and destroyed. The nine cities were forever gone, but the Queen swore to protect the five hundred villages that remained. It was the first day of her reign over all of Illium. The first day of peace.

The Queen had then planted fields of flowers around Regentium, in memory of the battle fought there: magic flowers that never died, come snow, sleet or hail. The flowers surrounded red walls that would never fall, and they were looked down upon from the Queen's Red Tower, tallest building in the land.

Fen knew the story well. The War of the Ten Cities against Mansren was a tale told by the Royal Historians at every public holiday. The villagers celebrated Servilia's victory once a year on Shattering Day, when the children smashed open stuffed Mansren dolls and ate the candy inside.

Even one-handed, Fen had gotten pretty good at smacking open those dolls and grabbing the sweets.

She scratched at the dried skin on her right arm. The stump still longed for the hand. Sometimes, if she were sleepy enough, she could feel her missing fingers. Today there was something more than an itch. It was tingling, as if her ghost hand had fallen asleep. She shook the stump until the prickles went away.

She pushed back the blanket on her sleeping mat, stood and dressed in the cool air, using her left hand to do up the cloth-knot buttons and to slip on the rectangular jade locket that had once been her father's. Fen stumbled out to the table, scraped the skin off the top of the rice porridge on the cookstove and filled her bowl.

Her mother came out of the other bedroom already dressed in grey mining clothes. The silk dust mask hung around her thin neck. She gently ran her fingers through Fen's hair. "It's still black," she said. "Be diligent with the dye."

Fen nodded. One red hair had appeared in her dark locks a month ago. Fen had yanked out the traitorous hair and burned it. No one in her village was ever born with hair of that colour. No one in the queendom, except the Queen and her guards, was allowed to have red hair.

Crimson hair was a sign of magic, and it grew one of two ways. Either the person had used the red dust to create magic, which was illegal, or else the magic had appeared within them on its own—this was known as wildmagic.

Only the Queen's most trusted artificers were allowed to work with the red dust. It could be formed into armour or swords; it could be used to strengthen a bridge, to build battlements or to invest a spell into an amulet. Most others who touched or breathed it died of the red cough.

But wildmagic was much more mysterious. It would appear in a person for no known reason and had nothing to do with the dust at all. One night their hair would turn a bright red and they'd wake with the ability to make rain or to levitate or to turn objects to stone.

A wildmagic had arisen in the village when Fen was a child. Chen, an ancient fisherman, had stepped out of his hut one morning with a full head of red hair and burning hands. He had been amazed at his newfound ability to shoot fire. He lit an oven. He lit torches. Even singed the eyebrows of his wife. But one greedy villager, seeing only the bounty on wildmagics, had sent a raven to Regentium, and by that afternoon Chen was being chased through the village by infernus hounds to the town square, where his head was removed by a Queen's guard.

Fen did not want to become a wildmagic—she had given enough of her body to the Queen. A few days after she plucked out that one red hair, a patch of red had appeared just behind her left ear. She'd gone to her mother but not spoken of it, for words had a way of crossing the leagues to the Red Tower. Lin had nodded, led Fen to the cupboard and mixed a perfectly shaded dye. Fen had used that dye every day for the last three weeks.

"I'm leaving for the mines," her mother said, patting Fen's shoulder. "The red dust waits for no worker."

"You should eat, Mama."

"I'm too old to eat." Lin gave Fen a squeeze and sipped from a chipped porcelain cup. "The tea will be enough." Until nightfall Lin would be scraping the red dust into bronze pails and carrying it to the royal wagons. The wagons would be covered with tightly woven tarps that wouldn't allow a speck of dust to escape. Soldiers would guard the wagons, guiding them to the Queen's Road and on to Regentium. There, the Red Artificers would take that dirt and invest its magic into blades or armour or staffs or lockets. Or it could be used to turn young men into

Queen's guards and to create corvuses, the Queen's giant raven-like messengers. And to do many other things that Fen had no idea about.

"We are digging so deep to mine the dust," her mother whispered. "The veins of red are smaller. If it runs out, what then?"

Fen didn't know the answer. The workers of Village Twenty-One had been mining the red dust for hundreds of years. Many of the other villages had their own mines. Were they running out too?

"Ah, those are worries for ancient toads like me," Lin said. "Forget them! Now, roust your sister and take her berry-picking. And be careful in the trees!"

"I never fall, Mom. Never."

"Such pride. Such confidence. Both are good, but wariness is better." Lin kissed her daughter's forehead. "You are more than Fen." Her mother said this every morning and it always made Fen shiver, for her mother was referring to Fen's secret name. The one they hid from the Queen. Her father had written it in their old language on a piece of vellum and stashed it under the floorboards. May had her own secret name too. Along with her mother and father.

Xi, her father, was the last of their family line to be able to read the old language, and he'd never spoken it aloud, in case the Queen heard him. He'd promised to teach it to Fen when she was older but had taken that language with him to his grave. If there were other villagers who could write or read in the old tongue, they never mentioned it. All the old languages in all the five hundred villages had been banned for over a thousand years. The Queen had declared that the only language to be used was Illish. It would unify the land. Other languages—other learning—had led to countless wars and the destruction of the nine cities. The citizens in Regentium were taught to write, but the villagers were not. The only thing Fen could write out were her numbers, which were needed in the market.

"And you are more than Lin," Fen said.

Her mother nodded and left, closing the slat door behind her.

Fen swallowed the last of her congee and went into her mother and sister's room. May was curled up on her bamboo sleeping mat, her head buried in her yellow pillow—their mother had sewn it in the shape of a cat. How May was able to fall back asleep after the Queen had awakened her, Fen would never know.

She poked her sister's shoulder. "Get up! Or I'll kick your porky hindquarters." It was how her father had greeted her every morning. It felt as if he were still home when she used his words.

"I *am* up," May growled without opening her eyes. "I'm just resting."

"Well, I could leave now and let the shirkers get you. They gobble up little girls." Fen knew May still believed that shirkers, the goblin-like creatures that served Mansren, actually existed. Even though she was eight summers old and should know better. Mentioning them was always a clever way to motivate her.

"There are no shirkers," May declared. Her confidence surprised Fen. "The Queen killed them all."

"She left a few alive. Just to chomp on lazy girls like you."

"I'm not lazy!" May stood slowly and dressed slowly, yawning the whole time, and then she shuffled to the table and ate her congee at such an abysmally slow pace Fen was tempted to clap her on the side of the head.

"Hurry! The sun will be up and we'll be late to the market."

Fen grabbed two baskets and pushed May out the door. Even then her sister walked with the speed of a sun-drenched turtle.

But May wormed her hand into Fen's and whatever irritation she'd felt faded. May was good at that. Worming her way into Fen's heart. Plus, she had such warm hands.

They walked past the town square. The executioner's block stood in the very centre. There was one in every village. Fen held her stump to her side as if to protect it. She could still see the Queen's guard clearly, the way his face had reflected the Queen's, the way the blade had caught the sunlight. Any whiff of smoke reminded her of the smell of her own flesh burning. Losing a hand hadn't seemed a fair penalty for stealing a glass butterfly.

Fen was old enough to be working in the mines, but one-handed thieves were not allowed near the magical red dust. Nor was it possible to harvest rice, as you needed to hold the stalks of rice in one hand and swing the sickle with the other. So the jobs no one wanted fell to her. She spent her hours sifting through the refuse pile for buttons or bits of cloth her mother could sew onto shirts, or helping the fishmongers scale fish. Some days she would conceal her father's small crossbow in her knapsack and hunt squirrels. At night, if there was need, she'd help her mother mend wounds or sell soothing ointments.

"Will I get to eat any berries?" May asked.

"Only the spoiled ones. The rest are for the market."

They turned a corner and came to the last row of bamboo huts. Fen saw a familiar face. Bay, the son of a fishmonger, was sitting in a chair, several large redfish on a table in front of him. He was scaling a particularly large fish by scraping the blade from tail to head. He jumped to his feet when he saw them. A cloud of fish scales drifted from his pants and shirt. "Fen-May! Fen-May!" He had a habit of repeating names and words. "Where are you off-off to today?" He was eleven summers old. By next year he'd be at work in the mines. "Where-where?"

"Picking sunberries," Fen said.

"Sunberries! I love-love sunberries!" Bay was slow-minded, but not so slow the Queen's Guard would come and take him away. Fen had seen that happen with a girl child a few years earlier. Her parents could only watch quietly. To resist would mean death. "I have to scale fish-fish today. But tomorrow, will you show me the best-best sunberry trees? The very best-best?"

"Yes, of course!" She clapped his shoulder and then rubbed the scales off her hand with her stump. "Tomorrow, we'll climb! I'll meet you here at sunrise."

"Good-good! Bye, Fen! Bye, May! Bye-bye!"

The sisters kept walking. "He talks funny," May said when they were out of earshot.

"He has a kind heart. So you should be kind to him."

"I am." May sounded a bit perturbed. "The other kids poke him—with words and sticks—and he doesn't get mad."

"You tell me who does that and I'll poke them, hard."

May kept silent. She'd always been good at holding in secrets.

They walked along the winding Vilia River and then climbed the green hill that was called Grandfather's Nose, stopping at a line of sunberry trees. The trees were tall, and the best berries grew at the very top.

"You stay here, May." She gave her a basket, and then tied her own to her belt. "Pick the berries from the ground that still look good."

"I know what to do!"

"And don't eat any unless they're broken!"

May put her hands on her hips. "I can climb with you."

"Not until you're older. You need longer arms."

"You only have one hand!"

Fen bit back the first reply that came to mind. It was a mean one. "But two strong arms and good tree-sense. Now do as I say."

Fen grabbed a bough with her left hand, climbed up a few feet and then curled her stump around a branch. Once she was partway up the tree, she set her feet, plucked a fist-sized orange berry and dropped it into the basket.

She ascended a little farther. The rising sun cast light across Village Twenty-One, outlining the huts and making the river glitter like a silver snake that had curled around one corner of the village. No, not a snake, Fen thought. A dragon. Her father had told her the river dragon was friendly and brought good luck. She knew dragons weren't real but hoped the luck they brought was.

On the western edge of the village was the vast pit of the red earth mines. A haze floated up from the layers of earth that had been stripped away, shovelful by shovelful. The miners marched in and out, little dolls from this distance, breathing that dust, their faces covered with flimsy flaps of silk.

Across from the mines was a collection of small obelisks marking the ashes of the dead—they cremated any who had worked there. There were legends that the red dust had brought ancestors back to life as demons, so it was better to be certain they stayed dead.

Her father was in that graveyard under a smooth green stone etched with a dragon. He'd come home one evening five years ago with the red cough and died by morning. He was cremated at once and buried. Her mother had burned a paper dragon in their fireplace that evening, but when Fen asked why, her mother told her to be silent. "Do the same when I die," she said. "Promise me." Fen promised, even though she didn't know what any of it meant.

Fen climbed ever higher in the tree, picking berries as she went. She'd step right into the air itself to get a better berry. She had a clear view of the small green Grandfathers' Mountains that crouched over the village. Many of the grain and rice crops were grown in their folds. The spirits of the elders went to those mountains when they died.

All around them were the other villages, each with their tasks for the queendom. In the centre of Illium were the wheat growers. In the north, the metal miners. There were villages, she was told, where people had black skin, and other villages where the people were white-, brown- or pink-skinned. She longed to see those places. But travel was only for the merchants and the officials or soldiers of the Queen. Fen would never have any reason to explore.

Whether there were actually five hundred villages, she didn't know. There were rumours that some villages had rebelled against Queen Servilia and been burned to the ground by her Queen's Guard.

Fen could not see the ocean from here. It was many, many leagues away in all directions. Illium was an island queendom. She had no idea if other lands existed across the water.

Fen's basket was nearly full—a dream haul. Her mother would kiss both her cheeks. And they would purchase meat— auroch or deer—with the coins the berries brought. She licked her lips, thinking of how much better her mother's noodles would taste with something other than squirrel meat.

She spotted a trio of plump berries on one of the uppermost branchlets. It was good luck to find things in threes. She clambered higher and clamped her stump around a thin branch.

The three sunberries were the biggest she'd ever seen! They might each fetch a crown. She set her feet and stretched. The first was so round and juicy she was tempted to taste it, but she set it softly in the basket instead. Then she laid the second beside it.

When she reached for the third berry, the branch beneath her feet snapped without even the slightest warning and she tumbled downward, casting out with her left hand and finding nothing to grab. She closed her eyes to slits to avoid having them poked out. She managed to catch a branch but slipped and, by instinct, reached out with her stump.

Useless! Totally useless! But something in that place where her hand had been grabbed a branch as though a ghostly version of her fingers were still there. Her fall slowed, the branch bent and then, before she could look up to see how this was even possible, it broke.

Fen dropped straight down and smacked the ground with her back. Her breath *whumped* out of her body. An eon later, she breathed in a hard, hurting breath.

Her hearing returned. Her eyes were not working properly—she saw only the brightest white light. Then, a small shadow.

"Are you dead?" May asked.

"Not yet," Fen said. She wasn't certain if she could move. A cripple with a broken back and a missing hand was more than useless; the Queen's Guard would take her away for sure. She lifted her one hand and shook her arm. Nothing was broken.

"Do you hurt?" May asked. "I mean bad. You must hurt."

"I hurt. Now, help me up."

May grabbed her hand. Fen sat up, her back creaking the whole way. The berries were scattered about her, squashed and split, their fleshy pulp looking like orange blood. Even her basket had smashed open.

"Stupid! Stupid!" Fen said. "Utterly stupid!"

"You mean yourself, don't you?" May asked.

"Of course! I should've tested that branch."

"Your tree-sense wasn't very good."

Fen spat a gob, expecting to see blood. "No. It wasn't."

"We can pick more."

The sun was lighting up the morning sky. The merchants would soon be in the town square. "There's not enough time. We'll have to come back tomorrow."

Fen looked up at how tall the sunberry tree was. She'd fallen from the very top. She should be dead. If not for the branches slowing her and—

It had seemed as if her right hand, her missing hand, had grabbed a branch. But that was impossible. And yet, she had felt contact. Not of her fingers so much, but something else that was invisible and attached to her arm.

She lifted her right arm. Her sleeve was torn, revealing her stump. Fen ran her hand across the scarred, mottled skin. On her second pass, she found a rough, dark patch and upon closer examination, she saw that something was sticking out. At first she thought it was a big green sliver, but she pulled on it to discover a vine. She gave it a good yank.

It was a part of her.

It was her.

"No," she whispered. She pulled again and it separated from her flesh—a short vine with small leaves. But it had grown out of her arm.

"What is it?" May asked. "Do you have slivers?"

Fen covered up her stump. "It's nothing. It has to be nothing." It was her imagination. The vine had been lodged in her arm. "Just help me pick up what's left of the berries." Fen gathered a handful. "At least we'll have something to eat."

CHAPTER TWO

A SUDDEN BURST OF CRIMSON

THAT NIGHT FEN DREAMED ABOUT REACHING UP AND plucking a golden star from the sky. The fingers on her right hand—her long-missing hand—grew warm with the power of the heavens. She was whole. Her body complete. Her feet were anchored to the earth as if she'd grown roots.

Then, as Fen stared at the glowing orb, the Queen drifted into the dark space. Her face was impassive and extraordinarily faultless. It was such a familiar countenance—as familiar as Fen's mother's or sister's. Fen saw it on coins, in paintings and it awoke her every morning. The Queen watched Fen silently.

"You are having a star dream," Queen Servilia said finally.

Fen, in all her years, couldn't remember ever talking to the Queen in a dream.

"Yes, I am," she said. "A star dream." The power of the star was coursing through her. Her bravery was rising from the ground.

"What's your name?" the Queen asked.

Fen looked from the star in her hand to the Queen.

"Am I really talking to you?"

"Tell me your name. That is a royal command." The glint of hardness in Queen Servilia's eyes made Fen tremble.

"I—I don't know my real name." It felt like the truth. And a safe answer.

The Queen pointed at her. Her long nails had been painted black.

"What village do you live in?" she asked. "Tell me."

"My village doesn't have a name either," Fen said. That, too, was truth. She wouldn't lie to her monarch. "It only has a number. The number you gave it."

"*Which number is it?*" the Queen hissed. "*I command you to tell me!*" With each word, the fabric of the dream tore at the edges. "Tell me now!"

The star vanished. Fen's hand vanished. And, finally, so did the Queen.

Fen opened her eyes. Her heart was beating rabbit-fast. She would not have been surprised to see Queen Servilia standing right over her sleeping mat.

How horrible! Had she been speaking directly to the Queen? Her body said yes. But she wasn't certain that was possible. The Queen visited her every morning, but that was a message sent to every citizen at once. This had been a conversation.

If it had been real at all, that is.

Fen reached to rub away the sleep from her eyes, but a sharp pain stopped her. Her neck, shoulders and back ached with stiffness. The fall from the tree had tried its best to break every bone. Despite an afternoon of scaling fish and pulling a rice cart, she hadn't loosened those muscles. Sleep had only made them tighter.

Fen sat up slowly. Small pieces of bark littered the bed. She brushed at them and then, in a panic, grabbed her stump. Even in the dim light, she could see the skin had turned a hue of green. *Is it septic?* She rubbed where her wrist used to be and discovered more short vines. Touching them produced a tickling sensation. When she pinched one, intending to pull it out, it was as if she were tearing at her own skin.

"What is this?" she whispered.

"Get out of bed, Fen!" her mother said from the kitchen. "You need to be first at the market to get the best fish!" Lin pushed open the slat door. "Oh, dear Zaoshen!"

The fear on her mother's face stopped Fen from spouting off about her privacy. Lin had just spoken the name of one of the old gods aloud. To even mention a god was a crime punishable by ten lashes.

"What!" Fen asked. "What is it?"

"Your hair!" Lin grabbed a handful and held it so Fen could see.

Red. Red. *Red!*

Her hair had gone crimson. Every strand had changed from dark black to red overnight. The dye should have lasted at least a day! She touched the traitorous hair. It felt thicker and glowed in the semi-dark.

"We must cut it." Her mother's voice was frail. "Right to the scalp. Quick! Get up!" She slammed the door. "We don't want your sister to see it."

"May wouldn't betray me," Fen said as she stood.

"One slip of her tongue and you'd be dead. Any who turned you in would dine for a year on that gold." She dug in the cupboard and came up with a pair of iron scissors. "Hold still."

"Mama!" Fen put up her left hand. "I don't want to be bald."

"You can say you had lice."

"Lice! Never!"

"Would you rather lose your head?" Lin grabbed Fen's hair so tightly that it hurt and snipped at a handful with the scissors. "It won't cut! Old gods! Why this? Why now?"

"Stop talking about the gods!" Fen took the scissors and tried a smaller clump, but she couldn't slice through one strand. How could it be so strong? She yanked and not a single hair came loose.

"Mama." Fen's voice trembled. "What's happening?"

"The worst! The very worst! You'll bring death to the family. Maybe even the whole village. Oh, Zaoshen save us!"

"Stop naming the gods!" Fen hissed.

Her mother took a deep breath. "You're right." She reached down and picked up a piece of bark from the sleeping mat. "What's this?"

"Nothing. Nothing." Fen scrambled to brush the bark away. "I went to sleep in dirty clothes."

"Well, don't do that!" The admonishment came out immediately. It was something her mother would say on a normal day. "Perhaps we can dye your hair."

Fen had never seen Lin's hands shake so much as when she brought the dye jar over to the bed. She dipped her fingers directly in and rubbed a dark jelly-like clump through Fen's hair. The dye hissed and turned to smoke.

"This is madness," Lin said.

Someone rapped three times on the window. "Fen," a young voice whispered. "Fen-Fen! Are you up-up?"

"Who's that?" her mother whispered.

"It's Bay," Fen said. "I told him I'd pick berries today."

"Send him away. Now!"

Fen stumbled over to the closed wooden shutters. She peeked through the crack. Bay was standing with a basket in his hand, fish scales glinting on his clothing like chain mail. "Please, Bay, go away."

"The sun—the sun is just about to rise. It's the best-best time to pick."

"I'm sick today!"

"You don't sound sick-sick." He squinted at her window and Fen pulled back a few inches.

"I am," she said, making her voice hoarse. "Please go."

"Go? Go? But you know where all the best-best berries are."

"Climb the Grandfather's Nose hill. There are plenty of good ones there. I'll help you tomorrow. I need to sleep now."

"Yes-yes," he said, but he slumped his shoulders. "I'll go-go." He trudged away.

Fen stood beside her mother, but before she could speak, there was another knock on the window.

"Bay!" she shouted. "I mean it . . . Go away!"

A sniffing sound followed.

"Bay?" Fen asked.

Worm-thin fingers reached between the blinds and felt around for the hook. The fingers were far too pale and thin to belong to Bay.

"No," Lin whispered. "Not one of them."

Fen took a step toward the window. "Stay out. I'm not dressed."

The fingers discovered the latch and slowly lifted it. There was a squawk and then the shutters swung open with a bang.

There, sitting on the windowsill, was one of the Queen's corvuses. Fen had never seen the royal messenger birds up close. This one had massive black wings and sharp claws, which it dug into the window ledge. Two dark eyes stared out from a pudgy face—a face so much like a human child's that it was disconcerting. Little arms with long, spindly fingers hung from its chest, its hands designed by the Red Artificers to hold messages.

The corvus sniffed a snotty sniff and cocked that baby head like a bird. It eyed Fen from head to foot and opened its beak. "Crimson," the corvus cackled. It pointed a long, thin finger. "Caw. Queen, hear this! Village Twenty-One, hut by river. Crimson."

Fen brushed past her mother to get to the closet. Reaching inside, she yanked out the crossbow, placed the end of it on the floor and, with her foot in the stirrup, struggled to pull back the string until it was locked in place. She grabbed a bolt.

The corvus watched her without any fear. "Crimson. Wildmagic. Village Twenty-One. Summon the guards."

Fen's hand trembled so much the bolt dropped to the floor. She snatched it up.

"Caw!" the corvus said. "Caw! Crimson."

Fen lifted the crossbow, laid it across her right arm and pulled the trigger, but the corvus flapped its wings and took off. The bolt sailed out the window and uselessly toward the river.

The corvus was a dot in the distance before she could load a second bolt.

CHAPTER THREE

THE GREEN
SECRET

MOTHER AND DAUGHTER STARED OUT THE WINDOW IN shock. Then Lin grabbed Fen's shoulder. "You must flee."

"Mama!" Fen said. "You need me here."

"You'll be executed if you stay." She clutched Fen's hair in desperation, staring at the redness. "Do you have magic? Can you fly?" There was a crazed look in her mother's eyes.

"Fly? No! I have no magic at all." Fen hid her stump behind her back. Those were just useless vines. They might even be her imagination. After all, how could they grow out of her arm? Ridiculous.

"Well, your hair wouldn't go crimson without some magic inside you. Maybe you just don't know what it is yet."

Lin grabbed a leather knapsack that had belonged to Fen's father and began stuffing clothes into it.

"Where do I go?" Fen asked.

"Helwood. Hide in the forest."

"That's three days' walk! The Queen's Guard will catch me long before I get there."

"Follow the river. Stick to the tall grasses and bamboo forests and avoid the Queen's Road. Don't talk to anyone! Oh, be quick, my dear."

Fen pulled on fresh breeches and a grey shirt. "And once I reach the forest?"

"I don't know. Your father heard rumours of hermits and thieves living there."

"Rumours about thieves? That's it?"

"There isn't time to argue, Fen. The Queen's Guard will come and they'll—"

"I know what they'll do." Fen finished buttoning up her shirt with her left hand.

Lin set the knapsack down. "Oh, Fen, I don't want to lose you. You have been so strong. I've leaned on you so many times."

Fen bit her lip. The truth was clear: "We don't have a choice."

"We never do." The words sounded bitter and Fen knew her mother was referencing the Queen.

Fen followed her mother into the main room. Lin wrapped up a steamed pork bun and some salted oxen meat and dried berries in rice leaves and placed them in the knapsack. Next came fresh carrots, snap peas and a turnip. That was followed by sewing needles, and a package of healing herbs and ointments. She tied a coiled rope to the back.

"I need weapons, Mother."

Lin lifted the floorboard and gave her a sheathed knife. "Take your father's knife for protection. Don't forget your crossbow."

May wandered in, one fist balled up to rub sleep from her eyes. She stopped. "Fen. Your hair! It's red!"

"You shouldn't see this!" Fen shouted.

"Go!" Her mother swatted May, nearly knocking her down. "Get back to your room! Forget what you saw!"

May held her head and glanced back at Fen, her eyes wide. She ran out of the room.

Fen hid the crossbow in her knapsack and slid the small quiver of bolts into a special pouch. Then she attached the sheathed knife to her belt.

Lin dropped three copper coins into her hand. As Fen was pocketing them, Lin took her by the face, caressing her cheeks. "Be strong, Fen. There must be others in the forest who hide from"—she looked over her shoulder—"from *her*. You can make a life there."

"With outlaws?" Fen said.

"You're an outlaw now." Her mother pushed Fen's hair back and deftly tied it with ribbon. "There have to be good people. Watch with your careful eyes, Fen. Then befriend them. You'll be safe."

It sounded like her mother was trying to convince herself. "I'll do my best, Mama."

"You always have. It's one of the many things I love about you." She gave her a quick hug. "When you're gone, I'll have May run into the street to proclaim you a wildmagic. We'll—we'll say you attacked us and fled. We must not be seen as harbouring you."

"I understand," she said. It only made sense. She didn't want her sister or mother to face one of the Queen's inquisitors.

Lin handed a grey hooded cloak to her daughter and helped her put it on. Then she suddenly pushed Fen aside, pried up another floorboard and retrieved four rectangles of vellum: each inscribed with a name in the forbidden language.

"Take these," her mother said, handing them to Fen.

Fen looked down at the soft leather in her hand. "But . . . but this is your name too. And Father's." The characters made no sense to Fen.

"The soldiers will search every corner of our hut. You guard our names." She helped Fen put them in the knapsack, choosing the pocket that was so well oiled it was waterproof. "As long as you have them, we'll always be with you." She hugged Fen again, tightly. "Be brave."

"I will," Fen said. "I promise." Then she added, "I love you, Mama."

"You are more than Fen. And I love you. I always will."

Fen felt tears forming in her eyes, so she pulled her hood over her head, opened the window and looked out. No one was within sight. She swung over the sill using her left hand and dropped to the ground. She waved but her mother motioned her away, mouthing something Fen couldn't hear. There was no turning back.

Their hut was next to the Vilia River, so within a few steps she was hidden by tall grasses. Close by, the river burbled. She walked along the edge. If only she had a cutter . . . then she could ply the water. But she would be far too easy to spot. And the river flowed the wrong way if she wanted to get to Helwood.

This turmoil was all happening far too quickly to comprehend. She had no magic.

But even with that thought, she couldn't help glancing at her stump. To see if some other green oddity had grown there. She rubbed and nothing felt different.

She doubled her pace. If she stayed, she'd be dead. The whole family: dead. And she had to keep their names safe.

Soon the sound of livestock and the *tink tink* of the blacksmith's hammer faded. Each step weighed on her heart. She got a whiff of a putrid scent that she knew came from the Great Salt Mire. When the wind blew from that direction, the smell of poisonous gas would fill the village, burning eyes and nostrils. It was a toxic place. No one ever went there.

She'd have to walk around that wasteland, cross the Queen's Road without being spotted and then turn south toward Helwood. It would be almost impossible to do without being seen.

One step at a time! She pushed her way through the tall grass and bamboo trees into a clearing.

"Who are you?" a voice asked from nearby.

Fen spun. A young man was sitting on a large stone. It took her a moment to recognize Kang, one of the rice harvesters. He was tying a red ribbon to his tightly braided hair. He finished the knot and let the braid fall over his right shoulder. His thin arms were taut with corded muscle. His rice sickle rested at his feet.

"Who are you?" he asked again.

"No one," she said.

"No one," he echoed. "A No One who can talk, that's a wonder. A No One who can walk. That's magical."

Magical? Had her hair shown? Fen touched the side of her head. No, the hood was tight.

Kang lifted his sickle and used it to clean under his fingernails. "Well, *No One*, I think you're a thief sneaking out of our innocent village. Are you a thief?"

"No!"

"You hide behind a hood. You're missing a hand. Your pack is bulging with goods. You *must* be a thief. The coin from turning you in would buy me a nice water-buffalo steak. And you would be handless."

"I'm not a thief!" She gripped the handle of her father's knife.

"Are you from some other village? Leaving with our rice. Our meat. Our trinkets."

"I'm Fen."

"Fen." His smile displayed a missing front tooth. Fen knew he'd lost it in a fight in the fields. "Why are you skulking away?"

"I'm going to pick berries."

"With a full knapsack? I could use a nice knapsack."

"It was my father's."

Kang stood. "He shouted at me once. He said I was worthless."

"You deserved it!" She regretted the words the moment she spat them out. But the man was lazy. Instead of getting to the rice fields at dawn, he was hiding in this hollow fixing his hair.

He slowly cut the air with the sickle. "Something odd is happening. Little girls don't hide their faces. I want to see your eyes, Fen."

"I have a copper coin. I could give it to you. Let me pass."

He weighed her offer only for a moment. "Not enough. Show me your face—it's pretty. Except for that smug look—your father had it, your sister, even your mother. Odd to see that sneer on a family so poor. Show me your face, Fen of the One Hand."

"No."

He crouched and then leapt across the space between them, swinging the sickle upward. It caught the edge of her hood, cutting the top and knocking it off.

"Crimson!" He covered his mouth. Then he lowered his hand and smiled. "You've gone crimson. Leave the knapsack and the coin. Leave everything!"

"No!"

"Do it or I'll kill you now." He raised the sickle. "You're dead anyway."

"No! The knapsack is mine."

"Then I'll have to take it." He swung the sickle and she ducked—it whistled over her head. He chuckled. Had he meant to miss? She dodged his second blow and thought of turning and running but he had blocked the path forward—her only escape was back to the village. Kang swung again and she stepped to the side, lost her balance and fell hard to the ground. He brought the sickle down and stopped a finger's width from her forehead.

"Take off the knapsack!"

"No!"

He took another swing at her. Fen raised her arms and with a flash of green, a blurring snake—a thick vine—shot out of the stump. In a heartbeat, it wrapped around his hand and over the sickle, stopping the blow in mid-arc. Another vine and another snaked along his arms, criss-crossing his chest. Kang's eyes widened. The vines encircled his throat and when he tried to yell, they dove into his mouth. His face turned red.

Fen felt as if there were something—a power—coming up from the ground into her body. That even the bamboo trees around her were lending her their strength.

The vines spooled out of her stump and she could actually feel Kang's face from where she was lying, feel the constriction around his throat. One vine had a hold on his tongue, a squished red chunk of flesh. The vines tightened and tightened.

Kang was purple now. His eyes so wide and frightened it was almost comical. He made a strangled sound.

"Stop it!" Fen shouted. "Stop growing! Halt!"

The strangling sound continued, growing weaker, and his eyes went dull. He slumped toward the ground but the vines held him in the air like a puppet.

"Stop!" Fen said. The vines slowly retreated back into her arm and Kang fell over. He didn't move.

She stood up, her chest tight, her breathing shallow. She had felt his face through the vines! As if the tendrils were a part of her. She looked at her stump and there, hanging out of it, were several finger-length vines.

"Oh, dear Zaoshen!" she whispered. It really was wildmagic. Her stomach clenched.

Kang looked too pale. And motionless. She didn't want to step near him, but she did so, peering down. She kicked his shoulder and he didn't react. His chest wasn't rising.

He was dead.

She had killed him. She stared at the vines again. No, *they* had killed him. The magic she felt glowing in them. In her veins.

Fen fled past him along the river.

CHAPTER FOUR

A BLACK BOLT

Fen ran. Her hood had been sliced by Kang's sickle, so she held it in place as she picked her way along deer paths. The vines in her arm rubbed against tall grass, brushed against bamboo trees and reeds. The sensations made her run faster. How could she feel through them? What was this thing growing on her? In her?

The vines had killed Kang. Right in front of her! Of course, he had threatened her life. But she hadn't meant for him to die.

After what seemed like hours, she stopped and sat down in the shade of an osmanthus tree, its orange flowers rich with the fragrance women often used for oiled perfume—her mother's favourite. It took Fen several minutes, one-handed, to sew the hood together. It was tight when she pulled it back on. The whole time, she ignored her right stump. She didn't even want to look at it. What if the vines decided to kill her?

But her stump itched and without thinking, she lifted up her sleeve and scratched. The skin was rough as bark and the collection of vines still hung there. They grazed against her fingers, almost like a greeting, and she yanked her left hand back.

When she'd attacked Kang, it was as if the vines had shot out of her arm and then retreated on their own. She would never forget the sensation of touching his face—grabbing his tongue!—with those tendrils.

Whatever power had made them grow had also made her hair turn red. Fen wondered if severing her arm from the elbow down would cut the magic out of her. Her hair would turn back to black and she could go home.

"Don't be stupid," she whispered, surprised by how raspy her voice was. "You'd bleed to death."

Well, I don't have to cut off my whole arm. She took out her father's knife and grabbed one of the longer vines. She used her foot to hold it to the ground so it was tight against a stone and sliced as close to her stump as possible.

"Ahh!" Cutting into the vine hurt as if someone had stabbed her finger. A few drops of blood oozed out of the piece she'd lopped off. Her blood inside a vine! It made no sense. It was wrong.

Wrong!

She gritted her teeth, but when she went to slice another vine, it jerked out of the way. They were a part of her and yet they had a will of their own. A chill ran down her back, despite the sweat.

She slid the knife into its sheath. It would take too long to cut the green growths off—instead she wrapped up her arm again. She needed to get leagues away from the village if she wanted to live past nightfall. Maybe there'd be a hermit in Helwood who could advise her on what to do with the vines. She stood and started hustling through the tall grass.

Fen had grown up next to the Vilia River and it ran in her blood. So much of her time, when not working, was spent fishing for carp. Or catching eels. Often she'd take May with her and they'd whisper stories about cherry trees on the moon or water demons frolicking at the bottom of the lake. Thinking of May made Fen shiver with sadness. She might never see her again.

She *would* never see her again. Ever. That was what being an outcast meant.

The river was swollen, making the banks soft and muddy, so Fen had to walk closer to the fields of sugar cane, keeping slouched down. There would be villagers tending the crop, waiting to harvest it into sugar and paper for Regentium's massive stone bins. She didn't want to be caught by any workers. She couldn't know if the vines would show themselves, couldn't trust anyone to keep her wildmagic a secret. Whenever there was a break in the cover, she'd glance skyward in search of corvuses or other winged creatures belonging to the Queen, but she saw none.

Fen's stomach started to rumble. She stopped and unwrapped the rice leaf and took a bite of the sweet bun. It would expand in her stomach and make her feel full the rest of the day. *This is one of the last times I get to eat my mother's cooking.* Why had she complained about overcooked noodles so often?

Fen walked, her arm still tingling. Hours passed and the sensation almost began to feel normal.

She came to the Queen's Road—a glowing, red-paved highway that ran in all four directions from Regentium. This was the southern section. There were shorter roads that stretched between each main artery, so that every corner of the queendom could be quickly accessed. The Queen had invested every paving stone with a magic that made her soldiers run, ride or roll faster than the eye could see, so that every corner of Illium was within a few hours of Regentium. If anyone were standing on the road as the troops came through, they'd be run over in a heartbeat.

Likely a squadron had already sped down this way and taken one of the side roads to Village Twenty-One.

All of the trees and grasses on both sides of the road had been cut away, so it was possible to look a long way in either direction. The moment she stepped out of the sugar canes, she would easily be spotted from the sky.

Citizens from the five hundred villages had built the road after the War of the Ten Cities. The Royal Historians spoke of how they'd volunteered because they'd understood the road would bring eternal peace to the realm. If the Queen's Guard could travel with such swiftness to any village, no one would ever break the law.

Fen sat down near a thick banyan tree and huddled in her cloak. It was still several hours before nightfall—the best time to cross. She looked back the way she'd come. A line of smoke snaked on the horizon. It was most likely someone burning a fallow field.

Her neck was sweaty, so she pulled her hood back and the cool air caressed her skin. This new red hair felt strange under her fingers. Her black hair—her *real* hair!—had always been coarse, but these locks were as soft as silk and long enough she could hold them in front of her eyes and stare at the luminescent red.

"Crimson," came a cry from above her in the tree. "Caw!"

Fen's heart skittered a beat. A corvus sat in the uppermost branches, glaring down at her. "Red hair. South Queen's Road. Caw!"

The creature pointed, and its thin, wormy finger seemed to reach right into her heart. Freezing her. "Red hair. Wildmagic. Near South Bridge. Caw." It would repeat those words when it found the nearest patrol of the Queen's Guard.

She carefully removed the crossbow from her knapsack, hooked the stirrup on her foot and pulled, setting the string. She slipped out a bolt, all the while remembering how she had missed the last corvus.

Not this time!

The bird-thing spread its wings but did not take to the sky. "Crimson. Caw!"

It stared down at her with owl eyes. For all she knew, the Queen or one of her minions was glaring through those orbs. Fen set the bolt in the slot and the corvus flapped its wings and took to the air. She raised the crossbow and, using her stump to brace the shaft, tracked the bird, loosing the bolt a short distance in front of it.

The bolt caught the beast in the chest. The creature made a loop as if to show it wasn't hurt, and then it plummeted from the sky like a black comet.

Fen ran, the crossbow still in hand. She found the corvus in a pile of flattened grass. It was on its back, wings curling and uncurling. Its wingspan was as long as her body. Tiny pale hands were wrapped around the shaft of the bolt. Green blood leaked out of its chest. "Red hair," it cawed softly. "Killed. Me."

The beastly thing did look a lot like a little boy who'd dressed up in huge raven wings. Its beak opened and closed. "Mama," it said. "Queen. Mama. Mom. Maaaaa." Then it gurgled and its eyes grew dull.

She waited several heartbeats before kicking it to be sure it was dead. Pressing her foot on its chest, she pulled out the bolt, wiping the green blood on the grass. She slid it back into the quiver.

Then she vomited. Hard. Took a deep breath and vomited again.

The corvus was an abomination made by Royal Red Artificers and yet Fen had killed it. With her own hands. And it had cried out like a child for its mother. The Queen.

Fen wiped her lips.

"Don't cough your guts out about it," a man said, close enough to make Fen stand up straight. "You just gave Servilia a glorious poke in the eye."

CHAPTER FIVE

THE VOICE BEHIND THE MAN

FEN STEPPED ON THE STIRRUP OF THE CROSSBOW, pulled back the string, slipped a bolt in and swung the weapon around. She pointed it at . . . nothing. The words had come from directly behind her, but there was no one there. She jerked her head left and right, and spun around again.

"Ithak is rather hard to see." The stranger's words had a slurred rice-wine tone she'd heard enough times in the village. He also had a different accent than hers. All citizens of Illium spoke Illish—the Queen had decreed that a millennium ago—but he sounded like someone from Regentium itself. And only the Queen and her most loyal subjects lived there.

"Show yourself!" She spun around until she was almost dizzy. "Right now!"

"Ithak doesn't want an extra nostril. Put down the bow."

"No!" Fen balanced the bow on her arm. "Go away if you aren't going to show yourself."

"Go away? A lonely red-haired urchin should be begging for friends. And Ithak is the very best kind of friend to have."

Was he crouched somewhere and throwing his voice?

"Don't try anything!" Fen pointed the bow at the ground. "I won't shoot you. Unless you deserve it." She was surprised at how confident she sounded.

"Ithak will have to trust you. Now look directly toward the tree. Ithak is about to reveal his humble self. Don't pee your britches."

"I won't!" She gritted her teeth but blushed at the same time.

His chuckle reminded her of clucking chickens. "Oh yes, you will. And now Ithak stands revealed!"

Nothing happened.

"You're toying with me." Fen gripped the crossbow tighter.

"Oh, darn. Ithak flubbed it. Now, here Ithak is!"

A shimmering occurred several yards ahead of her and then a grinning man stepped out of thin air itself. His arms and legs and torso were covered with bark—the same colour as the banyan tree. Then the bark shifted to a lighter shade to become white-skinned flesh. He was naked! No—he had pale short pants and wore a belt with a pouch. All equally pale. His eyes were owl-like. "You didn't wet your britches!" He clapped his hands. "Most fall down on their knees and worship me. Or chase Ithak from their kitchen with pots."

"Who are you?"

He bowed. "Ithak is the shadow in your footsteps. Ithak, who can hide in plain sight. Ithak the taker. The stalker. The finder and the keeper."

"You're a thief?"

His grin widened. "Ithak distributes the wealth of others into his own pouch." He touched the pouch hanging on his belt.

His hand lingered there. His hair, shorn so short it wasn't much more than fuzz, was red.

"You're a wildmagic!" she said. He was smaller than she first had thought—almost the same height as her.

"Ithak is the greatest of all wildmagics. Now, tell me your name."

"It—it's Fen."

He nodded as if she'd answered more than one question. He put his hand on his pouch again. She wondered if he was worried about losing some jewel inside.

"Is that your true name?" he asked.

"What do you mean?"

"Oh, Ithak knows you villagers. No matter what your colour, you all have other names you hide from the Queen. Ithak has listened late at night as you whisper the old names to each other."

"I don't know what you're talking about." Fen had a sudden urge to check to be sure she still had the pieces of vellum her mother had given her.

"Yes, you do. But Ithak doesn't care about your names. It was a pleasure to meet you, Fen. Now Ithak must go."

Her hand was sweating on the crossbow. "Where are you travelling to?"

"I'm hastening back to Helwood."

"Helwood? Truly? I'm going—" She stopped.

"You're going where?"

Fen clenched her teeth. Her mother had warned her to be careful. "I'm not going anywhere. H-how did you find me?"

"Ithak was, how shall Ithak put it, expeditiously fleeing a village."

"Which village did you come from?"

He pointed where the line of smoke rose into the air. "Ithak doesn't pay much attention to their numbers anymore. Just glad the simpletons unknowingly open their pantries to me. They were the same colour as you."

"That's my village!"

"It *was* your village." He rubbed his chin. "By now it's ashes."

"What do you mean?"

He pointed at her. "You're not overly gifted with brains. By morning you'll be bumping along the Queen's Road in a cage. Then off with your head and the masses will cheer."

"What happened to my village?" She was tempted to raise the crossbow. "Answer me!"

"It has met with a bit of a burning. Queen's Guard came in, their torches in hand, corvuses in the sky to guide them. People dead and all that." He raised his right hand and held his finger and thumb apart. "Ithak came *that* close to being trampled."

Fen's stomach churned with something worse than hunger. "Did they burn the whole village down?"

"Oh no. Someone has to mine the dust."

"I have to go back."

He crossed his arms. "Idiocy! By now several squadrons of Queen's Guard have arrived and they've released the hounds. In fact, since they're after you, those hounds may be along any moment now." He scratched behind his ear. "We should part company. Ithak doesn't like death. And Ithak can smell it on you."

"I'm going back," she said.

"Are you a dolt?"

"My family is there."

"Let them fend for themselves." Then he rolled his eyes. "Ithak sees that your mind is set. Be smart and cross the river. That way the hounds will lose your scent."

Fen knew her mother could be in the hands of a Royal Inquisitor right now. Her sister too. She hadn't imagined the Queen's Guard would burn the village! Fen put the bolt in the quiver and slid the crossbow into her knapsack.

She took a step and her foot bumped the wing of the corvus. She looked down. The image of its human face would haunt her.

Ithak picked his teeth with a piece of grass. "If they catch up with you, run right into a sword. A quick death is the best."

He was grinning so broadly she wanted to smack him as she strode by. Even as she thought it, she felt something move in her stump as though the vines would come shooting out again.

"You never told me what your magic is." He was walking backwards alongside her. "Each magic comes from an element. Mine is from air itself. To make myself unseen. But what is yours?"

"That's not your business." She didn't stop walking. "But to be honest, I don't know what it is."

"You mean you have no magic? You are so very doomed."

"Thank you for helping me," she said, unsure whether she was being sarcastic.

He shrugged his shoulders and waved, saying, "Farewell, corvus-killer."

Fen ignored him, slid off her boots, tied them to her knapsack and waded into the river. Hiding her scent was something she should've thought of herself. She dived in and began to swim.

CHAPTER SIX

BACK IN
THE VILLAGE

THE CLOSER FEN GOT TO HER HOME, THE FASTER SHE ran. Her clothes dried slowly. When there were no paths, she forced her way through the brush. The smoke got thicker, worked its way into her lungs and made her cough. She kept her hood tight—corvuses were circling above the smog, their large wings casting shadows. She was glad for the tall grass and much taller bamboo trees.

Fen skidded to a stop at a clearing. The smoke had taken the form of Queen Servilia looking down at the village. She glared as her head turned from left to right. Was she able to see through that apparition? Fen would be easy to spot from that height. The giant Queen blinked. Her movements were so jerky and repetitive Fen became certain it was a trick.

She crept up to the outskirts of Village Twenty-One. Several Queen's guards on horseback, swords drawn, were galloping between the huts on the opposite bank of the river. There was the occasional shout but no sign of the villagers. Her people. Her mother and sister.

She got down on her knees and crawled until she was right across the water from her hut. Flames were licking at the thatched roof and where one mud-brick wall had collapsed, the interior of their home spilled out like guts. May's yellow cat pillow sat torn in two in the mud. Several pieces of clothing were scattered across the grass.

Mama! May! Fen wanted to swim the river. If either her mother or sister had hidden in the hut, then they were dead.

Fen slowly removed her crossbow and loaded it. She painted her face with mud. Nightfall was coming, the sun already red and low in the sky. She lowered herself right to the earth and became two eyes and two ears.

A bark sounded, louder and more powerful than that of any dog she'd ever heard—a bark that had been designed by the Red Artificers to instill fear. Another hound barked and her insides went liquid. Moments later, she saw an infernus hound sniffing near her hut, its legs long and spindly, its snout stretched and dangerous-looking. The dog's eyes, though, and something in the shape of its face reminded her of a young boy. An angry, vicious boy. The hound was so lean it was as if someone had pulled on both ends to make it even longer, even faster.

Three more hounds joined the first. The pack sniffed through her hut, ignoring the flames. One poked its nose into May's pillow, another snuffled Fen's clothing. A Queen's guard yelled an order and the hounds gathered into a pack and raced along the bank of the river, right across from Fen. She'd heard stories of how they'd ripped traitors to pieces. By the look of the creatures, it wouldn't take very long.

One hound broke away from the pack, circled back and

found a scent along the riverbank. Fen held still. The hound pointed its long snout toward her, snorting in the air. The hound's angry boy-eyes glowed red.

"Get on with it!" a Queen's guard shouted. He thundered up on his charger. His armour glittered and his red hair was unruffled by the wind. He did not seem as if he'd ever sweated or bled. His purple cloak looked perfectly clean. Even his horse was spotless, as though the mud or soot failed to stick to it. "Go, Gripper. Hunt!"

The dog gave a low growl and then put its nose to the ground and worked its way west along the riverbank. The Queen's guard trotted up to the water and let his charger drink. Fen held her breath. Her leg twitched and the horse pointed its ears forward.

The Queen's guard looked directly at her. She ran a finger over the crossbow. The armour couldn't be penetrated, so she would target his neck. She had hit squirrels at an equal distance. A neck was larger than a squirrel.

Could I kill a man? she wondered. *I killed Kang! No. It was the vines—the vines did that.* It would likely be pointless to attempt to kill the Queen's guard—their wounds healed almost at once. Get him in the neck and he'd pull it out and a few moments later be charging after her. Her second choice would be to kill the horse. It didn't have any armour.

She'd always liked horses. They were so strong and stable.

Fen held her eyes open an impossibly long time, worried that even closing them would attract attention. The vines on her stump felt as though they were growing across the ground.

The Queen's guard spat into the river, and then yanked the reins and followed the hounds.

Fen slowly let her breath out between her teeth and blinked several times. Her stump was itching and, without meaning to,

47

she gave it a scratch. The green tendrils were longer and had wound themselves together. She felt the vines. The vines felt her. It was so odd to have sensations there again. She slowly pulled her hand away.

She waited. Not moving. The sun set. Flames from other burning huts lit the village. She knew who owned each one, hoped the families were alive and well. Her back started to cramp and her legs grew cold.

Something—a pig perhaps—crawled along the opposite bank. It dipped its head into the water. Only as it started splashing water onto its face, wiping off dirt, did she see it was a boy.

Not just any boy but Bay, the fishmonger's son. His face was more than dirty—there were bruises too. His eyes were red from crying.

"Bay," she whispered.

He was whimpering to himself.

"Bay," she said, a bit louder.

He looked up, startled. "Who-who is it? Who-who's there?" He wiped his nose with a muddy hand.

"It's Fen. I'm across the river."

He squinted, splashed a little. "Fen-Fen!" he nearly shouted. "It's just horrible. The guard-guards have attacked. They've attacked!"

"Yes, I see that." She put a finger to her lips. "Please, keep your voice down."

"They burned houses. Burn-burned them! And they have everyone at the square and they're shout-shouting."

"Did they hurt you?"

"One hit-hit me. With the flat of his blade. Then he chase-chased someone else and I crawled away. I hid-hid in the reeds. I rolled in pig-pig dung. I stink. Hounds can't smell-smell me."

"Brilliant idea, Bay." She took a breath. "Are my mother and my sister well?"

"Your mother," he said with a gulp. "There was so much blood-blood, Fen. Blood-blood-blood."

"What happened?"

"In the town square-square. Queen's orders. Death orders. A guard grab-grabbed your mother. They ask-asked her questions, Fen. She wouldn't answer."

Fen's breath was stuck in her throat. "What did they do?"

"They cut-cut off her head, Fen. Her head. Off-off."

"They killed her?" She nearly sobbed. "But she was supposed to tell them I'd attacked them. She was supposed to tell them."

"May's in a cage-cage. In a wagon. They say you-you're a wildmagic, Fen."

"No. No, I'm not." Even as she spoke the vines were curling in on themselves.

Across the river, a hound barked. Then another. "Run, Fen. They'll kill kill you."

"Where did they take May?" she asked. There was a hard edge to her voice.

"To the Queen-Queen's Road."

"Then I'll track them and I'll get May out of there." Even as she spoke the words, the task sounded impossible.

A hound growled and Fen saw a sleek grey blur racing across the ground between the huts and the river.

"Bay. Get out of there!" she shouted. "Run!"

He turned, terror in his eyes, and only managed a half crawl along the bank. The hound grabbed him by the leg. Another hound bounded through the grass and clamped onto his arm. Fen raised the crossbow and aimed at one of the dogs.

Bay looked directly at her. "Run-run!" he shouted. "Go! Fen! Go-go!"

He was right. Already Queen's guards were galloping toward the river. She crawled backwards and then clambered through a rice field, knocking over tall stalks in her hurry. Fen scrabbled until her knees were raw, her clothes caked with mud and dirt. Stump. Hand. Stump. Hand. Her stump seemed longer, softer. It dug into the ground and pushed her forward.

But she soon grew tired, her arms too weary to move, her heart like a stone in her chest. She collapsed into the soft earth, smelling the grass. *Mama. Mama.*

Her mother was dead. She had brought Fen into the world and now she was beyond it. By tomorrow Lin would be ashes. A few short hours ago her arms had been wrapped around Fen. She had touched her hair. Her face.

Mama!

It would be better to be caught here. To be taken away before anyone else was killed.

But then she remembered May was in a prison wagon. How far would it have travelled from Village Twenty-One? How scared would her sister be?

The road ran near the river. She might see them and, somehow, rescue her.

Fen lifted her head. She hoped Bay was alive—he had to be! The hounds usually only killed wildmagics. Bay would try to keep the fact he'd seen her a secret, but the Queen's guards were gifted at getting confessions. Especially if there were Royal Inquisitors. She hoped he would speak in time to save his life.

She rose to her feet and ran along the bank. Back toward the Queen's Road.

CHAPTER SEVEN

A DROWNING MAN

FEN FROZE EACH TIME A QUEEN'S GUARD EMERGED OUT of the fog on the opposite bank. Their armour glinted in the darkness, seemed to be on the edge of glowing. They were either shouting orders or silent and grim. She'd hold still until they galloped away. She lost count of how many she'd seen.

Well into the night, she spotted a torch on the opposite bank, and when she got closer, she saw it was burning from the box of a prison wagon. The torch cast enough light to reveal a pair of Queen's guards sitting on the wagon bench, their horses standing still, resting. There was an iron cage in the back, but Fen couldn't see inside. She watched for several minutes. The guards were talking and at ease. One even had his legs stretched out as if he were about to have a nap.

The Queen's Guard had killed her mother. *They had killed her!*

Her stump itched with a burning sensation, as though the vines were on fire, distracting her from what she needed to do. *May had to be locked up there!* In the light of day, when she had her sister by her side and they had safely fled, Fen could inspect her stump and see if she had to cut her whole arm off, but there was no time now.

One of the guards burped, stretched and then climbed down the side of the wagon and strode into the bamboo trees. *They're just like mortals! They need to pee!*

Touching her jade pendant for luck, Fen slipped off her knapsack, crawled into the water and swam smoothly toward the wagon. She chose a landing spot where the reeds were taller. One peek inside the cage was all she needed. Done stealthily enough, the guards wouldn't even know she'd been there.

She squirmed out of the water on the opposite bank, drew her knife and moved with as much speed as she dared, feeling heavy because of her soggy clothes. She did make the occasional squishy sound, but the remaining guard still had his legs stretched out. His eyes were closed.

Fen crept around the side of the wagon and stood on her toes to look inside.

The cage was empty.

The wagon creaked. The Queen's guard came down on her like a boulder, smashing the air out of her lungs and knocking her father's knife from her hand.

"Who in the blazes are you?" He lifted Fen to her feet as if she weighed nothing. His eyes were frightened, though; there was enough light to see that. The Queen's guards all looked young—not much older than eighteen summers—but this one seemed even younger. Newer. As if he'd just come out of the Red Forges where the artificers had shaped him.

"Get your hands off me!" She tried to push him away, but he had a tight hold. He flipped her hood, his eyes narrowed and he shoved her so hard she stumbled backwards several feet. Quickly, he yanked out his sword and swung.

Fen raised her arm to stop the blow. A flash of absolute strength filled her body, her stance solid in the earth. That strength moved through her and out her arm. She had an image of her missing hand becoming a long branch-like appendage.

This time, she was familiar with what was happening. She felt the vines, in a heartbeat, extending outwards. She could even partially aim them so they smacked the guard in the centre of his chest. He was knocked from his feet, his blade dropping to the ground. It lay right in front of her.

She picked up the sword with her left hand. It was deceptively light.

"Where's my sister?" she asked. The guard was standing already, but he backed away, reaching for a dagger.

"Don't move!" she commanded. "Or I'll—I'll skewer you!"

"Get into the cage." Even his voice sounded young. It would only make sense that the newest guards were on wagon duty. "Surrender to the Queen!"

"You've forgotten who has the sword!"

He had the dagger out now. "There's a whole regiment here." He sounded more confident. "You're surrounded. Things will go easier if you surrender."

"You killed my mother!" She spat these words out.

"I—I didn't. Now put down my sword." He took a step toward her.

Fen jabbed the blade in his direction to scare him, but it caught his arm, slicing through the armour.

He clamped his hand over the cut, blood running between

his fingers. Then his armour glowed and he removed his hand. The wound was gone. Even the red spatters on his armour had vanished in smoke.

The stories were true. The Queen's magic healed them within moments.

"We are quite hard to kill," he said. There was more confidence in his voice. Even cockiness.

"I don't want to kill you." She wondered if she could yank his cloak over his head. Then she could run. No, she didn't want to get that close.

A jaunty whistled tune cut through the air. The other Queen's guard was returning.

"Albus!" the soldier in front of her shouted.

Fen dared a glance behind her. No one was there, yet.

"What is it, Marcus?"

"Beware! The wildmagic is here!"

"You better not be imagining things, greenie!" Branches snapped and a nearby bush moved.

"She's right here!"

Albus burst out of the bamboo behind Fen, sword in hand.

She screamed a war cry—or as close as she could come with her hoarse voice—and darted at Marcus. He lurched back. She shot through the open space and sped toward the river.

Over her shoulder, she saw that Marcus was at her heels. She considered throwing the sword at him, but if he didn't have it, he couldn't kill her. She dived, but he grabbed her foot and she landed in a few inches of water. He overshot her, though, so she pushed him hard. The bank was steep and he fell into the deep water and was swept along by the current.

A crossbow bolt whizzed past her ear. She jumped as far as she could into the river, sword in hand, discovering it was light enough to swim with. She kicked her way toward the opposite bank under water, eyes open.

A bright light flashed below her. Marcus had sunk like a boulder to the river bottom. His armour was glowing, as if he were in a bubble of sunlight. His hand was at his throat, his eyes bulging.

He's drowning! The Queen's guard couldn't swim.

She dived down. He was flailing madly, and she knew better than to get tangled up with a drowning man. He saw her and reached out. She got as close as she dared and then lifted her right arm. As if following her bidding, the vines grew and a green blast shot through the water. It felt to Fen as if she were punching him. The vines lifted Marcus to the surface and threw him bodily toward the bank. The force of doing that propelled her in the opposite direction.

She let the current carry her along and swam the rest of the way across the river. As she crawled out of the water, she looked back to see the other guard bent over Marcus, shouting at him. Fen took a moment to plaster the blade with mud, and then she crept along the bank until she found her knapsack. She started to run.

A flare lit the sky, but she was far enough away that it didn't cast light on her. The two Queen's guards were standing by the wagon. The one who'd almost drowned—Marcus—was holding a crossbow. The other gripped his sword in one hand and a horn in the other. He let out three blasts.

"Are you the stupidest creature on earth?" a voice said right in her ear.

Fen nearly swung the sword but then recognized who it was. "Ithak," she said. "Stop following me!"

"Following you?" He was standing next to a tree, only half-visible. There was a sheen of sweat on his face. "Ithak is cursing you. They've cut off my path to Helwood. Guards and soldiers are racing up and down the Queen's Road. Servilia really wants you dead. Was the village in flames?"

"Yes."

"Ithak said so. But you didn't listen to Ithak."

She wanted to shout that her mother had been killed and her sister captured, but she guessed Ithak wouldn't care. She sucked in a calming breath. "And where do I . . . where do we go now?"

"We? Oh, all friendly now that you're friendless. Why would Ithak want such a stupid companion? Takes on two Queen's guards. Neat little trick you did there, throwing him out of the river. Stupid, though, as Ithak said. Their armour gets heavier in the water. Better to leave him as fish food. Why did you do it?"

She failed to come up with a good reason. Other than she couldn't stand seeing the look on his face as he drowned. "I didn't want him to die."

Ithak slapped his forehead. "Queen of idiots! They're here to kill you."

"Where do we go now?" she repeated.

"The guards are swarming like hornets. You'll be dead by sunrise, without my help." He pointed south. "We'll go into the Great Salt Mire."

"It's poisonous! No man can breathe that air."

"No woman either. Or girl. But better dead and beautiful in a marsh than torn up by infernus hounds and bleeding out next to this river."

He turned and began running in the direction he'd pointed. A moment later, she followed. She put her hand to her belt to touch her father's knife, but it was gone. She'd lost it in the fight. She hoped that wasn't a bad omen.

CHAPTER EIGHT

BECOMING
THE STINK

THE SUN WAS RISING. THE GREAT SALT MIRE spread out before Fen and Ithak, a flat, dead land as white as winter. Already, the stink made her eyes water and her breath catch in her mouth. Fen didn't want to imagine the stench once they were in the bog itself. Ithak marched forward.

Fen covered her nose and cast an eye to the skies. A corvus was high above them, travelling in a slow circle.

"The Queen watches," Ithak said. "But even her beaked children will die if they stray too far into this stench. They don't have my lungs."

"How can you breathe the air without choking?"

"Ithak was chased here by obnoxious villagers from the south. They used to be called Berbs." She saw, upon closer examination, that his skin was a series of small scales. "Whatever Ithak is faced with, Ithak becomes that thing. So Ithak became the stink. And the swamps became my hidey place, and neither the Berbs nor the Queen could follow me here."

She wondered how it was even possible to get accustomed to the smell. But something else niggled at her. "You called the villagers Berbs. What does that mean?"

"It was the name of their people. They had a city that shone like a jewel . . . Mazhig. It's dust now. At least that's what Ithak read."

"I thought only those who served the Queen could read."

"Ithak grew up in Regentium," he said. "My parents taught me. Plus, Ithak's brain is very, very big."

Fen drew in a breath, intending to ask another question, but suddenly she started coughing. She coughed and coughed until she thought she'd black out. She tried inhaling through her sleeve, but this only resulted in more coughing. A prickly sweat began to itch in every scratch on her body. Her eyes watered.

"It will be a shame when the stink kills you." Ithak ran a pale finger below his eye as if tracing a tear. "Ithak will miss you. Of course, Ithak will take your goods and eat your food. Which reminds me, do you have any food?"

Fen wiped spittle from her lips. "Half a sweet bun and salted oxen meat." She had eaten the last vegetables in the night.

"Oh, joy, more salt." He sniffed. "Ithak will take the bun."

"You meant to say please, right?"

"Oh, Ithak's humblest apologies. Please, Princess Fen. Please. Please. Please." He said the last three words in a mocking falsetto.

She dug into her knapsack and found the bread wrapped in a green leaf. The sight of her mother's baking made Fen swallow a sob. Before she could even offer the bun, Ithak snatched at it. She held on to a chunk, but he grabbed the rest and tossed it into his gaping mouth.

"Mmm. Sweet!" He chewed loudly. Fen carefully wrapped up the last bit of the bun.

Ithak motioned toward the Queen's blade that Fen had tied to her knapsack. "That sword is a rare find. Only a dead Queen's guard will give up his blade. In fact, that wetling you took it from, he's certainly headless now."

"Why?"

"Queen's law: immediate execution for any soldier who loses his blade to the enemy."

"But that's horrible!"

"No." He chuckled. "It's funny. You saved his life and you killed him at the same time."

Would they really execute that Queen's guard? She couldn't remember his name.

She broke off a piece of the salted oxen meat and let the rock-hard beef soak in her mouth. It was the way her father had taught her to eat it. *Don't chew until you count to sixty.* She counted inside her head.

"You could sell the sword. Those blades are forged by the Royal Red Artificers and will cut through everything. Stone. Metal. Even poke a hole in a Queen's guard's armour." He tapped his chin with his index finger. "It dawns on Ithak that Ithak will be the one selling it. You'll be dead."

"I won't die." She tried to say this without coughing. The air was so thick she felt she'd choke on it.

"Ithak doesn't share your optimism."

The soil grew soft and she stepped around a place that looked to be a sinkhole. Water as white as milk bubbled up from another hole beside her.

She glanced skyward again. The corvus had vanished. It likely couldn't stand the smell.

There was something Fen had been wondering about. "Does your clothing change with you?" she asked.

"Yes. Years ago, Ithak would have to take it off every time he made himself unseeable. Awkward! And dangerous—why, once Ithak had stripped naked but forgotten to remove his hat. He was running away from a pack of bakers. Hilarious!" He slapped his thigh. "It wasn't until an iron pot knocked the cap off Ithak's head that Ithak became aware of the mistake."

Fen smiled, but she held back her laughter for fear of coughing. "So your clothing does change?"

"My dear benefactor had the belt and tunic sewn for me. Pockets are so handy! Wish Ithak had a suit of armour that could do this."

"You have a benefactor?"

He patted his stomach. "He even feeds me. He dwells in Helwood. Very dependable and very, very ancient. He helps so many outsiders. He may even help you, if you survive the stink."

"Who is he?"

"He's too old for a name. Ithak gets items for him. Gold sometimes. Pieces of black stone. Pouches of magic dust. A small price to pay for his help."

Fen started to bark and hack and this time she spat up blood and stared at it in horror. Her father had coughed up blood the night he died. "How—how can I get used to this smell?"

"You won't."

"So you led me out here knowing I'd die?"

"You faced certain death by the river." He pointed back toward her village. But they had walked so far that she couldn't even see the green land behind them. "At least here you get to take a few more breaths."

And you get all of my stuff. She took an awkward step and

stumbled, landing on her knees in the soggy white mud. Ithak didn't offer her a hand up. He just kept walking. She wheezed as she pushed herself back to her feet. The knapsack was growing heavier.

They passed a leafless, dead white tree that was maybe twice her height. Most of the branches were broken off. "Why is this place so desolate?"

"Oh, to know nothing! What a blessing. Ithak aches to be a simpleton like you."

Fen gritted her teeth. "Just tell me."

"This was a kingdom once. It included one of the nine cities and all the surrounding villages."

"What?" She looked all around her. There wasn't even a sign of any buildings.

"Yep, we are walking where thousands of people would have walked. I don't know which city was here. Queen Servilia destroyed it with her guards and her red magic. Every wall, every sculpture, turned to dust. Every city dweller, too, of course."

"You're wrong!" Fen pointed at him with her left hand. "Mansren destroyed all nine cities. Queen Servilia defeated him and brought peace."

"You're rather defensive of the woman who cut off your hand. And you're stupid for believing the lies the Royal Historians spread. Your stupidity is understandable—you can't read . . . you wouldn't know any better." He lifted a handful of salt and let it fall from his hands. "Ithak has travelled every corner of Illium. There are nine wastelands like this in the queendom. That's not a coincidence."

The idea that they were walking over a dead kingdom—a whole kingdom!—made Fen feel sick.

"How can you know all this?" she asked.

"I read a really, really old book."

She put her hands on her hips. It felt as if her stump were slightly longer, but she ignored that sensation. "Only the Queen's servants can have books. How did you get one?"

"That's a long story I'll share later, if you live. I curse the fact that so many pages were missing. But believe me, this was one of the nine cities."

Fen suddenly coughed so hard she nearly fell over. When she was done, she spat another wad of phlegmy blood onto the white earth. Her vines began rustling around on her arm as if they wanted her attention. She ignored them.

"That's how it begins," Ithak said. "A dribble of blood, a drabble and then the torrent drowns your lungs. A particularly nasty way to die."

She took a step. Forced herself to take another. *I'm not going to die here!* She continued to follow Ithak, but as time passed, she coughed harder and more violently. She couldn't catch her breath.

"What is your magic?" he asked, indifferent to her predicament.

"I—I don't know." Her voice was rough. "At least, I don't understand it."

"You were able to throw that Queen's guard from the water. Are you incredibly strong?"

"No. I just imagined it and it happened. I—I used my stump."

Another hacking coughing fit blocked her ears. Ithak's lips were moving. She had the sense her lungs were somehow filling with water. Or was it blood? She spat out a mouthful of burning black bile.

"Answer Ithak: are there other times you've had the magic happen?" he asked. "Ithak tires of repeating himself."

"Yes." She gasped. "I was attacked by a man with a scythe and I . . . I grew vines."

"You became a plant?" He slapped his thigh.

She spat again. More blood! "They—they choked him and . . . and he died."

"Perhaps Ithak should fear the great green murderess." He let out another aggravating chuckle. "Ithak doesn't see any vines. Where do they go?"

She hid her stump behind her back. "They disappear."

"Into thin air?"

"No. They—they retract."

He rubbed his chin. "Any other times you've been . . . vined?"

"Once when I fell from a tree. The . . . the vines grew and grabbed a branch."

"You are a clumsy oaf! But it does seem the magic rises when your life is threatened."

"Yes." It was all she could spit out.

"Your life is threatened now. And yet your magic does not aid you. Interesting, isn't it?"

She leaned over to cough again and didn't stop until her face had turned purple. "You're talking me to death." The words were ragged in her throat.

"Stop whining. Let Ithak see your stump."

Almost ashamed, she lifted her arm. For the last three years, the stump had been the obvious sign she was a thief. That she was partially crippled. She untied the sleeve and brought her arm out.

Fen drew a deep, surprised breath. The vines had formed into a small green appendage. It looked to be made of soft, pliable wood. There were even fingernails of bark.

"You've grown a woody hand!" Ithak said.

She stared. She imagined the fingers moving. They moved! A hand—she had a hand again! "By the gods!"

"Oh, this wasn't the gods," Ithak said. "This was you." He poked at the hand. "Do you feel that?"

"Yes."

"If we break off a finger, will it grow back?"

"Don't try!" Her lungs were burning now, along with aching to cough. "New hand or not. I . . . can't . . . breathe."

"You must master your magic." He gestured and his skin changed to pure white in an instant before he vanished. Then he snapped his fingers and became visible again. "That took me years to perfect. Finding the side of me that mirrored the outside world."

"What . . . what should I do?"

"Picture something that'll help you breathe."

"I can't think of anything," she said.

"Then you'll die."

She coughed so hard she nearly retched. What would make the air clearer? New lungs? Gills?

"There's nothing," she said. She fell to her knees, knocked down by the force of her coughing.

What brought air into her? Her nose, her mouth. A cloth wasn't enough to block this smell. Whatever was in the stink, and was killing her, was invisible. Was impossible to stop.

"Ithak will take that sword and your food and your crossbow. And that jade necklace. And Ithak will eat the last of your pork bun. A bun your mother made, Ithak guesses. When you die, there will be no one left who cares for your sister. She will rot in a prison cell."

Fen wanted to punch him in the face, but she couldn't reach him.

"It has been somewhat pleasant knowing you, Fen of the Green Hand."

64

Her vision was fading. She had once scooped a codfish onto the banks of the Vilia and watched it thrashing as it tried to breathe. She was now that fish.

And she would soon be dead.

CHAPTER NINE

THE MASTER COBBLER-TO-BE

"Breathe . . ." Fen's voice was a raspy whisper. "Must . . . breathe . . ."

How could she change the very air? She pictured her mother's silk dust mask. It would be useless here.

Then Fen lifted her right hand—that new hand—to her mouth. Or had it gone there on its own bidding? The air was fresher in the bamboo forest, where there was so much green. And in their hut—her mother grew herbs and flowers, even small trees. Somehow, green was the answer.

It had been May's job to water the plants. Fen saw an image of her sister clutching the clay watering jar. She was holding up a leaf with her other hand. "Green . . ." May said.

"Green," Fen replied. She expected her sister to answer, but she only held the leaf. "Green," Fen said again.

Ithak was bending over her, his big eyes blinking. "Have you gone batty?"

"Green . . ." she repeated.

She rubbed at her face and could feel her cheek through those soft and supple wooden fingers. *Green means life.* A flash. A web of vines and leaves grew out of the wooden fingers and wrapped around her face.

Fen couldn't breathe at all now. She couldn't even cough— her nostrils and throat were blocked by the vines. Her hand was choking her.

Ithak looked amused by her panic.

Help me! Help! Fen yanked at the leafy growth with her other hand, but the vines didn't break. And they wouldn't stop spreading into her.

Her body so needed air. She felt a scratching down her throat, into her lungs. Tendrils of green, budding there. Maybe they were running down her very veins and up her arteries. She pulled away her wooden hand and the vines snapped, but they continued to grow and expand despite not being attached to her.

Air burst through the leaves and into her lungs, which filled and then deflated. She was drawing in clean air!

"Hmm, that's too bad," Ithak said. "Colour is coming back to your cheeks. Ithak thought that sword would be his. Can you speak?"

She tried, but only a muffled sound came out. She gladly gulped another breath of glorious air.

"You're silent now? Perfect! Can you stand?"

She did so, shakily. He grabbed her arm and steadied her.

"A very curious magic power you have. Leaves have saved your life. You are breathing, right?"

Fen nodded. She felt stronger. There wasn't even the slightest smell or stink, though her eyes still watered. She blinked until her vision cleared.

"Well, it's a long walk," Ithak said. "No sense standing around gawking at your greenery."

She stared in wonder at her hand of wood, opening and closing it. A moment later she noticed Ithak was already twenty paces ahead. She followed.

In time, the spiderweb of leaves plastered across Fen's mouth and nose began to feel like a natural part of her body. Ithak had filled the silence by talking about the weather, his sore feet, his favourite meal—which was, oddly enough, roasted squirrel— and, finally, he said, "Ithak supposes you want to know how he gloriously arrived in this world. It's a great tale of betrayal and courage and cunning. If you agree to hear this tale, just stay silent."

The leaves in her throat prevented Fen from making any noise.

"Ah, so you agree. Then Ithak will begin. Ithak was born in Regentium, the humble son of a humble shoemaker. My parents adored me. It was only natural. Ithak was a beautiful baby. And Ithak grew into a handsome young man. Extremely handsome and tall." From what she could see, he was not the most attractive man to walk Illium. And he certainly wasn't tall, though maybe through the years he'd been shrinking. "'You're going to be the finest shoemaker in the city,' my father would say. Ithak believed he would grow up to make velvet slippers for the Queen herself." He shrugged. "Anyway, one day when Ithak was twelve, he was stitching a cork shoe and suddenly he could no longer see his fingers. It gave Ithak a fright. The needle and thread were floating in the air—Ithak's fingers had vanished!" He shook his hand to show her, making them vanish and reappear. "The fingers returned. Ithak assumed it was just a hallucination caused by sausage gas. Ithak went to bed, and his parents both kissed him good night and told him how much they loved their perfect child."

Fen thought she heard a coughing noise behind them. She turned, but the flat salt mire stretched on forever. The air was obscured by salt dust. She was glad to be done coughing. In fact, she'd never before had fresher air.

Ithak was touching the pouch on the side of his belt. Then he nodded as if in answer to a question and looked up.

If she could have spoken, Fen would have asked what was in the pouch.

He gave her a smile. "Now where was Ithak? Oh, yes. In the morning, Ithak's mother strolled into his room and screamed. 'What is it, dear Mother, ye who birthed me into this world?' Ithak asked.

"'You are gone!' she shouted. She was correct. His body was the same colour as the sheets. Ithak patted his chest and arms. They were still there. 'I am here, dear Mother,' Ithak said in his most loving of voices. He grew visible, but he wasn't certain how he'd done it. 'Your hair!' she exclaimed. 'It's evil red!' Ithak's father bumbled into the room holding his cobbler hammer. 'Oh dear,' he said. 'Oh dear.' He brought the hammer up as though he were going to strike his beloved child from the world. 'This is just a momentary sickness,' Ithak uttered in innocence. 'I will get well and become the shoemaker you always dreamed I would be.'

"'Stay in your room,' Ithak's father said. He was still holding the hammer in a tight fist. 'Yes, don't move,' Mother added. She closed the door. Ithak lifted his hand mirror. His beautiful, boyish, long, blond tresses had become a cursed red."

He wiped at his face. Tears? Fen wondered. No. Just salt dust in his eye. She wished she could mention that she, too, had been overtaken by the magic during the night.

"Ithak was certain his parents were planning to hide him in their wagon and flee and live happily ever after far away.

"But Ithak's door was kicked open and a glittering Queen's guard crashed inside, sword in hand. Ithak vanished in fear. 'Show yourself, coward!' the guard shouted. Ithak threw the blankets off and leapt out of bed. His flesh had matched the room. The guard swung and cut Ithak's bed in half. He killed Ithak's shelves. Stabbed Ithak's dolls. Sliced Ithak's shoe collection from the dresser. Ithak darted past him into the hallway. 'He's here, right here!' Ithak's father said. The hand that had patted Ithak's head a thousand times was a vise on Ithak's arm. 'Oh, dear Father,' Ithak said. 'Release me in the name of love.' Ithak's mother was crying in a corner and Father shouted, 'The monster is here!' The Queen's guard burst out of the room—he'd slain all the furniture—and another Queen's guard charged through the front door. Ithak bit his father and he let go. 'The evil demon bit me!' Those were the last words Ithak heard from his father's mouth. Ithak dived out the window and ran into the streets." Ithak took a deep breath. "Ithak can see you are moved by my story."

Fen was, though she didn't think she was showing it. The poor man, to be betrayed by his parents.

"Well, the Queen's guards pursued and Ithak knew they'd soon have the hounds out. So Ithak had a brilliant thought. A survival thought. Ithak dashed through a pigsty. Oh, the stench. Oh, the ignominy. The guards soon lost him. Ithak eventually found his way out of the city gates and, in time, after many grand adventures and thrilling events, Ithak came to live in the great forest of Helwood. A very stirring tale, was it not?"

Fen nodded. It was all she could do.

"Ithak hopes they gutted his parents," he hissed. "How dare they betray Ithak? Their prince. The master cobbler-to-be."

Fen wanted to say something to comfort him. Her mother had attempted to save her and was killed for it. Fen stifled a sob imagining her mother's execution. To see the sword coming . . . Perhaps her mother had been spared the sight of May being flung into a cage bound for Regentium. Fen clenched her right fist.

The wood felt strong. She had a hand again. A hand! It was soft and green. Its five tiny branches were covered by pale bark, but they opened and closed as easily as the fingers on her original hand. She was no longer Fen of the One Hand. The thief.

She was tired of not being able to speak. She imagined the leaves clearing inside her throat and mouth and found they responded to what she pictured in her head. To test her theory, she breathed in through her mouth and the poison air burned. She coughed. Then she sucked in sweet air through her nose. She took several more deep breaths.

"How—how long ago did you leave Regentium?" she asked. Her throat was dry, the words crackled.

Ithak glanced her way. "Hmph! You can talk again."

"I'm breathing through my nose."

"Clever! Ithak left Regentium seventy summers ago."

"You're over seventy summers old!" She couldn't hide the incredulity in her voice. "But you . . . you look no more than thirty."

"Thirty! Oh, hurtful child! Ithak has applied wagonloads of moisturizing clay to his skin, rubbed buckets of green tea leaves under his eyes, all to look twenty-five summers old." He ran a hand through his hair. "Well, to be specific, Ithak has been in this world for eighty-three springs, eighty-three summers, eighty-two autumns and eighty-two winters."

"But how can you have lived so long?"

"Not all of us wildmagics are gifted with long lives. Some

have such great powers that they are burned out quickly. Or their heads get chopped off. But some will live centuries. The good ones, Ithak humbly adds. You might even live for ages if you're part tree. Several wildmagics have lived longer than the Queen herself. Ithak has not met them in the flesh. Well, Ithak may have met one. But he . . . well, he didn't quite have his head." Ithak put his hands on his belt. It was the third time she'd seen him tap the pouch, as if it held some sort of good luck trinket.

"What's in your pouch?" she asked finally. He gave her a sharp look, holding his hand tight against it.

"A chunk of history," he said. "Would you like to see it?"

"I suppose."

He flipped open the pouch and pulled out a dark object, about four inches long.

"It's a finger," she said.

"A stone finger. It's my good luck charm. There was a statue once of a . . . a poet. A dreamer. A statue that was made before the Queen was born. The rest of it is broken to bits. But Ithak found its finger. Ithak carries it to remember there was a time before the Queen. It also carries me." He chuckled. His laugh made her think he spent far too much time alone.

"May I hold it?" She reached out, but Ithak shoved the finger back in his pouch.

"It's my finger. Not to be pawed by—"

He fell over. At first, she thought he'd tripped. But he squirmed on his back and gasped in pain. A crossbow bolt was sticking out of his right shoulder. A hissing swept past her head and at the same moment a sharp sting jolted the side of her face. She put her hand to her ear and felt blood.

"Get down, fool!" Ithak shouted. "Before you become a pin-cushion!"

CHAPTER TEN

THE VOICE
INSIDE HIM

FEN THREW HERSELF TO HER STOMACH, LANDING HARD. Salt dust shot into her eyes, making them water.

"There's someone loosing bolts at us," she said.

"Oh, you're clever!" Ithak had crawled to hide behind a small rise of earth. He glanced at his shoulder and grimaced. "The bolt has the Queen's markings on it."

"What should we do?" she asked.

"We? I'm wounded. You go kill the archer." He clutched the injury, blood pumping over his fingers. "Can you see our enemy?"

She raised her head and a bolt flew just inches above it. She dropped down again, but not before she'd glimpsed a red-haired shadow about twenty yards distant.

"A Queen's guard is directly ahead of us," she said.

"Ithak has a brilliant plan—lead him away from me."

"What?"

"Whenever their chicks are in trouble, a bird will draw the cat away. You be the bird."

"I'll get a bolt in my back!" She pressed herself more closely against the ground. "Just make yourself invisible."

"It's hard to do when you're bleeding." His flesh was quite pale, and he was looking like he might pass out. It dawned on her that the Queen's guard likely wasn't alone. They could soon be surrounded.

"Fine. I'll go."

Fen slid off her knapsack, took out her own tiny crossbow, grabbed the quiver and crawled to her left. She expected a bolt through the head. But with each passing moment, none came. She wriggled in a wide circle, staying behind the ridge or tufts of dead grass.

Eventually she heard a wheezing that sounded like leaky bellows. Several heartbeats later, the bellows let out a hoarse breath. She edged forward, dragging herself by her fingernails. Her wooden hand felt particularly strong.

She would have to aim for the heart. No—if it was a Queen's guard, the armour would be impenetrable. Her best target would be the head. He'd heal, but maybe the injury would distract him long enough for her to tie him up. Or she could use the sword to behead him.

She wasn't certain she could do that.

She peeked over a small hump of pale earth. A Queen's guard was caught in a sinkhole, only his shoulders and head showing above the liquidy brine. His red hair was coated white with salt. He pointed the loaded crossbow toward where she and Ithak had been standing. The man let out another raspy rattle of air. Whatever magic he had was fighting to keep him alive in the poison atmosphere. And failing.

"*Kill. Kill. Kill,*" he whispered. The anger in his voice sent a chill through her innards. "*Kill the girl now. Kill. Before you die, my son. Obey your Queen. Obey your mother.*"

The voice was his and not his. It sounded feminine. He was poised to shoot, but if she waited quietly he would sink out of sight and die.

Her mother had told her to watch with careful eyes. But this was not a time to sit back. Fen stood and looked all around. This was the only enemy and he didn't notice her. He was perhaps wheezing too loudly to hear her. She pointed her crossbow directly at his head.

"Queen's guard!" she shouted. "Turn around very slowly."

He spun and cried out, "*Die for me! Die!*" He loosed a bolt. Fen's wooden hand shot out with impossible quickness and caught it only an inch from her forehead. She let it fall to the ground.

Fen blinked. She should be dead. How stupid of her not to shoot him right away.

"You missed," she said. No, that wasn't right. "Your bolts can't harm me." She had caught an arrow in flight—a feat only heroes in old stories could perform. But none of them were girls, let alone girls with wooden hands.

The Queen's guard threw the crossbow at her and then tried to crawl in her direction, succeeding only in sinking faster. "*Come closer and die! Die for your Queen! I command you!*"

"Stand up, Ithak," Fen said. "The Queen's guard is no longer a threat."

The guard continued to churn and sink. It was madness! He'd be lost in the mire in moments.

Ithak limped over. Blood was running along his shoulder and down his pale body.

"Well," Ithak said. "Let's take a seat and watch the rat die."

"*Traitor! Kill you too. Both of you. Die. Die!*"

"You'd think he'd be asking us to toss a rope," Ithak said.

"He's gone mad," Fen said quietly.

She had such a clear memory of the guard who'd severed her hand. Of how calm and perfect he'd been. This one was nothing like that.

"*Kill you! Cut off your heads. Traitors!*"

"Queen's guards *are* usually more level-headed than this," Ithak said. "They are intelligent. Begrudgingly, Ithak admits they even have some majesty. Perhaps the salt has rotted his brain."

"*You must die! For the Queen. For me. Me. The Queen.*" The Queen's guard rattled in another ragged breath. He was turning a pale, pale white. Only one eye was focused. "*Get up and kill them for me, son! Kill them for the Queen!*"

"He thinks he's the Queen," Fen said.

"You're wrong." Ithak couldn't keep the wonder from his words. "This is the Queen herself."

"The Queen?" Fen lifted her crossbow. "Here?"

"Yes. Yes! Hello, Queen, can you hear me?"

"*You mock me?*" The Queen's guard slammed his fist against the white mud, splashing himself. "*You'll be choked with your own entrails.*"

"Why don't you come and try," Ithak responded. "See if you like the stink out here—a stink you made. Your guard doesn't."

"Should we be taunting her?" Fen asked.

Ithak grinned. "She's taunted and hunted me my whole life. This great mire is one of the few places she cannot reach."

"*I'll eviscerate both of you.*"

"That's the Queen all right," Ithak said. "If you had any pity, Fen, you'd just give him a death blow with your sword. Don't waste a bolt. She'll keep using him until he's dead."

"I can't stab him."

Ithak shrugged, then winced and held his shoulder. "Good. He'll struggle in the mire, the magic invested in his armour—his blood—resurrecting him each time he dies until he grows too weak. Eventually, painfully, he'll perish."

"*You are worm food. Both of you are marked!*"

"Ithak has been marked since the day Ithak turned. You tried to get Ithak then. You failed."

"*I will torture your sister,*" the Queen's guard said.

Fen went cold.

The voice was growing more hoarse. "*My Royal Inquisitor will summon May to the red chambers this very hour. He will pluck her toenails one by one.*"

"You—you. Can't."

"*I will.*" The guard's voice sounded so certain, so powerful. And so much like the voice Fen had heard on waking every morning. "*I am the Queen. And May is very frightened. She will be crushed, bone by bone, crying out your name. And the name of your mother.*"

"Don't you dare touch her!"

"*Come before my walls and fall on your knees. Only that will save her. I promise you safe passage to Regentium.*"

The Queen's guard was up to his neck now.

"Your sister is in no more danger now than she was before," Ithak said.

"*Kneel before me in Regentium,*" the Queen commanded. "*If you love your sister, you will come.*" Then the Queen's guard fell silent. His eyes closed.

"Drat!" Ithak barked. "It looks like he'll die before he sinks."

Clumps of salt mud were stuck to the guard's face. He shuddered. Once. Twice. A third time.

"Death throes," Ithak said. Fen found the joy in his voice disgusting. "At least this part'll be entertaining."

Then the Queen's guard opened one eye. It focused on Fen. He coughed and riding on that air were the words *Help me.* It did not sound like the Queen. "*Help. Meeeeee.*"

Fen stood still for a moment. Was it a trap? The man had said such horrible things only moments earlier. Or the Queen had. And he *had* tried to kill her and Ithak.

"*Pleassse help.*" His voice wasn't much more than a hiss. It would be better to let him die. Safer.

She waited another moment. And another. *Mama would never let him die,* she thought. Then she let out a huff, undid her belt and tossed one end to him.

"What are you doing!" Ithak shouted.

"Something stupid," she said.

The Queen's guard didn't grab at the belt. She flipped it so that the buckle slapped against his arm. "He'll be of use to us," she said.

"As a chair?"

She ignored him. The guard's hand closed slowly on the belt, but when she pulled, it slipped out of his grasp. She got down on her stomach and crawled toward him, spreading out her body so she wouldn't sink. The closer she got, the more clearly she saw how badly he was doing. Maybe he was already dead. She looped the belt around his wrist, her own hand sinking into the salt mire. She wiggled back to more solid ground and pulled. There was a sucking sound, but he was too heavy and too deep in the mire to move.

"Give me a hand," she said.

"Ha! This vile weapon has been sent to cut us in two. Unless . . . are you hoping to strip his armour and sell it?"

"No."

"Then you are the most dull-witted child Ithak has ever had the displeasure to meet."

She pulled. And pulled. The guard slid slightly toward her.

"Help me!" she said.

"Ithak is wounded."

"All I need is one of your hands. Just take the belt and pull."

"Mansren preserve us from this madness," he said, but he grabbed the belt. They tugged the Queen's guard forward, bit by bit, until his shoulders were free. In time they were able to drag him to more solid ground. He lay completely still. Fen scooped briny mud out of his mouth. It felt odd to touch his lips, dry as they were. But it had to be done.

"As Ithak mentioned before"—Ithak huffed and puffed—"he's dead."

"No. They heal themselves."

She thumbed another lump out. He'd swallowed a pailful. He was still somewhat warm. Both eyes were closed. "He will not die," she promised. "If there's a way to my sister, it's through him."

"Madness! Your sister is in Regentium. She's dead. We wildmagics have a saying. *The dead are dead.* It's not the deepest of sayings, but it—"

"No!" she shouted. "She won't die!" Fen put her hand over the guard's face and pictured him somehow healing and breathing . . . yes, breathing just as she was breathing. The thought became a warm emotion, a movement in her mind. Tendrils of vines grew down into his mouth, up his nostrils. "I won't allow his death."

"You are incredibly stubborn," Ithak said, but there was wonder in his voice.

She felt a part of her was pushing his lungs open, pulling them shut, bringing the air into him. Bringing life. She sensed the energy coming from the ground itself. From far below the salt mire.

The Queen's guard coughed. He rolled over, spat up a wet, briny liquid and moaned. The vines separated from her, but continued to do their work. His chest was rising and falling. His eyes stayed closed but he grew less pale. She felt his neck and discovered the faintest pulse. "He lives."

"Wonderful," Ithak mumbled. "Now he can poke us full of holes."

"He won't," she said, with more certainty than she felt. Then the Queen's guard opened his eyes and grabbed her tightly by the arm, his breath still ragged, his mouth full of leaves. She swore she heard him say "Thank you."

CHAPTER ELEVEN

YOUR LIFE
BELONGS TO ME

THE GUARD'S HAND FELL TO THE GROUND. HIS EYES slid shut.

"Tie him up," Ithak said. "Before he strangles you."

She unknotted the hemp rope from her knapsack and tied his wrists, and then she looped it around his midsection. She noticed his scabbard was empty.

"He has no sword," she said.

"Perhaps it was lost in the mud," Ithak said. "Or . . ." He rubbed his chin. "*You* have his sword. He was sent to get his weapon back."

There was no way to tell the Queen's guards apart. "He might be the same one." She finished tying him and removed the scabbard, attaching it to her own belt. The sword fit perfectly in it. She turned to Ithak. "Now, what about you?"

"Me?"

"We can't leave that bolt in your shoulder."

"It's a decoration." He gave a pained smile. Fen saw he was barely standing on his own.

"The wound will widen each time you move," she said. "Then it'll go septic and you'll die."

"Since when are you a healer?"

"My mother was gifted in that art." She clenched her jaw. The best way to mourn would be to survive.

She convinced Ithak to lie down and then easily cut through one end of the shaft using the sword.

"Oww," he said. He'd grown even more pale and had started shivering. "Don't just yank it out. Ithak will tell you when to pull. The best way is to—*aaaah!*"

Fen was holding the now-free bolt in her hand. She tossed it away. "There."

"Ithak told you to wait!" he whimpered.

"We would've waited until the end of the world." Fresh blood pumped out of the wound. The puncture wasn't too wide. "You're lucky. It missed bone and any big arteries."

"Ithak doesn't feel lucky. Ithak feels very pained."

She found a small collection of healing leaves and one of the sewing needles her mother had packed for her, as well as several strips of cotton and some ointment. Her mother had thought of everything. She lifted the needle and thread. "I'm going to stitch your wound. You might want to bite a stick."

Ithak stared at the needle. "Have you done this before?"

"I've watched my mother do it."

He groaned. "Oh, go ahead."

Carefully, she stitched the flesh together. It was easier than she'd thought it would be and her wooden hand was adept at holding the needle. Ithak stayed surprisingly still.

"There." She smeared on some healing ointment and tied the cotton strips in place. "With luck, you won't go septic."

Other than rasping through his gritted teeth, Ithak was silent. And for the first time, Fen had a moment to think. She was uncertain what to do. The Queen had promised safe passage as long as Fen knelt before her. Fen was certain it would mean her death, but wouldn't that be a fair trade for May's life? Unless the promise was a lie. Or she could travel on to Helwood and hide there and hope, somehow, to find another way to save her sister. Either way she had to get to the edge of the salt mire and then she could—

Fen heard a noise.

The Queen's guard was stumbling her way. He half-lunged, half-fell toward her and she stepped out of his path. He missed and, since his hands were tied, his face struck the salty soil.

"The best Queen's guard is a dead Queen's guard," Ithak said.

The guard rolled onto his back and glared at her. Fen drew the sword and pressed the blade against his throat.

"Are you there, Queen?" she asked.

The Queen's guard tried to speak, but his voice was caught by the leaves.

"The Queen is gone," Ithak said. "She's left this husk of a soldier for us to feed and water. If you don't have the guts to slice him up, Ithak does. Ithak will be slow about it."

Fen shot Ithak a dirty look and then turned to the guard. "Don't move!" she shouted. "And don't bite me!"

She yanked the vines from his mouth, leaving the ones in his nostrils intact.

"Breathe through your nose," Fen said.

He sucked in through his mouth and coughed.

"Listen to me! Breathe through your nose."

The Queen's guard snorted in fresh air. He coughed again but soon settled.

"Good," Fen said. "Now tell us your name."

"Do not give me commands!" he rasped.

"It wasn't a command." She put her hand to her chest. "I am Fen, the person you want to kill. And you are?" The sword in her right hand did not waver.

"Marcus." The name sounded familiar to Fen.

"Is this your blade, Marcus?" she asked.

He nodded.

"So you are the same guard I met at the river!"

"You attacked us."

"You attacked me! I was only looking in your wagon. And I saved your life. Three times! Once from drowning, once from sinking into the mire and once from choking on the very air around you. Do you agree that I saved you?"

He gave her a wary, trapped look. "You threw me into the river."

"Oh!" Ithak said. "This guard is part solicitor."

"Forget the river. Today, I pulled you from the mire. Your life belongs to me." She had no idea whether he'd accept that statement. "Now, stand."

Marcus rolled over on his knees and stood. She poked the sword against his chest. "What do you swear by?"

"By the Queen, my mother," he answered.

"Then swear you will not attempt to harm us."

He narrowed his eyes. "I've already sworn to execute you."

"He won't break his vows to that vile witch," Ithak said.

"Don't call her a witch!" Marcus leaned ahead and Fen poked him in the chest with the sword. It easily cut through his armour. Blood dripped out. He grimaced.

"Stay still," she hissed.

"He'll heal." Ithak waved his hand as if waving away her worries. "Though Ithak is curious what will happen when he runs out of his blood wine."

"What do you mean?" Fen asked.

"They've spent their whole lives drinking the blood of the Queen."

Since childhood, Fen had heard rumours about this. "They actually drink her blood?"

"Yes. Or something like it. They carry flasks of red blood with them wherever they go. It keeps them forever young. It also makes them think like her. Look like her."

Marcus glanced down at his still-bleeding chest. "I should have healed."

"You'll be more careful now," Fen said. "You bleed just like us."

He stared at her right hand. He couldn't hide the disgust in his voice. "The wildmagic. It—it grows out of you."

"Yes, it does," she said. "You never finished your oath. You owe me your life."

"I can't owe my life to a wildmagic."

"You do. That's the truth of it. So swear you will not harm us over the next three days."

"Three days?" Ithak said.

"I need time to think about how he can help us," she said. "Do you swear?"

He spat on the ground. "I do."

At first she thought the spittle was part of his oath. "He'll hit you with a great big gob the next time," Ithak said.

"Swear on the Queen," Fen said. "That's the only oath I'll trust."

There was anger in his eyes. But no guile. "I swear on the blood of the Queen, she who rules over all Illium, she who is my mother, my wife and my sister."

"Yeouch!" Ithak said. "That's an odd and disturbing oath."

"We are all one with the Queen," Marcus said. "In all ways."

"Slaves to her, you mean," Ithak said.

"Enough." Fen put the sword away. "He has sworn. For three days, he'll leave us untouched. But remember two things, Marcus. One—you have sworn an oath on your Queen. And the second is that with a flick of my hand, I could pull the vines from your nostrils and you'd choke on the poison air." Marcus nodded, though he didn't look frightened. "Ithak, will you lead the way? I'll follow behind Marcus."

Fen waited until the Queen's guard had started walking before she fell into line.

THE GODS
I DON'T BELIEVE IN

FEN STOPPED TO CHECK THE KNOTS ON MARCUS EVERY hour. He had kept up a good pace, even though his wound still bled slightly. During one of their breaks from marching, she rubbed more ointment on and packed healing leaves against it. The armour was hard as metal—a shell around him—but not thick, so she could see the rising and falling of his chest. She'd expected its surface to be cold, but she could feel his warmth through it.

"Hold still." His purple cloak was getting ragged at the bottom, so she tore off a strip and tied it around his chest to keep her poultice in place.

"That is kind of you." Marcus sounded sincere. Some of the glow was coming back to his hair and face. She thought of the Queen's guard who had cut off her hand and how she'd been awed by his beauty yet afraid at the same time. Marcus could have been that guard's twin, but the salt and mud stains on his armour and face also made him look more mortal.

"I wouldn't want you to die too soon." She smiled as she said it. He responded with a blank stare. Maybe they didn't teach guards how to laugh.

"How far are we from the other side of the salt mire?" she asked Ithak.

"About two days' march. We'll get caught then."

"Caught?" Fen asked.

"Yes, they'll have corvuses patrolling the outskirts of the mire in all directions. It's a massive border, but we'll be dragging this extra glittering weight"—he gestured at Marcus—"so we'll be very visible. Well, you two will. Ithak will just make himself unseeable." He spat a wad of white bile. "There's a long stretch of land to cross before we reach Helwood. Guards will most likely ride us down. Well, they'll ride you two down . . . Ithak will—"

"Make himself unseeable," Fen interrupted.

"Don't hate Ithak for his talents. If we move with enough sly speed, you have a slim chance of making it to Helwood. Our enemies will not follow us inside. It's the only forest the Queen couldn't cut down for her forges."

"She tried to cut it down?" Fen asked.

"Three hundred years ago, every Queen's guard was given an axe and camped at the edge of the forest, planning to do their chopping in the morning. But that night Helwood stretched and grew around their tents and . . . well, only a quarter of them emerged."

Fen shivered. "Are you certain *we'll* be safe in Helwood?"

"Absolutely. As long as Helwood likes you."

She crossed her arms. "You talk about the forest as if it had feelings."

"Oh, you'll see." Ithak had a smug, knowing smile. "You'll see."

That answer didn't make her feel at all comfortable. Each step they took was a step farther away from her sister. "Shall we stop for the night?" Fen asked. "We can time it so at least we are leaving the salt mire under darkness." She didn't mention that she still wasn't certain whether she'd go to Helwood or to Regentium.

"Good thinking! And here Ithak assumed you were all muddled up by the handsomeness of the Queen's guard."

"I am not muddled!" She pointed several feet away from them. "Sit over there, Marcus."

"As you command," he said. The Queen's guard was smiling now. Fen didn't like that smile. She slumped down on a dry spot of ground.

"Ithak still has no idea what your grand plans are for your toy," Ithak said.

Neither did Fen. She would sleep on it.

"Should we take turns on watch?" she asked.

Ithak stretched his arms and yawned. "You take both watches. Ithak insists." He closed his eyes and moments later began to snore.

Only when she was sure Marcus was asleep did Fen start crying silently. She pictured her mother the last time she'd seen her, looking out the window of their home. Fen also imagined the fear May was feeling. Was she being tortured? The Queen had promised to do so.

Cold descended on the salt mire. Fen shivered for the next few hours. At some point she fell asleep, snuffling awake after several minutes. She glanced at Ithak and Marcus, but neither had moved. She shook her head. Attempted to stay awake.

In the morning, as the sun began to rise, the Queen appeared inside her head. "*Arise, your Queen commands it. Be fruitful and obey my laws.*" The words and the image of the Queen drew Fen toward waking. And just as she was about to open her eyes, the Queen looked directly at her and hissed, "*I'll disembowel your sister!*"

Fen huffed out a breath, clutching for the sword. The Queen's words echoed in her ears. Ithak was on his feet, pulling at his hair. Even Marcus was awake, looking perplexed.

"Did you hear her?" she asked.

"A mind trick!" Ithak shouted. "It's a stupid trick! Seventy years of her waking Ithak up. How Ithak hates it! The only time Ithak doesn't hear it is when Ithak is in Helwood."

"But did you hear her threaten my sister?" Fen hadn't let go of the sword hilt yet.

"Aye," Ithak said. "It means nothing, though."

"I also heard it," Marcus said. His brow was furrowed. "My mother has awakened me every morning of my life. But I have never heard her utter a threat."

"She's toying with you," Ithak said. "We have to carry on. In Helwood, the Queen's voice will be silenced."

Fen let go of the sword. Despite her worry and fear, her stomach rumbled. She opened her knapsack.

"Are you looking for the dried berries?" Ithak asked. "Ithak finished them last night. And the turnip. You fell asleep on the watch. Thus, a midnight snack for Ithak."

She discovered her waterskin was also empty. "I should have tied you up too."

Ithak pointed at his bandages. "Ithak needs sustenance to heal."

"Well, with no food and no water, we won't last long, will we?"

Ithak could only offer a shrug.

Soon, they were following him across the white marshes. Only occasionally would the stink make its way into her nostrils. She walked beside Marcus.

"Did—did the Queen give birth to you?" That was one of the stories she'd heard from other children. They'd imagined that, like some ant queen, Servilia had birthed each of the seven thousand Queen's guards.

"No!" Marcus said. "That's disgusting."

"Ithak started that rumour years ago," Ithak said. "Glad it still makes the rounds."

"We were gifted to the Queen, and in her infinite mercy, she made us immortal and raised us," Marcus said. "Well, the sergeants raised us. My only childhood memories are of holding a wooden sword."

"So there were no wet nurses?" Fen asked. "No one held you?"

"Now that's a girl's question!" Ithak pointed jauntily at Fen. "She's imagining you as a babe in her very own arms. Silliness! The guards were abandoned by their parents and given poky things to hold and poky things to shoot and so they love poking people like us. That's all they know."

"We learn numbers," Marcus said. "And maps."

"A smart killer is a glorious weapon," Ithak said.

"So you haven't left the barracks since you were a baby?" Fen asked.

"The first time I walked through the gates to Regentium was to hunt for you," he admitted. "I long to return to my brothers."

"And your mommy Queen," Ithak added. "You want to run back to her arms."

Marcus clenched his jaws. Then he said, "*She* spoke through me." Fen thought he sounded angry. "The Red Artificers promised if the Queen spoke through us, it would be the greatest honour. The greatest joy. But . . . but she *controlled* me."

He didn't seem pleased about that. Perhaps he would be a bearable companion.

And without any further thinking, Fen announced: "I'll go to Regentium with Marcus."

Ithak drew to a stop and his eyes became so wide his face seemed to disappear. She nearly laughed. Marcus looked equally shocked.

"You'll die," Ithak spat out. "The moment you meet another Queen's guard. If Marcus doesn't behead you himself."

"He swore an oath not to harm me."

"For three days!" Ithak said with such force spittle flew from his lips. "He also swore an oath to kill all wildmagics!"

"I would not kill Fen." It was the first time Marcus had said her name. "I would escort her safely to the walls of Regentium. I swear it. On my life. On my Queen. *Your* Queen."

Fen regarded him. His eyes were set. Was it the Queen talking through him? Again, she didn't see any guile, but she'd only known him for less than a day.

"It's the best way," Fen said. "I need to get into Regentium and free my sister."

"Don't be doltish!" Ithak pointed at her. "Do you plan to fight your way out of the city with your crossbow?"

"I have my magic," she said.

"Oh, great! You can leaf them to death!"

"Can you suggest a better way to get my sister?" Her right hand had formed a wooden fist. She was tempted to pop him over the head.

"Bah! You're a foolish child! You'll die. Then your sister will die." He rubbed at the bandage on his shoulder. "Ithak will tell you the truth of it. She's as dead as your mother. Your best vengeance is to flaunt your life in the Queen's face. From a distance—flaunting should always be done from a distance."

"You want me to hide!" Fen said.

"To live is the greatest revenge."

"No. I'm going." She turned toward Marcus. "When we near Regentium, you could summon a corvus—or whatever it is you do—and offer my life in place of my sister's."

"This is ridiculous!" Ithak actually forced his way between them, holding his shoulder. "You're worth nothing, Fen. Your sister is worth even less. The Queen would kill you and that would be the end of the deal. We wildmagics are a threat to her." His eyes grew wide and thoughtful. He stabbed his index finger in the air and tapped his forehead. "You've been thinking about this the wrong way. Even Ithak has. Your sister is not dead. She's maybe not even in the dungeon beneath the Red Tower. She is likely working on the upper levels in a kitchen, slopping soup."

"What does it matter where she works?" Fen said. "The Queen promised to torture her."

"Empty threats. The Queen keeps your sister alive to lure you back. Ithak has seen her do it with other wildmagics. They miss their mothers. Their wives. Their children. They get so distraught they dash to Regentium and are captured and gutted. But picture this through your sister's eyes. She was living in horrible drudgery in a dung hole of a village."

Fen crossed her arms. "Village Twenty-One is not a dung hole."

Ithak blew a raspberry. "It was a dung hole. Believe me! The truth is, your sister would've worked her fingers to the bone like your mother. She'd have died of the red dust cough. But right now, she's fed the best food from the queendom. Sunberries every night! She's getting plump! As long as you live, Servilia will keep your sister alive."

Ithak certainly had a silver tongue. There would be no way to test his version of May's life. But that image of May in fine robes, eating fresh, good food . . . it was powerful. Fen so wanted it to be true.

"Your sister fattens as we speak," Ithak said. "Imagine if you came marching in and tried to take her away from a glorious life."

"May would not be angry," Fen said. Her sister was only eight summers old. She understood very little about the world. Maybe she *would* get upset.

"You are the elder sister," Ithak said. Fen wanted to slap the clever grin off his face. "It's your duty to care for her. If you surrender, she'll die. If you live . . . she has a chance. Ithak won't lose you now. Ithak wasn't sent here to do that."

Fen cocked her head. "What do you mean by *sent*?"

Ithak put his hand on his heart, grimacing a bit because the movement tugged at his wound. "The gods sent Ithak to you."

"You don't believe in the gods."

"Ithak does when Ithak feels lucky. Now don't you worry about that slip of Ithak's tongue." He put his hand on the pouch. "Don't worry about it at all."

"He's hiding something," Marcus said.

"Shut your mouth, Queen's guard." Ithak tapped Marcus's nose with a pale finger. "Ithak will cut out your tongue and toss it in a salt pool. You don't have enough Queen's blood in you to grow it back." Marcus tried to bring up his hands, but they were bound.

Fen edged away. How much did she know about Ithak? He'd stumbled across her by that banyan tree. Had he intended to find her? That was impossible. Even she hadn't known she'd end up there.

But his argument was solid. If she went to Regentium, both she and May would die. It was a fool's errand. There was only one choice she could see. "I'll go with you to Helwood," she said.

"You are so wise," Ithak said. Then he turned and stomped forward. "We don't want to waste another moment talking."

Marcus looked at her but was silent. She wasn't certain what his glance meant. He was getting stronger. She would have to keep a closer eye on the knots.

And on Ithak too, she decided.

CHAPTER THIRTEEN

A STONE THAT FLOATS

THEY LEFT THE GREAT SALT MIRE IN THE MIDDLE OF the night. The moon was a sickle in the sky, not quite bright enough to reflect off Marcus's armour. Fen took her first step onto land that was not covered in salt and felt more steady. The mire had been shifting and soft and dead—a place where so many thousands had lost their lives. This ground was solid and alive. She wanted to kick off her boots and scamper through the grass. She imagined doing just that and grinned at how shocked Ithak and Marcus would be. She squinted skyward, but could not spot any corvuses.

Fen pulled the vines from her nose and throat. Her first breaths still burned from the salt mire air. Using the plants to breathe had been a good trick. But how many of those magic tricks did she have?

"I'll take your vines out," she said to Marcus. He leaned over and allowed her to remove them. They were sticky with goo, perhaps snot, so she quickly tossed them to the ground. "The first few breaths will not be pleasant," she warned.

He breathed in and his eyes watered. "The air smells like the barracks' latrine. Even magic can't make a Queen's Guard fart smell sweet."

Fen couldn't help but laugh, and she was surprised to hear Ithak chuckle along with them before he whispered, "Now shut up, both of you. Corvuses have big ears."

In time they came to the Queen's Road, glimmering red in the night. She expected there to be guards racing up and down it, but the lane was empty. After a signal from Ithak, the trio ran across the red paving stones. Fen worried that even stepping on those stones might somehow warn the Queen.

"We are several leagues from the welcoming branches of Helwood," Ithak said. "It would be better if we weren't dragging this hunk of meat."

"I'm going no slower than you," Marcus said.

"Well, you can't keep your pet forever," Ithak said to Fen. "He wouldn't survive a minute in Helwood."

"When it's safe," Fen said, "I'll free him."

With each step the ground was growing rockier and hillier. Her muscles burned. She ignored the hunger pangs as best she could. It wasn't like a bowl of noodles would fall from the sky.

A horse whinnied. Ithak raised his finger to his lips. Then came the sound of wings far above them. Fen watched as Ithak grew invisible except for his bandages. "Leave the boy behind," he whispered. "We have to flee. Now!"

"I won't leave him," Fen replied.

"You must!"

"He's right." Marcus was nodding his head. "Leave me. My

brothers will rescue me. If not, I'll walk until I find aid. Cut the bonds that bind me and give me back Biter."

"Biter?" Ithak said. "You named your sword Biter! How infantile!"

"It's a good name!" Marcus said.

"It doesn't matter what you named your sword," Fen whispered. "You cannot have it."

"They will kill me if I've lost my sword."

That gave her pause. She pulled Biter out of the scabbard with her wooden hand.

"What are you doing?" Ithak asked.

"I can't leave him tied up." She sliced the bonds. "But I need your sword. I hope they let you live because you survived the salt mire. I'm certain no Queen's guard has done that. Now run, Marcus."

Marcus's only movement was to rub his wrists. "Thank you. You have a conscience and kindness. I didn't know that was possible for a wildmagic."

"Nor did I think a Queen's guard could laugh," she said.

"Oh, this is too sickly sweet." Ithak grabbed Fen's arm. "Leave the oaf and flee."

Fen pointed the sword at Marcus. "Don't follow us."

She ran alongside Ithak. Marcus stayed next to the tree. There was an odd look in his eyes and she hesitated to think it was respect. She glanced back a few more times until he was little more than a glittering figure. Then he vanished in the darkness.

"You are too soft," Ithak said.

"I was only being honourable."

"Surviving is the only honourable thing to do." She still could only see the bandage. It was getting red.

"Your wound has reopened," she said.

"Proof of your clumsy healing skills! Wait . . . be quiet."

At first Fen didn't hear anything and wondered if it was Ithak's imagination. Then came a whisper of wings swirling in the air above them. A child's voice screeched, "Wildmagic. Wildmagic. Here. Caw!" Fen saw the wide, glowing eyes of a corvus, its wings outlined briefly by the moon's light. Then it was gone.

"It'll be croaking our whereabouts to the guards," Ithak said. "They're on horseback. We are on foot. Our odds are horrible."

The two of them scrambled up a hill and through a line of bushes. The branches snapped and stabbed at Fen's legs and arms. "Is this the start of Helwood?" she asked.

"Ha! We're still a league away. Faster! They'll make good time on this land. There is some rocky earth somewhere in this darkness that'll slow their horses down. We just have to find it."

But the moonlight revealed a gently rising landscape. No rocky hills, nor the sign of another tree or any cover.

"Sheath that blade!" Ithak commanded. "You might as well light a torch."

She did so and discovered she could run faster without it in her hand. She kept her eyes on the moving patch of blood.

A horse neighed in the gloom. "They're getting closer," Fen said.

Ithak had vanished. She panicked for a moment before spotting the bandages floating off to her left. She hurried to catch up. "Quiet now," he said. "Let's hope they don't have any infernus hounds."

She and Ithak stumbled up a gravelly incline, thankful that it would be harder for the horses to climb.

There was another neigh. Then came the pounding of

hooves and a shout. Fen's heart was beating so loudly in her ears she could no longer hear properly.

"They're almost right on top of us," Ithak whispered. "Change into a tree and hide. Try that."

"Truly?"

"No, you fool!" He ripped his dressing off and tossed it away. "Ithak wishes he could aid you," he said softly. "Ithak has come to enjoy your inane thoughts. But we must part now."

"You're deserting me!" Fen tried to grab him, but he'd already moved.

"Think of it as the smarter one surviving," he whispered from a few feet away. "Ithak will sing your praises to all Ithak meets."

"Stay and fight!" she said.

"Stop whining!" He was now a good distance away. "You're just drawing attention to yourself. Keep running and they may not find you. Pull your hood up!"

He was gone. She cursed him for a moment and then ran straight up the rocky incline, urging her legs to push harder. Forcing her lungs to suck in more air. The horses were getting closer. And so was the thumping of wings. A corvus cried out, "She's here. Caw! Wildmagic! Here. Here. Caw. Here."

Glittering riders came into sight only ten yards away.

Fen backed up against a large boulder, drew her crossbow from her knapsack and loaded it.

The riders approached slowly, chargers snorting and fighting against their reins as if they wanted to trample her. She raised the crossbow.

Something feathery brushed her face as a corvus dived down and grabbed her bow in its talons, dragging her up into the air. The weapon was ripped from her hands and she fell hard to the ground.

As Fen got to her feet, the Queen's guards rode up. There were two horses, but three guards. Marcus was seated behind one of the riders. She hadn't seen him at first because his armour was still dull.

"You're cornered," a guard said. He pointed his crossbow at her. "Raise your hands or I'll put a bolt through your heart."

Fen slowly raised her hands. Marcus and the other guard dismounted.

"This waif held you captive?" the guard on the ground asked. He drew his blade.

"Yes," Marcus said. "She took me unawares and stole my sword."

"You lost your blade to a girl!" snorted the guard with the crossbow. "This tale grows in the telling. Remove your hood, child." He motioned with his crossbow and the moonlight caught the sharp metal point of the bolt.

Fen drew her hood back. Her red hair glowed in the moonlight.

"So she is a wildmagic!"

"Loose your bolt," the other guard commanded. "Before she bewitches us."

"No!" Marcus shouted. "I demand the right to slay her."

Fen swallowed. "Marcus . . . don't . . ."

He strode toward her and she wondered if she should raise her hand to strike him with vines as she had in the river. "Don't try your tricks on me," he hissed. "He'll put a bolt through your eye."

"But you swore an oath!"

"My oath to the Queen takes precedence over all others."

Ithak had been correct. Her ideals would be her death. And her stupidity in trusting Marcus would mean May would die too.

Marcus reached toward her and she raised her hand to fend off a blow, urging her vines to grow and choke him. Nothing happened. Stupid vines! Marcus knocked aside her arms, drew his sword from the scabbard on her belt and held the blade in the air, letting out a small cry of triumph. "My sword! Biter!" He sounded like a child finding a lost toy. He spun around to show his companions. "I have my blade again!"

"We can see that!" the mounted guard said. "Now run her through."

"Too easy! I'll behead her," he announced. "I thank you, brothers, for giving me this vengeance. For three days I've waited."

"Be quick about it!"

"Stop!" Fen said. "Take me to my sister. The Queen promised safe passage. I beg you."

"How long should I let her beg?" Marcus turned his back on her and stepped toward his companions.

"There's nothing like the sound of a wildmagic begging," said the guard on horseback. "What's her magic?"

"She grows twigs," he said. "As far as I can tell, she only uses them to pick her nose."

"Ha! All this fuss for nothing!"

"Behead her," the other man said. "Then cut off her hands. I've seen girls this size turn soldiers to stone."

Marcus spun around and fixed her with a look of hatred. "You are going to die now, Fen."

"My blood will be on your soul," she said. "I—I, Fen of—" She wanted to say her real name. The one written down. To speak it just once in her lifetime. But she'd never heard it. "I curse you. I curse all of you."

"I've been cursed by hundreds of wildmagics," the guard on horseback said. "I still breathe and all who have cursed me are dead."

"It's time to die," Marcus said.

Then he spun and struck the guard next to him right through the heart. The man fell to the ground. Fen stood completely still, in shock. Marcus leapt toward the mounted Queen's guard. "Traitor!" the guard shouted. "Traitor!" He loosed his bow and the bolt caught Marcus in the leg. Marcus charged on. The guard dropped his bow and drew his sword, and when Marcus took another staggering step, the man pulled back on his charger's reins and shouted, "Up, horse!" The massive creature reared and struck Marcus with its front hooves.

He fell down and didn't move. Fen ran to his side. "Get up, Marcus!" He opened his eyes, tried to rise, but failed. Fen struggled to pull him to a seated position.

The Queen's guard dismounted. "I don't know how you got inside his mind, but I'll take your head to the Queen. And his."

He raised his sword.

She pointed her wooden hand. "Get back or I'll strike you down."

The guard hesitated and she tried to imagine something growing from her hand. Anything. But again, nothing happened. The vines didn't seem to want to grow when she beckoned them. "Grow! Grow!" she shouted. A vine flitted out and fell to the ground.

The guard laughed. Then his diadem flew from his head and he dropped his sword. A stone had smashed into his temple and was now floating in the air. "This isn't twigs!" he shouted. The stone struck him again and he crumpled. It hit him once more in the head and he lay still.

The stone fell to the ground. "Well, that was perfect timing," Ithak said, sounding completely pleased with himself.

"Thank you!" Fen answered. "I mean, it would've been better if you'd stuck around the first time. But thank you."

"My pleasure. Ithak missed your nattering." He put his hand on his pouch. "And this Marcus appears to suffer from kindness. Very curious."

Fen pulled on Marcus's arms, but his leg collapsed before he could properly stand. "Help me get him up," Fen said.

"First Ithak will behead these Queen's soldiers. Otherwise they'll be up and around and chasing after us."

"Let them live!" Marcus said. "They're my brothers."

The one he'd stabbed through the chest was already moving. *They healed so quickly!*

"Oh, the soft hearts have the day," Ithak moaned. He undid the sword belt on the nearest guard and took it. Fen helped Marcus up, and once he was standing on his own, she stole the other sword.

"I must get this out." Marcus grabbed the crossbow bolt.

"No, don't—" Fen started.

But he yanked out the bolt and tossed it to the ground.

"You've just made the wound worse!" she said. "I could've cut the bolt head off and pushed the shaft through."

"There's no time," he said. "And I couldn't ride with it in my leg." He limped over to one of the horses.

"Ithak will get the other nag," Ithak said. The second charger, which had stopped several yards away, raised its ears and shied back. Then the reins lifted and moved in the air. The horse reared up several times, but the reins continued to float. "Stupid beasts never did like me."

Fen helped Marcus onto the horse and then climbed up herself and took the reins. The charger did not seem to mind having a new master. Marcus clasped his arms around her.

"Follow me," Ithak said. His horse cantered ahead. Fen followed.

"Traitor!" the Queen's guard yelled after them. He was sitting up and holding his head. "We'll get you."

Fen urged the horse to a slow gallop. "You didn't kill me," she said after they'd been riding for several minutes. The corvuses followed high above in the air.

"No, I did not," Marcus answered. "I owe you several lives. And besides, we both have magic in our veins."

CHAPTER FOURTEEN

PIGHEADED

FEN GLANCED BACK TO SEE THAT MARCUS HAD HIS hand on the wound, trying to hold back the blood.

"Should we stop?" Fen asked.

"No," he said. "I'll heal." She didn't want to argue. Whatever magic had healed him before was obviously failing now.

She urged the horse on. She had only ridden the mine ponies, and it hadn't been an easy thing to do with one hand—her stump couldn't grab the pommel or the horse's mane for balance. This charger was huge in comparison. It moved with fluid grace and controlling it gave her a sense of power. She held the pommel with her left hand and clutched the reins in her wooden one.

That new hand was still such a great mystery. It shot out vines when it wanted to, but it didn't come to her defence when requested. Yet she could open and close the fingers at will. Her right hand had been dominant until the Queen had taken it away. So she'd learned how to use her left. Now, as if no time had passed, her right hand was dominant again.

"Ride harder!" Ithak shouted. "Shove the Queen's guard off and you'll be as fast as me." He galloped ahead.

The horse was stained with sweat and had obviously been ridden hard by its previous master. Yet the charger continued ahead, easily climbing a hill. Despite its strength, Fen's horse did have two passengers and soon Ithak was outdistancing them by several lengths.

"Here! Caw! Here!" A corvus squawked. The cry was picked up by several other corvuses. When she glanced up, Fen was shocked to see ten of them circling in the sky. "Wildmagic. Here, brothers and sisters! Caw!"

"They could attack us at any moment," she said

"Just gallop." Marcus waved his sword above his head. "They are not the bravest of fowls."

They charged over the next rise and looked back to see something much worse: the sun cresting the horizon revealed hundreds of riders in pursuit.

"By Zaoshen!" Fen pointed. "There are so many of them."

"It's two regiments," Marcus said. "My mother—the Queen—wants to be rid of you for certain. But we may make it. Look!"

In the distance, like hands reaching up from the ground, were the first trees of Helwood.

"Hurry! Hurry!" Ithak shouted. "Safety is near!"

Fen glanced back again. The pursuers were gaining, and she guessed they'd soon be in crossbow range. Their formations were perfect, wheeling in and out between each other at full speed.

"The distance is too great," Marcus said. "I'm too heavy! Ithak is correct. Be sure to tell him so."

He jumped off. Fen looked back with horror as he collapsed and then slowly used his sword to raise himself to his feet.

"Fool!" she shouted. "Arrogant, stupid fool!" She yanked the reins, circled the horse and, ignoring Ithak's shouts, rode right back to Marcus. She thudded to a stop only a few inches away. "Get on!"

"No! You're faster without me. Ride! I'll slow them down."

"I'm not leaving you here."

"It's my choice! I owe you a life. Now begone!" He waved his sword at her as if she were an annoying fly.

"Don't you dare dismiss me!"

Ithak galloped up. His voice carried like a trumpet: "You idiots! You'll both die. Come, Fen. The Queen can't have you! You're far too valuable to lose."

"Heed him!" Marcus shouted.

"No." Fen dismounted. "You run, Ithak! It's me they want."

"You foolish, pigheaded girl," Marcus shouted. "I told you to leave."

A crossbow bolt thudded into the ground between them. It was followed by two more that struck to either side.

"Damn the both of you!" Ithak yelled. The stirrups snapped up and down and he raced off.

Another bolt stuck in the earth next to Fen's horse.

"Go!" Marcus shouted. "I command you."

"Get on the horse, I command you!"

There were now countless bolts thudding into the earth. It was only luck that none of them had struck home.

"I'll come," Marcus huffed. "But I don't owe you a life for this!"

She leapt onto the horse and extended her hand. He sheathed his sword and grabbed the back of the saddle instead, struggling to pull himself up into place. "Ride!" he shouted finally.

She slammed her heels into the horse and it shot forward. The gap had been closed and the thunder of the Queen's Guard on horseback was echoing around them—a sound that would make even the strongest army quiver. It was like a storm descending.

After several minutes of hard riding, their charger began huffing and coughing. A bolt struck its haunches and it let out a strangled sound. "I'm so sorry," Fen said, patting the horse's neck. "But go! Go faster."

Fen felt an inkling of hope when she saw that the line of the forest was within striking distance.

Five riders came out of a gulley, directly in front of them. They were clad in leather jerkins—common soldiers. Not immortal. But obviously dangerous. They drew their blades.

"They sent the speediest ahead to outflank us," Marcus said.

In the distance, nearer to the forest, several Queen's guards were pursuing Ithak and loosing bolts at the horse. Was a bolt floating in mid-air, shot through Ithak? His charger tumbled and fell to the earth and guards encircled it.

"Go right at the soldiers," Marcus said.

"Are you mad?"

"No. Go straight!" he shouted. "Our horse is bigger than theirs."

The soldiers were on mounts that were lithe and meant for speed. Not power. The charger was a good four or five hands taller, and it bowled right into the soldiers, scattering them. Only one had enough wits to swing his sword, but it broke when Marcus met the blade with his own.

The trees were now within reach! They were so big it was like Fen and Marcus were riding toward a line of wooden giants.

The charger, finding a last burst of speed, carried the two of them into the embrace of those giants. Right into the arms of Helwood.

CHAPTER FIFTEEN

HELWOOD

Fen held herself flat against the horse as crossbow bolts hissed through branches, sticking into trees. Mounted Queen's guards were crashing through the forest only a few horse-lengths behind them. She didn't dare look back; instead she kicked her heels harder into her charger's side and shouted, "Go! Go! Go!"

Long fingers of wood poked at her, slicing her face. She ducked even closer to the horse. The sun was swallowed up by leaves and it was getting harder to see the path. Several moments later, the pursuit grew quiet. Even the sound of her own horse's galloping softened. Fen risked a glance over her shoulder. There was no path to be seen. It was as if the trees had formed a wall.

She urged the horse onwards. Soon the only sound was the hard, desperate wheezing of her mount. She turned the charger left, and then right, following a narrower and narrower trail.

A cry of pain came from far behind them. It was followed by a shouted order a great distance away. The words were garbled. A distant trumpet sounded three sharp notes.

"They've sounded a retreat," Marcus said. His voice was full of wonder. His arms were still tight around her. "But the Queen's Guard never retreats."

"It's a trick." She kicked the horse's side. The charger sped up for several moments, bubbled out a blood-spattered breath and collapsed beneath her. Fen jumped and tumbled across the ground, avoiding the trunk of a large oak tree. Marcus rolled to a stop near her with a grunt of pain.

The horse had ended up a few feet away. Its eyes were wide—it exhaled a massive breath, shuddered once and was dead. Fen went over and stroked its mane. "Thank you," she whispered. There were five bolts in its side and another had sunk deep into the horse's neck.

"It was a good mount." Marcus had limped over to join her. He got down on his haunches with a grunt and reached for the saddlebag, steadying himself by leaning on the horse.

"I'll do that," Fen said, untying the saddlebag. The first thing she found was a thin golden flask marked with a *QS*.

"It's blood wine." Marcus licked his lips. "Keep it stoppered. You carry it."

"If you drank it now, you'd heal faster."

"Yes. But I might become *hers* again. Please, put it away."

Fen placed it in her knapsack and returned to the saddlebag to discover a small loaf of bread wrapped in red cloth. It smelled of carrots. The Queen's Guard actually ate the same food as mortals. There were no bandages, but that didn't surprise Fen. They wouldn't have any need for them. She also pulled out a short knife and a playing card with a golden cat on the front.

"It's a gilded cat," Marcus said. "For luck."

"Queen's guards believe in luck?"

"Arms don't grow back in a day. Or even fingers. And we can die, despite the stories the Royal Historians tell."

She slid the knife into the sheath that had held her father's knife. "It's as if our pursuers have vanished," she said.

"Even the corvuses can't get through all these branches. We'd better keep moving and hope that Ithak, if he lives, can catch up with us." Marcus tried to stand and fell to the ground.

"Just stay still," Fen said. The armour on his leg was stained red and he looked paler. "You aren't healing at all."

"The Queen's blood in my veins is mostly gone. I guess this is what happens."

He closed his eyes. A moment later, she realized he had passed out. This gave her a chance to swaddle the wound, using yet another section of his cloak. At least the tourniquet seemed to be holding the blood in. Her mother had taught her how important it was to wrap a wound tightly.

As she wiped the sweat from her forehead, she noticed the blood on her hands. She spotted a large fern leaf and wiped her fingers clean. With the motion, she realized that her wooden hand felt stronger here. As though being in the forest gave it even more strength. She opened and closed the hand, held it near a massive oak tree. Could she talk to it? Nothing happened.

She wasn't certain she could make sense of her magic.

Her hand may have been stronger, but her body was tired. And her cheeks ached where the branches had scratched them.

She sat down and huffed out an exhausted breath. Marcus's face looked as if the sheen of magic had been wiped off. His pale cheeks might even have been slightly pudgier. And he seemed younger. Would he someday not look like the Queen?

"Just put him out of his misery," a voice said.

"Ithak," she grunted. She was too dog-tired to shudder. "You really do love sneaking up on people."

"Your tone suggests you're happy Ithak survived. No thanks to you and your plaything."

"He's not my plaything," she said. "He's my friend."

A patch of dried blood was floating in the air. "Ah, you see me." He made himself visible. "Don't become a healer. You'll kill all your patients."

"I saw your horse taken down. I thought you were dead."

"Well, Ithak slowed his horse and jumped off. The simple soldiers pursued the riderless beastie. Ithak darted into the forest like a handsome and clever fox." He sat on a tree stump. "Ithak did see your valiant charge. Then it was just a matter of walking in this direction."

"But what stopped the Queen's Guard from pursuing us?"

"Helwood has a grudge against Her Majesty. Which reminds me, don't try and chop down any trees."

"You still speak as if the forest has a mind of its own."

He knocked on the trunk of a tree. "Ithak doesn't think forest thoughts. But she's a bitter old biddy." He jabbed a finger at Marcus. "Ithak doesn't trust his suddenly deciding to save you."

"He wounded his own brothers. And when he jumped off the horse and stood to ward away all of those Queen's guards, it was rather brave."

"Brave? It was the height of stupidity!" He rubbed his chin. "But he may have been following someone else's command."

"What point would there be to have him thwart our pursuers and accompany me into the forest?"

"You are such a self-important child! The forest hides hermits, wildmagics, even whole tribes . . . all the people who have fled the Queen in the last one thousand years. In numbers she cannot even guess at."

"How many?"

He held up all his fingers. "It's more than ten. The Queen may be using Marcus to find her enemies. This lump"—he gave Marcus a kick in his good leg—"would be her eyes and ears in Helwood."

"Don't kick him! And why wouldn't the forest reject him?"

"Does Ithak look like a tree? Ithak cannot read Helwood's thoughts." He licked his pale lips. "Do you have anything to eat?"

She remembered the bread she'd found in the saddlebag. Her stomach rumbling, she retrieved the cloth-wrapped loaf. She gave a lump of the bread to Ithak.

"Straight from the Queen's ovens," he said. "Ithak wonders how many children she's burned up in there. Oh, of course Ithak is not including your sister. Ithak is certain she's alive and well."

"Don't joke about that!" Fen said, but Ithak was already obliviously chomping on his bread.

She took a couple bites too, finding it dry and tasteless. She checked the dressing on Marcus's leg and discovered that blood had pooled on the ground. But it wasn't enough to cause her concern.

Marcus opened his eyes. "I am not healed," he said. He sat up slowly and grimaced. It made him look years older.

"Can you stand?" Fen asked.

He nodded, though he had to lean on her. There wasn't a new spurt of blood through the dressing. "There's still some magic in you," she said. "You should be bleeding more. Do you think you can walk?"

He limped around a bit. Then he nodded. "Yes. Not with much speed, though."

"Then let our motley group make our way into the heart of the forest," Ithak said. "My benefactor awaits."

"Which direction?" Fen asked.

Ithak opened his mouth. She expected a quip, but he placed his hand on the small pouch on his belt. Then he pointed. "That's the direction to warmth, safety and heartwarming accolades." After a few steps, he said over his shoulder, "I'm joking about that last one, of course."

CHAPTER SIXTEEN

A TRAIL OF WORDS AND BLOOD

"The sooner we are with my benefactor, the better," Ithak said. "Though Helwood has often been Ithak's home, she still makes Ithak shiver."

"Marcus can't walk a thousand leagues!" Fen said. She'd let him lean on her. He was growing heavier by the moment.

"It's not much farther. Ithak told you that."

With each step, Fen felt the forest close around them. Helwood was nothing like the smaller forests near her village. Here the trees reached into the heavens and blocked the light. There were no sounds of birds or other animals.

They passed a section where the leaves on every plant were red. It smelled like decay. Ithak guided them around it and deeper into the forest. Some trees were so thick and large it took several steps to pass them.

In time, the path opened up into a glowing grove with three throne-sized stones in the centre. Each bit of flora was a ghostly, luminescent white, as if someone had painted every leaf. The place smelled sweet.

"Let us rest here. Ithak needs to air his dainty feet." Ithak sat on one of the rocks and removed his shoes. He picked some green substance from between his pale toes and wiped it on the stone. "Nap if you can. Ithak will watch you."

"I don't think I can sleep." Fen sat on a nearby stone.

"Perhaps you need a sleepy-time tale." Ithak rubbed his hands together.

"Honestly, I've had my fill of tales," Fen said.

"Indulge me. Ithak wagers that our little Queen's guard didn't get too many bedtime stories."

Marcus nodded. He'd chosen to lean against the largest stone. "Lights were snuffed out after last trumpet."

"Well, well." Ithak leaned back and cupped his hands behind his head. "What do you two know of Mansren?"

Fen shrugged. "Only what the Royal Historians told us. He started the War of the Ten Cities. He was a creature born purely of magic. A god."

"Yes, a god. That's closer to the truth. And you, Marcus?"

"We had a statue of Mansren in our latrine. We peed on it every day."

Ithak guffawed so hard he nearly fell off his stone. "Oh! Mansren as a target for boys with full bladders. What else can you tell me?"

"Just that the Queen was the only one who could defeat him," Marcus said. "After he sacked the nine cities, she ordered the Queen's Guard to charge his shirker army. She came down from the skies on an equusa and turned him to stone. Marcellus, the first and greatest Queen's guard, broke Mansren into a thousand pieces."

"Ithak assumes you heard a similar story," Ithak said to Fen.

She nodded. "Every Shattering Day the Royal Historians would tell the tale. After we smashed the Mansren statues, we'd gather up the candy and eat it while we listened."

"Do you ever wonder who tossed the stories, like seeds, into your minds?" Ithak asked.

Fen shifted her position on the stone. "The Queen did. I'm starting to wonder how many of them are true."

"Oh! You're getting wiser! The Mansren you know came from the Queen's imagination. She writes all the histories. Lies, each and every one. And yet there are bits and pieces of the past, of the *truth*, let us say, that still exist. What if Ithak were to tell you Mansren was a hero?"

"Impossible!" Marcus nearly spat out the word. "He was pure evil."

"Those who win wars write the histories. But Ithak was able to find a few passages written in an old book that told a different tale. Ithak got it from a stinky old librarian."

"A what?" Marcus asked.

"Librarians are those who cradle books like children. No magic in their heads but the magic of stories. Long ago there were librarians who collected knowledge in tomes. Stories about love. Poems too. The history of the last ten thousand years. Did Ithak just enlarge your mind? Yes, ten thousand years of history. Ithak stole inside the librarian's hut and found a thousand-year-old book that had secrets inside its rotted pages. For instance, do you know where the corvuses come from?"

"The hatcheries in the Red Temples," Marcus replied. "The winged creatures were discovered in the north and trained by the Royal Falconers."

"Wrong! Wrong! Wrong!" Ithak shook a finger at Marcus.

"The corvuses are spawned from the children given up to the Queen. She keeps the people poor and they can't feed all of their offspring. So they give her the ones who are a burden. Obedient children become servants, strong ones become soldiers, the best—like Marcus—become Queen's guards. But the unluckiest of infants—or should Ithak say pluckiest—are melded with the wings, bodies and brains of birds. Given beaks and talons. They become the corvuses. The Queen's eyes."

"That's—that's horrible," Fen said. An image of the corvus she'd killed flashed in her brain.

"Not the worst, though. The children they have no use for become the wine they call the Queen's blood."

Marcus swallowed. "Is—is that true?"

Ithak sniffed loudly. "It stinks of truth. Ithak found so many truths in that book. Ithak read a different history of Mansren. It, too, stank with truth."

"But what did it say?" Fen asked.

"Oh, there was a lot of *thus* this and *thee* that. Ithak supposes neither of you would know. You can't read."

"I can read," Marcus said.

"Yes, Ithak forgot. For you must read the execution decrees and battle orders."

"Who needs those squiggles on paper," Fen said. "Did they ever feed a family?" But the moment after she spoke, she thought of the pieces of vellum inscribed with her family's names. How she wished those lines her father had created made sense to her.

"The right squiggles could feed a family for a hundred years," Ithak said. "The book was written by a historian. A real one, not like the royal fakers. The book spoke about how Mansren was found as a child over a thousand years ago. He'd been born in one of the magic pits inside a rare black seam. No one understood how he was created. He was raised by Sophos, a philosopher—that is someone who thinks the deepest thoughts. They are all dead now, so don't worry about them.

"Ithak won't bore you with Mansren's childhood or how he formed the first shirker out of his blood and magic dust and pee." Ithak scratched at his nose. "The Queen heard tell of him and came to see this Mansren, now grown. Sadly, his philosopher father died. Or perhaps Ithak should say *conveniently*. Ithak suspects poison stopped his heart. And speaking of hearts, Mansren fell in love with the Queen."

"That can't be true." Marcus shook his head. "They were always sworn enemies."

"Everything she's told you is a lie. Servilia may have been able to hide her darkness from him. So he helped her to conquer the nine cities, believing she would set the rabble free. Ithak even memorized some of the book: 'And Mansren saw the evil in the queen's heart, her plan to subjugate the people and to rule for all time. And he rebelled. And was cast down.'"

"That's all?" Fen asked.

"Oh, there was so much more!" He gestured around him. "The land from one side to the other was once called Irthra. But she changed it to Illium after her own name. That's how big her lies are. And the dominion Mansren believed Servilia would create was to be a place where there were no kings or khans or emperors! Where we learned to read, to shout out our thoughts, our dreams to each other. No queen skulking in your mind every morning. Freedom."

All Fen's life, the Queen had been watching her. Waking her up.

"That's traitorous talk," Marcus said.

"Ithak is a wildmagic. Just by existing, Ithak is a traitor. But this is the simple truth. Mansren wanted the people to be free. When Servilia is gone, the people will finally be liberated."

"And you found all of this in a book?" Fen asked.

"Oh, not the book alone. Ithak saw wondrous creatures that made me believe."

"What creatures?" Marcus asked.

"Shirkers."

"The magical army of Mansren?" Fen snorted. "They sneak into your room and steal your stockings. They eat the last piece of salted pork. At least that's what my mother told me. They don't really exist."

"They are as real as you two." Ithak pointed at both of them. "And they are watching us right now."

Marcus grabbed the hilt of his sword. "What game is this, Ithak?"

"It's no game." He stood and raised his hands as though he were about to embrace the air. "Show yourselves, my friends. You have been following our trail of words and blood. Ithak names you shirkers. Flesh of Mansren's flesh. Ithak calls you forward into this dim light."

Fen stood slowly, tightening her hands into fists. "There's nothing there. This is a stupid joke."

A branch several feet away creaked. Something dark and tall was moving alongside the tree. It touched a leaf, which turned black, and the leaves next to it also went black. The darkness swept across the white grove in a heartbeat.

What magic could do that? Fen's breath was tight in her throat. She, too, put a hand to her sword.

A shirker stepped into the open and revealed itself.

CHAPTER SEVENTEEN

THE CHILDREN OF MANSREN

FEN COVERED HER MOUTH IN SHOCK. THE SHIRKER WAS a tall and lanky creature. As it blinked its amber eyes, it seemed to float toward the centre of the grove, where it stopped. Its arms and legs were muscular and lean and each had an extra joint. It had smooth humanoid features, but wore no armour or clothing. There was nothing to indicate whether it was male or female. Its shadow fell in five different directions at once.

No. Not shadows. They were smaller shirkers. They walked as high as the thing's hips, hissing as they moved. They'd been cut from darkness. From the fabric around the stars. From the gloom inside Mansren's heart. That was how the Royal Historians had described them.

"See!" Ithak jabbed his finger at the tallest shirker. "Ithak was right! The shirkers exist. Though the once-great army of Mansren is shattered, these few have survived for over a thousand years."

Fen's heart was beating rapidly. This was not like seeing a wild animal. This was a creature of pure magic. It had an intellect. It had will. But it wasn't human.

"It's real." Fen kept one hand on her sword hilt and touched the jade necklace to be sure it was still there. "They're real."

"Ithak told you!" Ithak repeated. "They are his children. And they will not die."

"The Queen's Guard killed many of them," Marcus whispered.

"Yes, countless numbers were destroyed. But they are even harder to kill than Queen's guards. These ones can be cut in half and they come back as two."

The shirkers looked from Ithak to Fen to Marcus. Did she see consternation on the tallest shirker's face?

"*You brought two,*" the shirker said. Its voice was a hissing of air. "*One is the number asked. One is all that is needed.*"

"Oh, you shirkers and your numbers," Ithak said. "Don't count the Queen's clown. Ithak has brought the sleeping one. Ithak did as he was told."

The sleeping one? "What are you talking about?" Fen asked. "You know these shirkers?"

"They saved my life when Ithak was wounded by an irritable wildmagic. So Ithak has aided them."

The tall shirker was looking her up and down, making her feel naked. "*Her hand is wood.*"

"Yes!" Ithak clapped his hands. "Living, magical wood. My benefactor will be so pleased to see it. To see her."

The shirker was now directly in front of Fen. It hadn't moved a limb. It was just *there.*

"Stay still," Ithak suggested. "He likely won't hurt you."

Likely? The shirker's face was a black pool. Its eyes were full of tiny pinpricks of floating stars. There were no pupils. It reached out and touched her wooden hand.

A shock moved up her limb. It wasn't painful but it made the little vines stand up and, farther along, the hairs on her forearm. Her wooden hand began to itch terribly. "*You have felt such misery,*" the shirker said. "*We are sad to know that.*"

Then, in an eye-blink, the shirker was ten feet away and pointing at Marcus.

"*He is an enemy.*"

"As hard as it is to believe," Ithak said, "this one is a friend. His name is Marcus. Without his help, we would not have escaped the Queen."

The shirker narrowed its star-filled eyes. "*The essence said only two. He makes three. So I will kill him.*"

"No, you won't!" Fen said. She threw herself in between the shirker and Marcus.

"I can defend myself!" Marcus tried to push her aside. "Step away." Fen didn't budge.

"Listen to him," Ithak said. "Back off! Do not anger it."

The shirker's body was rippling. It seemed to elongate. "*He must die. Only the grower and you will be brought inside the walls. Only two. The essence said so.*"

The shirker lifted its hand and shoved Fen. As she fell to the forest floor, she put out her arms, but she didn't land. The little shirkers had caught her. They hissed into her ears as they pushed her up to her feet. Her flesh felt burned where the creatures had touched her.

Marcus had barely enough strength to swing his sword. Sparks flew and she remembered a story that the swords of the Queen's Guard were forged to cut magic itself. But his blade failed to slice the shirker's flesh. Marcus swung again, grunting.

Blood was leaking out of his wound as if the shirker was causing it to flow.

"I won't let you kill me," Marcus said.

The shirker struck out with a swift blow and Marcus deflected it but was knocked onto the forest floor. A heartbeat later the shirker stood over Marcus, yanked him up and drew back its arm. The hand on that arm was now the shape of a blade.

"No!" Fen leapt, slipping on the wet leaves. She grabbed the shirker's arm with her wooden hand, both righting herself and stopping the blow. There was no pain. No sensation of burning.

Again Fen felt as though her legs had become roots and a power was flowing through her from the earth below. Even stronger than she'd felt outside the forest. She squeezed, and the thing actually grimaced.

"Release him," she said. "He's my friend. My burden. I vouch for him."

The shirker blinked. It stared at Fen's hand and then into her eyes. It was unlike meeting the gaze of any mortal. She felt those eyes boring right inside her spirit. Again, the shirker looked down at Fen's hand. Her fingers had grown to encircle its arm.

The shirker dropped Marcus to the ground. He landed with a *thump*. When the shirker tried to pull away, Fen set her feet and held on. She could not be uprooted. "*That is curious,*" the shirker said. "*Release me.*"

"Promise you won't hurt him."

The shirker seemed to smile. Its teeth were red and sharp. It closed its eyes as though it were thinking—or receiving a message—and then it opened them again. "*I will not hurt him now. In this moment. In a future moment, I cannot promise that. But at this time, this moment, I shall not harm him. The essence has willed it.*"

That would have to be good enough. She couldn't stand being this close to the thing. She let go.

There were five lines where her fingers had gripped him. *"You touched me. No human has touched me and not been burned."*

"She's interesting that way," Ithak said. He had not budged from the stone. "Such powerful magic."

"Three is a good number," the shirker said. *"Audience has been granted."* The shirker turned away and gracefully moved into the forest. It vanished into the leaves. *"Come."* Its voice trailed behind. *"Come now . . . the essence awaits."*

Ithak rubbed his hands together. "Ah, a brilliant day! Audience has been granted." He grabbed Fen by her wooden hand. "Ithak touched a shirker twenty-five years ago. Just poked it with a finger. It still throbs at night. You greatly impressed me with that trick."

Fen's hand had not yet shrunk to its original size. It was almost a human hand, if not for the brown bark. Ithak let it go.

"Get up, Marcus," he said. "Fen saved your carcass again. Stick close to her."

Marcus stood and limped over. "Your wound," Fen said to Marcus. "We should re-bandage it."

"There's no time," Ithak said. "We don't want to miss our audience. Let's go!"

"I'm not going anywhere." Fen pointed toward where the shirkers had gone. "Those . . . those things are evil. At least, I think they are."

"Oh." Ithak shook his head. "Did you not listen to Ithak's tale at all? The shirkers are not evil. They are instruments, plain and simple."

"You've guided us into a trap," Fen said.

"Not true! Ithak brought you to the safest place in Illium."

"But that creature knew you," Marcus said. He had sheathed his sword but was keeping his hand on the pommel. "You have some sort of pact with it."

"Not true. There's no pact. Ithak is just friendly with many of the forest creatures. They like him. Come now, children, for an audience is not granted often."

"An audience with whom?" Fen's hand was still tingling. The shirker had been so beyond her knowledge. The very air had vibrated around it. If it had wanted to slay any of them, it could have easily done so.

"The essence, as they call it," Ithak said. "Or my benefactor, as Ithak likes to say. If anyone can save your sister, it is him."

That made Fen bite her lip. "I'm not that easily swayed, Ithak. I want to save her. But I need to know more."

"Ask. But be quick!"

"Who are they taking us to see?"

"A friend. An old, old friend." He glanced over his shoulder to where the shirkers had disappeared. "Ah, already this is taking too long." He began striding away. "Ithak grows tired of explaining the simplest things to you. Come now, or find your own way through Helwood."

Fen exchanged glances with Marcus. He shrugged. "What can we do?" he said. "We have to trust him."

"Finally, words of wisdom from the boy," Ithak said from several feet away.

Fen nodded. *He could save my sister.*

Each leaf that the shirkers had touched had turned black, which left a clearly marked path. Soon the three were passing trees that had grown thicker and more twisted. She couldn't imagine how many centuries it would have taken for each of them to sprout from a seedling to this massive size.

Just when Fen was about to ask how much farther, the path of dark leaves ended at a wall of overgrown trees that had somehow sprung up side by side without a space between them. The living barrier was at least a hundred feet tall, if not higher.

The shirker appeared a few feet along the wall. Or it had been there all along, and she just hadn't seen it. It rested a hand on one of the massive trunks, seeming to be stroking the tree.

"What is this place?" she whispered.

"This is my benefactor's sanctuary," Ithak answered. "As Ithak said, it's the safest place in Illium."

With a creaking and rumbling, the trees in front of the shirker began to part. An opening appeared. It was just big enough for them to walk into. "*Follow*," the shirker said. The shirker and his brethren entered without looking back. There was only darkness inside.

"Come along," Ithak said. "Once we enter these walls, you will no longer be a simple country girl and grunting boy. And along with knowledge, there will be wonderful food. At least there was the last time."

He walked in. Fen gripped her sword hilt and followed, Marcus behind her. Her wooden hand was tingling again, as if it were trying to send her a message—though she had no idea what that message could be.

The tunnel was at least fifty strides long. A regiment of Queen's guards armed with axes couldn't cut its way through in a hundred years. Then the tunnel opened into an emerald-green place that glowed with light.

What she saw stunned her to the core.

CHAPTER EIGHTEEN

THE BENEFACTOR

WITH A CREAKING AND GRINDING, THE TREES CLOSED behind them. Fen's gaze was drawn to a round table, set with the most abundant selection of food she'd ever seen—more food than everyone in Village Twenty-One would have eaten in a month. There were roasted potatoes, carrots, bowls of steaming noodles and seared venison. Cream balls, strawberries, cakes and sugar biscuits sat on another group of tables. And finally there were grapes, oranges and countless other varieties of fruit. She wiped saliva from her lips.

"Glorious!" Ithak said. "Ithak's last meal here was the greatest of his life."

Fen swallowed. The food had so attracted her attention that she hadn't seen the magnificence of the interior. The trees had curved together two hundred feet above them—a natural temple. Stars were floating in the vaulted ceiling . . . or were they perhaps massive fireflies? In the very centre of the open space was a large black oak tree.

"Don't look for Ithak's benefactor yet." Ithak had stuffed several cream balls into his mouth and was spitting out gobs of cream with each word. "Eat! Eat! One meal here will fill you for a week."

Marcus lifted up a rack of ribs and then dropped them. "It might be poisoned."

Ithak drew a roasted turkey leg from the table and shook it. "Poisoned? Ha! Then this is the world's best way to die. Eat up, Queen's guard. You too, Fen. Stuff your cakeholes!" He took a huge chomp of the turkey leg and tossed the rest to the ground.

Fen tentatively touched a bun. It was real. She picked it up. It had been buttered with a swirled pattern. "How can this food just be waiting here?"

Ithak wiped his mouth. "Don't ask questions, you fools. Eat!"

The morsel of Queen's Guard bread was all she'd had in days. Her stomach had withered. Fen picked up a star-shaped fruit and bit off one section. It was sweet and fleshy and tasted like it had been grown in honey. She shoved the rest in her mouth. Once she'd had one bite, she couldn't stop. She grabbed a square of yellow cheese and ate it. Then chomped down a slice of venison that was warm, perfectly roasted and spiced with cinnamon. Marcus began shoving food into his mouth too.

There were several bowls of noodles, just as Fen's mother would make them, but they had large pieces of chicken and pork. Not the bits of rabbit or squirrel she'd grown up on. She tasted one bowl and was certain it was her mother's recipe.

How? she wanted to shout. But her ravenous hunger led her to gobble up the noodles. She paused only to drink from goblets of lemon water.

Fen thought of all the meals her mother had cooked. There was always a little less than enough to fill her and May up.

But this was opulence even the richest in Regentium couldn't imagine. The Queen herself might not have such choice.

One delight followed another. Fen gulped blueberries and cherries covered in chocolate. There was a plate of sunberries larger than any she'd ever picked. She ate three of the berries and sighed. No wonder the rich paid so much for this delicacy. It already felt as if a year had passed since she'd fallen from the tree. It took her a moment to calculate that had happened only five days earlier.

Marcus bumped into her, in a hurry to grab a piece of cake. His cheek was stained with chocolate. She chuckled and pointed at his face, and he used his cloak to wipe himself clean. "You don't look much better, village girl," he said.

She couldn't think of a clever reply, so she took another swig of water. This time it tasted like mangoes.

"Fill your waterskin," Marcus suggested.

"Good thinking!" Fen did so. Then she went back to devouring food.

Finally, she pushed away from the table. Her stomach was so full it felt close to bursting. If only May could be here to taste this food.

Marcus joined her. He looked healthier.

"I've stopped bleeding," he said. She checked his bandages to see that it was true. She glanced up at Ithak, who was face-deep in the food. His shoulder no longer had any sign of a wound.

"Does the food heal us?" she asked.

"You had cuts on your face from our ride through the trees," Marcus said. "Now it's back to looking proper again."

"Proper?"

"Well, in-interesting," he mumbled. "Not messy."

She wasn't certain if any of those words were meant as compliments.

Ithak, meanwhile, hadn't slowed his pace of consumption.

"He must be all stomach," Marcus said.

There was a slight hissing in her ear. Fen turned to see the shirkers were right beside her. She shuddered.

"*Come*," the tallest said. Or had all six of them spoken at once? "*The essence summons you.*"

"Oh, time's up." Ithak grabbed a goblet, took a swig and then tossed it to the ground. "Let us hear from my benefactor."

They followed the shirkers to the giant oak tree in the centre of the fortress. Several large branches had grown together into a series of steps that circled upward. They began to climb. Soon Fen saw that they were approaching a throne set on a floor of woven branches. Whoever was sitting motionless on that throne was too high for her to see. But the hair on the back of her neck began to rise. When she'd made it around the first circle of steps, she glanced down to see that the tables of food had vanished.

Ithak halted, and then he belched. "Ithak is a stuffed pig," he admitted.

They came to the area that held the throne. A buzzing grew in Fen's ears.

The throne was made of thorns. The dark man sitting there would have been seven feet tall if he'd had a head. He did have a broad chest, strong arms and powerful legs. There were cracks all along his body—it was made of stone. Still, the headless body was a chilling sight. The tallest shirker motioned for the group to stop.

A small shirker clambered up the body and sat on the neck. A thought was niggling in the back of Fen's mind. This was familiar. A story she'd been told. But what was it?

"Yes, it's the body of Mansren," Ithak whispered. "Turned to stone and shattered by the Queen's first guard. Those stones were strewn across Illium and thrown into the ocean. The shirkers found each pebble, each chip, each grain and brought them here."

"How is that possible?" Fen asked.

"With patience anything is possible," Ithak said.

"But I have seen only six shirkers." Marcus was staring with a wide-eyed look of terror.

"Yes, as Ithak just said, with patience anything is possible."

Marcus had tightened his hands into fists. "The Queen would burn the forest if she knew of this."

"Which makes it a wonder you are allowed to stand here." Ithak patted him on the shoulder. "Best for you to keep your queenly mouth shut, boy."

The smallest shirker had folded itself up into a ball so it seemed to become nothing more than two huge, blinking eyes and a slit of a mouth. That slit moved.

"Ithak, you havvvve returned, my loyal friend. You havvvve brought me the grower."

Fen shivered at the sound of the powerful voice coming out of the shirker. *He means me.*

Ithak stepped forward and bowed. "Yes, my liege. Ithak has brought her. It was no easy journey. Many were the leagues crossed and troubles faced. Ithak struggled valiantly."

"Ssspeak not of hardship. Only know you have my thankssss." The voice sounded as if it were coming from far away. *"Ssstep forward, girl. Do not fear. I am a friend. Let me know you."*

Fen took a hesitant step. The shirker's head turned slowly so that its unblinking amber eyes stared at her. That look unnerved her to the core. Something was looking at her through the shirker. This body was stone, but it held something ancient and powerful inside.

"*I ssssee you now. Your name?*"

"Fen," she said.

"*Not your full name. Not your real name. But a ssssstrong name. Ssssstrong flesh. Sssstronger spirit. Sssstep closssser.*"

She took a small step.

"*Closssser,*" it commanded. The voice was a decree inside her skull. She crept ahead. The farther she got from Ithak and Marcus, the more vulnerable she felt. "*That'ssss closssse enough, my dear. Please don't fear. I know this issss all very odd.*"

"Are you truly Mansren?" she asked.

"*No. I am not. I am just a part of his esssssence. Of his will. A ssssmall part. I act on his behalf. Now, touch my sssshoulder.*"

Fen looked back at Ithak and he nodded eagerly. "Do it," he mouthed.

She reached out her right hand and laid her wooden fingers upon the nearest stone shoulder. She expected a tingling like she'd felt when she grabbed the shirker. But there was nothing. Nothing at all.

No, not quite nothing. A vibration. A sense of being measured. Of being known. Of being understood.

The shirker's head nodded. "*Oh, my dear, dear mortal. You are missssing something, aren't you? Your hand. Yes, sssshe took it. But you lost something more. Someone. Sssssomeonessss, that is.*"

I lost everything.

"*Mother dead. Your ssssister. Sssstolen.*"

How could it know that? Just by her touch.

"Yes." Fen's voice was raw. "My sister was captured by the Queen. My mother was executed."

"*Would you like to ssssee her?*" it asked.

"My mother?" She nearly drew back her hand.

"*No. Sssshe'ssss beyond where I can look. But your ssssister. I can show her to you. A friend would do that for a friend.*" Friend was an odd word. How could she be friends with this . . . this . . . essence. Especially someone whom, up to only an hour earlier, she'd considered pure evil. "*You musssst be wracked with worry.*"

Fen nodded. "Yes. Yes! I want to see her."

The shirker nodded. "*Of courssse you do. You love her.*" One of the other shirkers stepped forward and drew a rectangle in the air with a long finger. The rectangle stayed, as though outlined in red chalk. Then, with sharpened nails, the shirker grabbed at the top of that rectangle and pulled upward. The very air itself peeled away as though a blind were being raised. And in that space were colours—brown, red and black—that slowly came into focus.

Fen was hit by the stink of excrement and body odour. She nearly gagged. There was crying and a distant but horrible squeal of agony.

She was looking into a prison cell. A bundle of rags had been tossed on the floor near the wall. A bowl of water and a honey pail sat next to them. Outside the bars was a guard station, with what looked like several physicians' instruments. Beyond that were cages, each holding a dirty, starving child. Fen shivered.

The rags moved, coughed. A girl with dark, ratty hair raised her head. The cage itself wasn't even tall enough for her to stand in.

"*Your ssssister,*" the voice said. "*Ssssshee livessss.*"

"May?" Fen murmured. "May, is that you?" Her sister was over a hundred leagues away. Deep in the dungeons below the Queen's Red Tower. And yet, she was right in front of Fen.

May blinked and looked toward the glowing window. Something black stained her face. Blood?

"Fen?" Her voice crackled. "Fen?"

Fen took a step forward and broke her contact with the statue. "It's me. I'm right here! Can you see me?"

"I—I hear your voice. Oh, Fen. Fen. *It hurts.*" Fen saw for certain it was her sister's face. Her pug nose. Her dark eyes. Her hair was a mess of rattails and she looked a year older.

"What hurts?" Fen forced the words out.

"Everything. She hurts me every day. She asks questions. She wants to find you. Oh, Fen. And Mama. She's gone. I saw it happen." May wiped at her face. "Is this a dream? Where are you?"

"*Do not ansssswer that,*" the voice said. "*Pleasssse. Do not let the Queen know about ussss. About you.*"

"I'm hiding. But I'll come to you, May. I'll take you home."

"It hurts so much." Her sister's voice became a painful whine. "The horrible, horrible things they do." One of her teeth was missing.

"*Tell her the pain will end. I promisssse this as a friend.*"

"The pain will end," Fen said.

"*Tell her to be sssstrong.*"

"Be strong. Be strong." Tears poured down Fen's face. How could she be this close and not touch May?

"*Tell her sssshe will soon be free. Everyone will be free.*"

How could that be possible? "You'll soon be free, May. Free. Everyone will be free."

May rubbed her eyes. "I think I see you, Fen. You're right there. Pull me out of here."

"*Don't touch the opening,*" the voice commanded.

Whether he was talking to her or to May, Fen didn't know.

"Get me out of here," her sister began to shriek. "*Getme-outofhere!*"

May shot out her hand and Fen stumbled toward the glowing rectangle. She reached in with her wooden hand and for a moment she felt her sister's fingers in her own.

She squeezed.

"Oh, Fen," May whispered. "You're really here."

Then came a shout. And a bright blinding light. And Fen was thrown back as the window shattered into black fragments that floated down to the ground.

Her fingers tingled. She had actually touched May. If she'd been strong enough, she could have pulled her through.

Marcus helped her up. "Open it again," Fen said. "I could grab her."

"*I am ssssorry. It is not possssible. The dissssstance issss too great. You both would have been torn asunder. I cannot have that. Not you. My friend.*"

Her hand still tingled. She stared at it. "Why did you show me that?"

"*Becaussse I have a tiny request. If you complete it, you will free your ssssister.*"

"Then tell me what it is!" Her words were sharp. Even angry. "Make your request!"

The voice did so.

CHAPTER NINETEEN

THE TINY REQUEST

"You will go to Velchan'ssss Forge and bring back *that which you find there.*"

Fen had no idea where or what the forge was. But it didn't matter. It was the best way to get to her sister. "What am I bringing back?" she asked.

"*You will know when you ssssee it, Fen. The answer is sssssturing you right in the face.*"

Fen couldn't see the answer. She still felt the warmth of her sister's hand. And smelled the horror of that jail cell. May should not spend one moment longer than necessary in that place.

"Your head," Marcus said. "You want her to bring back your head." Fen glanced over at him, impressed by how quickly he had put things together. *I should have figured that out.*

"*Ssssmart Queen's guard. Yesss. That isss it.*"

"And why can't you get it?" Marcus asked.

"*All of my shirkerssss who have tried have died. And others I've sent.*"

"You've sent others?" Fen fixed Ithak with a gaze. Ithak shrugged. "Other wildmagics?"

"*Yessss. They were very brave. Good friendssss. But they failed. And died.*"

"And why would I survive?"

"*Survival is not a certainty. But only I can ssssave your sister, and only you can save me. Again, it is ssssomething friends would do for friends.*"

The voice was not as overpowering as it had been before. She wondered if she were just growing accustomed to talking to a dead man. No. A dead god. "And how will you save my sister?" Fen leaned a little closer.

The tree rumbled with the voice's laughter. Leaves fluttered around them. Fen backed up a half step. "*I will tear down the walls of Regentium and kill my dearest love, the Queen.*"

"Your dearest love?" She wasn't certain if that had been said in jest. "How can you defeat Servilia? I've seen her armies."

"*I will manifesssst the conditions. And all will be free, including your ssssister. That is my solemn promise, Fen. One thousand yearssss in chainssss issss too long for you mortals.*"

The voice spoke with such absolute confidence. "And what will I need on this journey?" Fen asked.

"*Your hand.*" Her hand tingled at the mention. "*Take the Queen's guard. He cannot live here. Though I see his good heart.*"

"If he will come with me, then he is welcome."

Marcus looked Fen directly in the eyes. There was more emotion on his face than she'd ever seen. "Our fates seem to be intertwined. I have nowhere else to go. And I do owe you one last life. Of course I will come."

Fen wanted to hug him. Instead she turned to the statue. "Tell me how to find your head."

"*Ithak, come clossser.*"

Ithak shuffled up. He looked to be almost bowing. "Yes, Mansren."

"*I am not him yet. I am jusssst his aspect.*" If he was only an aspect—a portion—then Fen wondered what it would be like to be in the presence of Mansren himself. "*Give the girl the pointing ssssstone.*"

Ithak hesitated before reaching into his pouch and pulling out the black stone finger.

"*Take a piece of mysssself with you,*" the essence said. "*It will lead you to Velchan'ssss Forge and guide you home. To me. Your dear friend.*"

Fen had never heard the word *friend* sound so ominous. But she had made up her mind. As she took the stone finger, her gaze travelled to the right hand of the statue . . . its index finger was missing. *So this really did belong to Mansren,* she thought, as she dropped it into her belt pouch.

"*Now go. Complete this tassssk and your ssssister will be free. Take my besssst and kindesssst wishes with you.*"

"But what can you offer me?" Marcus said.

The shirker gave him a long, baleful gaze. "*I will take the Queen out of your heart. I know you long for her. For her commandssss. Her pressssence. And you will for the rest of your life. But I will banisssh her from your heart. You'll be your own man. That is my promisssse to you, Marcusssss of the Queen's Guard.*"

Marcus nodded, a hard set to his eyes. "That will be enough."

"*Now go. The three of you. Go.*"

"Three!" Ithak squawked. "But Ithak thought he was finished. Ithak has been fetching for so many years."

"*One last mission, dear Ithak. They will need your wissssdom and your guile. Go. Go. I ssssleep now.*"

The shirker stepped off the statue and the sense of being in the presence of true power vanished. No, Fen decided, it hadn't vanished, but it slept in those stones—something deep and dark and forever.

The tall shirker led them down the circular stairs and toward a section of the wall that slowly pulled apart and formed another tunnel. It gestured with a long hand and stood there silently.

Fen marched through the tunnel, Marcus and Ithak a few steps behind. She glanced back. The remaining shirkers were standing at the throne tree, watching them.

When the trio stepped out of the fortress, the wall of trees groaned as it grew back together.

"Well, girl," Ithak said. "It looks like you're our feckless leader now. Which way are you taking us?"

She reached down into the pouch and brought out the finger. It was three times as thick as her own. And so dark.

"I'm not feeling—*aaaah!*" Fen dropped it. A shock had shot through her hand.

She grabbed the finger again with her wooden hand and held it in an open palm. The finger straightened and pointed northwest. She flicked it and it rotated and pointed the same direction.

"It's a compass," Marcus said.

"Oh, it's far more than that," Ithak said. "It is our guide."

"Then we go this way." Fen pointed. "But I have no idea what Velchan's Forge is."

"Of course you don't." Ithak crossed his arms. "You villagers don't know anything beyond the length of your noses."

"It's a mountain in the northwest." Marcus's voice was kind

and patient. "It belches smoke, I am told. And spews fire and liquid rock. The first suits of armour for the Queen's Guard were forged in the fires there."

"The Great Salt Mire is a garden of splendour compared to Velchan's Forge," Ithak said. "Ithak has only looked at that mountain from a distance. Ithak has never dared to climb it."

Fen tightened her hand around the stone finger. She took a deep breath and said, "Then we will have to dare."

CHAPTER TWENTY

THE
RED ROAD

FEN WANTED TO DASH TOWARD THE MOUNTAIN. BUT she also wished she could run straight to Regentium and hold her sister again. Fen had touched May. Actually touched her! Her sister had said she'd been questioned by the Queen. Any questioning would involve torture, and the thought of that made Fen want to weep. May was a tough little squirrel. She didn't mind banging her knees and bruising her arms, but that youthful toughness would break under the attention of a Royal Inquisitor. Fen shuddered.

The Queen might discover that Fen had reached out to her sister. Would May be further punished for that?

"You look worried," Marcus said.

"I'm thinking about my sister," Fen answered.

He didn't say anything, but patted her shoulder. It was an awkward gesture—slightly too hard—as if he was only used to smacking the shoulders of his fellow Queen's guards after some victory. But she appreciated it. He wouldn't have any idea what it was like to have a sibling.

"I have lost brothers," he said.

Perhaps he did understand. "I just want May back. I want something in my life that I used to have. Before this." She pointed at her red hair with her wooden hand.

He cracked his neck—it was a habit of his she'd noted. "We will do everything to get your sister back."

After only a few hours of walking, they came to the edge of Helwood. The land before them was a flat prairie covered with dry grass. Ithak sniffed and looked around. "This is the western flank of the forest. We are on the opposite side of Helwood from which we entered."

"How can we have gone that far?" Marcus asked. "That's at least a fortnight of walking."

"The doors of the fortress open wherever Mansren wants them to. So they opened in the west this time."

They were safe under the canopy of trees. Fen had grown used to the feeling of the ancient, hulking woods guarding them from prying eyes and searching enemies. Once the group was outside Helwood's shadow, they would no longer be protected.

"We must keep going," Fen said. She stepped into the open. The sun was bright enough to make her squint, and the sky didn't hold a single cloud. A corvus could spot them from a league away, but thankfully none were visible.

She set a quick pace and the other two followed. The stone finger was sometimes so heavy it slowed her down, the next moment so light she had to check to be certain it was there. But it urged her to travel northwest. As if it, too, were a tiny portion of Mansren's will.

They climbed a small hill to discover more and more hills beyond it. "How far do we have to travel?" Fen asked.

"Ithak's mind is part map." He counted on his fingers. "It should take at least two fortnights. If we walk fast."

Fen paled. "Almost thirty days! We can't evade the Queen for that long."

"We'll have to," Ithak said.

A whole month of torture for her sister. Of being locked in that cell like an animal. May would be broken. Or die. Then it dawned on Fen that she wasn't even counting the time it would take to get back.

"Is there a faster way?" she asked.

"You could grow wings." Ithak flapped his arms.

"There may be another path," Marcus said. Fen couldn't read the look on his face. Was it reticence? Fear? "We could take the Queen's Road. We are not that far away from the south-western section."

"That's madness!" Ithak said. "Utter, brain-numbing madness."

Fen put up her hand. "Let him speak. Why do you suggest it?"

"Because all Queen's guards can travel at great speed on that road," Marcus said. "We could cross the queendom in hours."

"But wouldn't the Queen know?" Fen asked.

"I'm uncertain about that," he said. "And to be honest, I'm also uncertain how to unlock the road's swiftness."

"Oh, great! The boy has never done it." Ithak threw up his hands.

"No, I haven't. But when my regiment travelled from Regentium to Fen's village, we went at speed. It seemed a simple manoeuvre from where I sat in the wagon. My brother just stared at the road and—and we were suddenly racing. Maybe I have enough Queen's blood in me to work with the magic. He told me you just had to find the road in your mind. It would shorten our trip by at least three weeks."

"Then we'll try the Queen's Road," Fen said.

"What is Ithak hearing?" Ithak pulled at his ears. "You're both idiots. The road will kill us!"

"It's final, then," Fen said. Ithak had teased her so much in the last few days that she enjoyed the shocked look on his face. "We'll go."

After some discussion, they came to the conclusion that Marcus still looked too much like a Queen's guard. They would never make it to the road if a corvus spotted his red locks—they had to assume the Queen was looking for a guard with two companions. Other than for executions, the guards always travelled in their squadrons. So Fen quickly cut up the last of his cloak and stitched it into a loose garment that hid his armour. Then she took her sword to his hair. It sliced through easily.

"I haven't had my hair cut since I turned thirteen summers." Marcus examined a tuft of red. "From that day, it was always the same length."

"At least yours can be cut," Fen said. "My hair defeated even the sharpest shears." She tried to slice off a lock of her own hair, but the Queen's blade wouldn't cut through it. "See!"

"That mop might make it harder to chop off your head," Ithak said. "You should grow it long enough to cover your whole body."

"At least I have hair," Fen said. "All you have is fuzz."

Ithak was rubbing his chin. "It is interesting that yours can't be cut. Does that mean your magic is stronger?"

"Who knows what it means." She got back to her task. Marcus's hair was soft to the touch. She was surprised how she'd already forgotten that her right hand was made of wood. It acted the same as a normal hand. She made a few more careful slices. "There! You're finished." She sheathed her sword.

Marcus ran his hand through the stubble and looked at the blood on his fingers. "You nicked me about ten thousand times."

"Only because you moved!"

"You look like a dumb pig farmer," Ithak said. "It's a good look for you."

Fen touched a darker patch near Marcus's temple. "Your hair is starting to change colour."

"What colour is it?" Marcus asked.

"Raven black. And it looks like it will grow out curly."

Marcus scrunched up his face. "Curly? I have curly hair?"

Ithak was stuffing some of Marcus's hair into his pouch. "Ithak may be able to sell this," he explained. He held up a tuft. "If your hair is dark, it makes one wonder who your parents were. The farmers in the north have curly dark hair. They were called the Ostros, or something like that. So perhaps your parents were from there. Makes sense: they're legendarily dumb people."

"Ithak!" Fen said.

"He's only kidding," Marcus said. "There was much banter between me and my brothers. This is Ithak's way of saying he respects me."

"What?! Ithak has no respect for either of you." As if to prove it, he got up and tapped Marcus's chest. "So did they paste the armour onto your skin?"

Marcus shook his head. "No. When a Queen's guard dies, a green recruit is summoned from the youth barracks to the Red Artificer's forge. They made me drink a particularly strong draft of blood wine. Then put a wooden bit in my mouth, laid me in a mould and poured the molten armour onto me."

"That sounds torturous," Fen said.

"It was painful," he admitted. "But the blood wine healed me and the armour became a second skin."

"I wonder when your armour will fall off," Ithak said.

Marcus looked down at his chest. The metal looked tarnished but still impressive. "Let's hope that doesn't happen." He stood up from the stone he'd been sitting on. "We should find that wagon now. I can't carry the two of you on my back."

"Oh, let me summon one out of thin air," Ithak said.

"We'll find one," Fen said. "And borrow it."

Ithak rubbed his hands together. "Ithak is an expert at borrowing."

By the late afternoon, they saw the red line of the Queen's Road to the west. It was as if the Queen had drawn a bloody stroke through the prairies. Crops had been planted in long, thin strips alongside it. In the far distance was a collection of round mud-walled huts.

"Do you know which village that is?" Fen asked.

"Does it matter?" Ithak said. "We just need a wagon. Oh, and we don't want to actually meet any villagers. They are wary of strangers and will send a raven to the nearest guard post. And then we'll die."

"Then let's try our best to hide," Fen said. It would be hard to remain unseen. The land was flat. But she didn't spot anyone in the fields or along the Queen's Road. A sign of good luck!

Their luck held when they came across a wagon half-full of cordwood next to a small copse of trees. The sound of chopping echoed inside the copse, but they couldn't see the woodcutter.

"Well, this is fortuitous." Ithak rubbed his chin. "Let's strike like sneaky lightning." He turned invisible and was gone. Fen and Marcus waited quietly. The chopping stopped for a moment. Then it began again.

"You know he's using you," Marcus whispered.

"Ithak?" she asked.

"No. Mansren. If that voice truly was Mansren. For some reason only you can retrieve his head. What if—what if that window you looked through wasn't real. What if it was some sort of spell that reflected what you wanted to see."

"No." She said this quietly, though she had been tempted to shout it. "I held May's hand. I touched her."

"I just wanted you to know my thoughts."

"I appreciate them. But this is the only way to get my sister."

Ithak coughed and reappeared. He looked from Fen to Marcus. "What were you two talking about? Hair? Anyway, the woodsman is alone. And portly. So we can outdistance him easily. We'd better take his wagon now . . . he was sweating like a hog but will likely catch his breath soon."

Marcus was the first to the wagon and he took a moment to let the horse smell his hand before stroking its mane.

"Finished making friends?" Ithak said from the wagon's bench. "We should be off."

Marcus nodded and climbed up. Fen hesitated. She knew losing the wagon would be a hardship for the farmer. She took one of the copper pieces her mother had given her and placed it on the ground.

"Why are you leaving money?" Ithak asked. Each time he spoke, the horse twitched its ears backwards, looking angry.

"To pay something for the wagon."

"Well, it's paid for. Let's go."

She climbed up and sat beside Ithak. "This is too crowded," he said, getting into the back and sitting on the chopped wood.

Marcus flicked the reins but the horse stood still. He flicked them harder. "Is there a whip?" Ithak asked. "Or twist its tail."

"It'll kick your head off," Fen said. She was pretty certain the chopping had stopped. Her father had cared for ponies in the red earth mines. He used to make a loud kissing noise to motivate them.

She made the sound. The horse raised its ears. She made it again and the mare walked forward and soon was trotting. Fen looked back but there was no sign of the owner.

"This is the slowest escape ever," Ithak said. The horse didn't speed up, no matter the form of encouragement, but soon they were far enough away that Fen felt safe. They followed a rough trail that led them to the Queen's Road.

Fen had expected warning flares or bells to ring the moment they rode onto it. This road was a symbol of the Queen's power. Instead, nothing happened.

They rolled ahead. Marcus stared at the road.

He no longer appeared to be a guard. The beauty the Queen instilled in each of her minions was still there, but it was fading. There were enough changes that he could be just a normal boy.

Well, a normal boy in armour.

"Why aren't we moving?" Ithak asked.

Marcus gritted his teeth. "I need to concentrate."

"Can you concentrate harder?" Ithak said. "It's going to take us a thousand years."

"You're not helping," Fen said.

Marcus raised his hand, quieting them. "I can feel the road inside my veins but I can't reach it." Marcus turned to Fen. "I need the blood wine."

"Are you certain?" she asked.

Ithak knocked on the bench. "Hello? Ithak thinks this is a bad idea."

"It's the only way," Marcus said.

Fen dug the golden flask out of her knapsack, paused for a moment and then handed it over. When Marcus unstoppered it, she caught a whiff of rancid stink. He took a small swig and his body shook. He stared at the road for a few seconds. Sweat formed on his forehead. He took another swig.

"The road is closer," he whispered. "I see it now. Like a line through the maps. It will work. I'll make it work."

The horse was trotting along at the same speed, but the land started to shift—it was as if the road were spooling faster underneath them. Then faster and faster. Fen grabbed the side of the wagon. The wind cooled her forehead. The bushes and stones along the side of the road were a blur. The horse acted a little spooked, but kept going in a straight line. Fen tried to spot landmarks, but she had only the barest impression of trees, then hills and then shacks.

"We just passed a village," she said.

They shot ahead, but within the bubble she felt safe. Even Ithak seemed pleased by the speed. Or at least he had stopped complaining. He stuck his tongue out, as if testing the air for rain.

"So this is how it works," Fen said. "Excellent, excellent work, Marcus."

Marcus was either grimacing or grinning, she couldn't tell which. It was clear he didn't want to break his concentration. Fen decided not to do anything to distract him. They were traversing leagues with each beat of her heart. Had a mountain range passed them on the left? A forest on the right? It was at least a week's travel in a few minutes. Then two weeks'. Three.

"It feels so powerful," Marcus whispered. He was smiling. "We could fly right to the ocean and skip across the water. To another land."

"Just keep us on the road," Ithak said.

"I wish you could feel this, Ithak. I wish—" Marcus straightened. "*Who uses my road without my permission?*" he hissed.

Fen drew in a deep breath.

"*Answer me. Who uses my road?*"

Marcus shook his head back and forth and nearly let go of the reins. "There is trouble," he said in his own voice.

"What can I do to help?" Fen said.

"*Answer me!*" Marcus shouted. His voice sounded so much like hers. "*Who uses my road?*" Then a moment later. "*It's you. The renegade and the wildmagic. You're alive!*"

Marcus squeezed his skull, dropping the reins. Fen grabbed for them, but they fell to the ground and were dragged behind the wagon. Marcus let out a short yell.

The horse whinnied and made a sharp turn, swinging the wagon off the road at full speed. There was a bump. Then they were in the air and the wagon smashed into the ground, falling to pieces.

All three of them catapulted forward.

CHAPTER TWENTY-ONE

THE
HORRIBLE WAY

FEN CLUTCHED AT THE AIR AS SHE FLEW, THE HORSE rolling below her. She tucked herself into a ball and tumbled across the wet, marshy ground, eventually landing in slough water. She struggled for breath for several moments and then lifted her head out of the muck.

There was a face looking down at her, only inches away. She recoiled at first before recognizing the horse. It was completely free of the harness. "Hey," she said. "Stay still, horse. Stay still."

The mare snorted, spattering Fen with snot, and then reared up and galloped away.

Fen stood, holding her head. She'd been deposited a long distance from the road. The wagon was rubble. Marcus had landed face down near a pool of water and was pushing himself up. She limped through the sticky mud and helped him.

"You're a horrible wagon master," Ithak said. Algae was hanging from his forehead.

"The Queen got into my head!" Marcus banged his fist against his skull. "She recognized me. She was there!"

"Calm yourself!" Fen grabbed his hands. "She's not here now. We're safe."

Marcus nodded, but even those two sips of the blood wine had made his face look more pure again. More perfect. Was she correct in thinking his armour sparkled more brightly than before?

"You're right," he said.

Fen released his hands. "We need to get as far away from the road as possible. Guards will be here soon. Does anyone have any notion of where we are?"

"We're in a swamp," Ithak said.

"I mean on the map!"

"Ah." Ithak raised one finger and sniffed the air. "My nose tells me it's the Stagnum of Crathis—Servilia must have been drinking when she chose that name. We've cut out at least three weeks' worth of walking during our short time on the road."

"Ithak is right." Marcus was now holding his head with one hand. "We are in the Stagnum."

"You did well to get us this far," Fen said. "The question is which direction to go next." She felt for the pouch, glad to discover it hadn't been torn from her belt. She took Mansren's finger out. It was vibrating and when she placed it in her palm, it pointed farther into the swamp.

"There's our answer," Ithak said. "The one thing we can trust."

Trust was not the word that Fen would use.

The trio worked their way deeper into the swampland. With each step, the ground grew softer, and Fen's feet were soon making an annoying *squash-squash* with each step. She pressed on, despite the wetness in her boots.

"My brothers will have difficulty travelling in this terrain," Marcus said. She noticed that he sank much deeper than she into the mire.

"The infernus hounds won't, though," Ithak added.

Fen glanced at the sky, knowing the corvuses would arrive first. The tall reeds and occasional moss-covered trees provided some cover. The tracks the three of them left were quite clear, though.

For the first time, she realized she wasn't yet hungry. But it'd been a full day since they'd walked through Helwood. The food Mansren had provided was still in her stomach. Did it have some magic property that would keep her feeling full?

They struggled through the muck. At times it was hard for Fen to find earth solid enough for them to cross. It was just water and mud. She expected to be sucked down at any moment.

"Find cover!" Ithak said.

They threw themselves under a large tree, which seemed to have no trunk at all, only a wide collection of branches and roots open to the air. A corvus swept through the distant sky, coming directly toward them. Ithak obviously had good eyes, Fen decided. "Stay still," he whispered. "Pretend you're roots. Or dead rodents." The leaves and roots gave them a good amount of protection. They waited silently. The creature circled lower and then veered northward.

"The Queen's Guard won't know exactly where we were on the road," Marcus said. "They would have to slow down in just the right place to see what remains of the wagon."

"Ithak hopes you're right," Ithak said. "And that the horse will be long gone before they arrive."

After waiting for several minutes, they continued their journey. Flies landed on every part of Fen, defying her slapping and swinging arms. They bit, drawing blood. Ithak spent as much time swatting them as he did walking. None landed on Marcus.

Mansren's finger continued to urge Fen onwards, pressing against her side and entering her thoughts. If she changed her direction to avoid a large bog, it almost felt as if the finger would compel her to walk straight northwest. "Was this finger always a difficult thing to carry?" she asked Ithak.

"Never," he said. "It should be light as a feather. Well, unless it becomes upset with you. Just go where it says and all will be well."

She thought back to the first time she'd noticed him touching the pouch at his belt. "You used the finger to find me," she said.

"You're not the quickest brain in Illium," Ithak said. "But you're correct. The shirkers brought the finger to me and told me to meet you. Somehow, my benefactor knew you'd found your magic. Then Ithak found you."

"How would he know?"

Ithak shrugged. "A wildmagic isn't born every day. My guess is that my benefactor was sensitive to that sudden burst of magic. Many others, of similar sensitivity, would be too. Especially the Queen."

"She knew?"

"Of course! Her Red Artificers likely have ticking and tocking machines that measure the appearance of magic. The corvuses can sniff it. Why else would the Queen's Guard make such a pleasant visit to your village?"

Fen remembered seeing Servilia in a dream, the morning she had gone crimson, asking who and where she was. "She knew. Not exactly where I was, but she knew."

"When the magic finds a wildmagic, it's a great moment. Just think: you were wanted. Finally."

"My mother always wanted me!" She said this so harshly a little spittle flew from her lips. "Even when I lost my hand. I was always loved by my family! Unlike you."

Ithak responded with a grin but there was a hard edge to his eyes. He made her so mad! *Don't let him get under your skin. He enjoys it too much.* As she took a breath in, she realized she maybe shouldn't have said such a mean thing to him. But the moment to apologize had passed.

Soon night fell and they took cover under a massive tree. Even then the stone finger wiggled like the tail of a snake in her pocket. And her hand was itching like crazy. But she slept.

It seemed moments later that the Queen's voice sounded in her head. "*Arise, your Queen commands it. Be fruitful and obey my laws.*"

Fen woke up. She was neither angered nor frightened by the visitation. Both Marcus and Ithak were awake and looking at her.

"One day her voice will be gone," Fen said. It almost sounded like a promise.

They continued walking. In time the land became harder, more solid and rocky. The sun cleared the mist, revealing huge, dark shadows in front of them.

"We're in the Carpenthi mountains," Ithak said. "The way should be horrible from here to the forge."

"You mean it wasn't horrible already?" Fen said.

These mountains were nothing like the soft, green, rounded mountains of her village. They were hard-edged, like angry and unforgiving stone gods.

The mud soon dried on their clothes. The brief glow in Marcus's armour after he'd had Queen's blood was fading. This was good; he'd be harder to spot.

Ithak did have a keen eye for finding goat paths, which helped ease their way somewhat. The trio climbed higher and higher, but they were soon away from any trees or vegetation and out in the open.

"We have to sleep during the day to remain unseen," Ithak said. "And travel at night."

"That'll make it impossible to spot handholds." Marcus glanced down the cliff face they'd just climbed. "We're risking death."

"Winged death will strike us if we travel in daylight."

They both looked at Fen. "We'll travel by night," she said.

They stopped and got what rest they could on the rocky ground. When night fell, Ithak led them. The moon was near to full, making the climbing easier. Twice they had to switch back when they found an impassable rock face.

At one point, they came to a plateau that revealed an impressive waterfall, glowing with moonlight, splashing hundreds of feet down. The water roared into a deep canyon that widened into a lake.

Fen wished she could stay and watch the water, but they had to press on, and soon the sound of the falls was far behind them. Fen's wooden hand didn't tire. She could have climbed for hours longer if her whole body was wood. Each time she grabbed an outcropping of rock, it felt as if the vines were helping her grip.

"Ow," Marcus said. He was looking at his right shoulder.

"What's wrong?" Fen asked.

He peeled away a small section of his armour and stared at it. Even in the moonlight, she could tell there was bare skin beneath. "My armour is coming off."

"We may soon be wishing we'd brought more clothes for you," Ithak said.

"What am I without my armour?" Marcus's voice cracked as he spoke. It made him sound younger.

"You're Marcus," Fen said.

Ithak chuckled like a clucking hen. "Perhaps not all the philosophers are dead."

Marcus dropped the piece of metal and it floated to the ground. He continued climbing. Fen stopped to pick the metal up. The armour was paper-thin and so easily bendable. She slid it into her knapsack.

Ithak eyed her but said nothing.

The climbing grew even harder. The air colder. But they had travelled what felt to be a great distance. Soon there was a red light in the sky. A flame burning atop a great height.

"It's Velchan's Forge," Ithak said. "We've climbed right up to a blazing oven."

A LAKE
OF FIRE

THEY SLEPT AT THE BASE OF THE SUMMIT OF VELCHAN'S Forge but woke up after only a few hours. Except for the occasional burst of flame, the mountain had been hidden by cloud and fog and darkness and only now did it become completely clear to Fen how hard her task would be. The sun revealed that the final section to climb was a black rock as smooth as glass and at least five hundred yards tall. It looked like a massive, wide chimney, with smoke pouring out the top.

"That's what impossible looks like," Ithak said, pointing upward.

"And we came all this way without climbing gear," Marcus added.

"It would be useless with the forge." Ithak put his hand on the stone wall. "Perfectly smooth. And for some reason beyond Ithak's feeble understanding, only Fen can retrieve Mansren's head. She'll have to go up there on her own."

"How?" she said.

"Perhaps you can grow a branch from here to there." He pointed to the top.

"It's too great a distance." She took off her knapsack and placed both hands on the wall.

"What are you doing?" Marcus stood near her and did the same with his own hands.

"Looking for even the slightest crack."

"I can't see any at all," Marcus said.

"I have good climbing sense." Even saying it reminded her of that day picking sunberries with May. Her last day before becoming a wildmagic. Her hand snagged on something. "There's a crack right there."

"You're imagining things," Ithak said.

"It's there." She pulled herself up. "Wish me luck." Fen tried to grab with her other hand, lost her grip and tumbled to the ground.

Marcus helped her stand. "Are you hurt?"

"Bruised pride," she said, brushing off her breeches.

"You certainly are brave." He was looking directly at her. She almost blushed.

"A brave person can ride a tiger, a coward fears a little mouse." It was something her father used to say. Despite her words, it was intimidating to stare straight up to the top. "I must admit, I'm not looking forward to this."

She found the crack again. Mansren's finger was rattling inside her pouch. Urging her: *Go! Go! Go!*

"If anyone can climb this wall," Marcus said, "it'll be you."

With those words in her head, Fen found another handhold—a crease in the stone. The roots of her wooden fingers were clinging more strongly than flesh fingers would. She pulled herself up and then swung out with her feet and pressed into the tiniest toehold. Then she discovered a fingerhold with her left hand that allowed her to move her wooden hand higher until it had worked its way into a gap. Soon she was ten times her own height up the rock face. In time, the motions became natural and she stopped thinking of falling.

"You must really love your sister," Ithak shouted from below.

Fen slipped, let out a small scream and fell. She lashed out with her right hand. *You are a foolish girl for even trying this!* She banged her hand again and again against the smooth black surface. Her wooden fingers somehow found a cleft in all that rock and gripped tightly enough to stop her fall, a few feet down. It felt as though the fingers were stretching out. She looked up. It was exactly the case! Her fingers were at least three times their normal length. The wood began shrinking back, pulling her up. Now *that* was a clever trick.

She chose not to look down and swear at Ithak, instead taking a deep breath and getting back into her climbing pattern. Right hand. Then finding a toehold and handhold with her left and moving the wooden hand higher.

Anytime she paused to rest, she used her right hand. It was tireless. If she had two hands like that, she would've been up the side of the mountain in minutes. It was harder to remember what it'd been like to be handless. Or to not have this magic in her blood. She was so different than she'd been only a few days earlier. So much stronger.

It was an eon—her muscles beyond exhaustion—before she pulled herself onto the summit of Velchan's Forge. She lay on her back, catching her breath and closing her eyes. The sudden onslaught of heat from the mouth of the volcano was enough to nearly drive her back down.

Her strength slowly returned. She got on her hands and knees and peeked downward. Marcus and Ithak were little more than dots. She waved to them, stood and stumbled toward the mouth of the volcano. The plateau was smooth for the first twenty steps or so. She came to the opening.

What she saw set her teeth on edge. In a round chasm below her was a large lake of liquid fire. The sulphurous stink and heat blasted her face. Already her hair was slick with sweat. She threw her hood back, certain any corvus wouldn't be able to see her in all this smoke.

This was why no one had ever been able to retrieve Mansren's head. Nothing could fly into such fierce heat without burning up. And no one could walk on lava. Her father had told her stories of mountains belching fire when Illium was formed. Perhaps this liquid rock had been there since the very beginning, older than even Helwood.

She sat on the edge. Where would Mansren's head be? Her own head was beginning to ache. The air stank. That, of course, she could deal with rather quickly—she put her hand to her mouth and willed the vines to grow there. She was soon breathing clean, hot air through her nose.

The interior wall above the fire lake was as smooth as the rock she'd just climbed. If she attempted to descend . . . one slip would mean she'd fall to a horrible death. There were sections at the bottom where the lava had hardened, but that would just break her skull.

Mansren's finger was urging her to jump.

The sun was beginning to set. It had taken her much longer to reach the top than she'd thought it would. She drank the last gulp of water from her waterskin.

Her sister was in a prison cell in Regentium. Each moment

of delay meant an equal moment of pain for May. So even though the rock was hot enough to burn her hands, Fen lowered herself over the edge. Maybe if she only went down a few feet and stood on a hardened outcropping, she'd see a way across. The last bit of sunlight revealed handholds—places where the rock had been broken. After clambering down for a short time, she stopped to rest on a ledge. The heat pressed against her, slowing her muscles. And her thoughts.

From this new vantage point, a few more patches of hardened rock were visible in the lake. One or two might even be large enough to stand on. The sight didn't give her much hope. How long would her boots last in such heat? It wasn't like she could strap stones to her feet.

Her wooden hand didn't grip as strongly as it had before. *What if it burns up?* She ignored that thought and eventually lowered herself to another narrow ledge thick enough to take her weight. She crouched down and squinted—there was no way to stop the smoke from stinging her eyes.

Fen saw now that there were definitely several rocky places where she could step on the lake. They even led partway across the molten rock. A black lump sat in the centre. It might very well be Mansren's head.

Was Ithak right that Mansren had been a hero? That he intended to bring freedom to the land? That type of benevolence was not what she sensed in the voice she'd spoken with at the throne tree, despite the fact that it kept calling her a friend. Instead, she'd felt awed by the presence of an overpowering will. Even the finger in her pouch was another piece of pure will. Of desire.

But perhaps being in the presence of powerful people or creatures was always like that. And what if he were telling the truth? Mansren could win a war and May would be free, and the nine cities rebuilt. The land would return to the way it had been. What had Ithak said Illium's name used to be? Irthra? That was a much better name—it had nothing to do with the Queen. Only Mansren could bring it all back. Servilia never would.

Fen inhaled to fill her lungs with clean air before lowering herself down. The heat was almost unbearable as she neared the lava. She hesitantly set her foot on a rock on the edge of the molten lake.

Her boot burst into flames.

She jumped back and slapped at it until the flame went out. Her toes were hot, but the fire hadn't burned right through the leather.

She couldn't even step on the stones!

With a sinking feeling, Fen wondered if she'd even have enough strength to climb back out of the pit. It was a long way to the top and the walls were slightly angled over her.

May! Tears came to Fen's eyes, but she wasn't certain if they were from frustration or sorrow or sweat. Then she turned and looked back across the lake. The stone in the centre had to be his head. Why couldn't she walk across to it?

Because your feet will burn off.

What can I do to prevent that? Strap flat stones to her shoes? There were none. And she would likely sink—there was no way to know whether the rocks jutting out here and there in the molten lava were solid.

Then she nearly smacked herself in the head. The heat was melting her thoughts! She had vines in her nose, giving her air. Would she be able to use the vines somewhere else? She touched her foot and imagined her hand growing. A sense of creation coursed through her body and vines laced around the bottom of her foot. She pulled until they detached from her hand.

She stared. A perfect green sole for her shoe. And the tendrils continued to grow around her foot, as though they now had a life of their own. She did the same trick with the other side and then lowered her foot down onto the rock. It burned, but she willed that section to grow again and it did.

She slowly and carefully put her weight on the nearest stone. The rock sank a little but the lava didn't spill over the top.

She took another step onto a larger stone, farther away from the banks. The heat was burning her legs and she feared her clothes would catch fire. She took another step. She was far enough away that she couldn't leap back to the ledge. The black rock sank deeper into the lava the longer she stood there. *I have to go faster!* The farther she went toward the centre, the hotter it became, and the faster her protective vines were burning. The vines in her nose were shrivelling up, too, falling out of her nostrils. New growth replaced them, but it took energy from inside her to keep this going.

She squinted, clearing her watering eyes enough to see there really was something black and oval in the centre of the lake. It had facial features. The head!

She stepped on a larger stone that began to sink and quickly leapt to another, the lava splashing away from her.

Her throat was parched and dry. She needed a drink. A drink. A river to swim in. Ice. Snow. Anything to combat this heat. Her hair was curling up, sweat plastering it against her forehead.

But with each step, the dark head in the molten rock became clearer. It had a flat nose, an aquiline aspect. The finger in the pouch willed her forward as though it could pull her there.

The head even seemed to be smiling.

Something moved in the corner of Fen's vision. She turned to look behind her.

Twelve helmeted skulls were rising out of the lava.

CHAPTER TWENTY-THREE

A HEAD
IN HAND

Rising all around her were twelve skeletons clad in armour, clacking their teeth, mouths opening and closing in silent screams. Of course! The Queen wouldn't leave Mansren unguarded.

In a few heartbeats, flesh and veins grew on these guardians, snaking around their bones. Their airless screams became grunts and horrible gurgles. Eyes gelled in those sockets.

They were Queen's guards! Taller than any she'd ever seen. They could be the original guards, before Queen Servilia started making them all the same. They were clad in similar magical armour, but it looked thicker and heavier. How much red dust had it taken to keep them alive for a thousand years under the lava?

They unsheathed their swords.

"You. Must. Stop," one said. It was difficult to look directly at him—he had no skin yet. But his goggling eyes glared at her. "You. Will. Die."

"Stay back!" She coughed, for she had let some of the sulphurous smoke into her lungs.

They lumbered toward her across the lava, making the circle smaller. One guard's foot slipped into the molten rock, turning back into bones, but he pressed on.

Fen jumped to another stone. The last leap toward the centre was a long one and she landed squarely, but the lava splashed against her leg, burning her skin. "Arrgh!"

Fen gritted her teeth, bent over and picked up the head with her wooden hand. It was much lighter than she had expected. She guessed Mansren's head would burn her flesh as deeply as touching a shirker would.

"*Ah, you have arrived,*" the head said. The voice was ragged. She looked down. Fen had assumed Mansren's skull would be made of stone, but his amber eyes glittered with humour. He winked, and she nearly dropped him. The head was alive! Somehow all this heat wasn't burning him. Perhaps this one part of his body had never been turned to stone. "*You are the third to try to reach me. I do hope you won't be the third to die.*"

"Help me!" she said. "Tell me how to get out of here!"

"*I believe you must avoid the guards,*" he said.

"That's no help at all!" She'd climbed all this way to find a jester.

The Queen's guards were getting more lithe as their ligaments grew in. Some had grown straggly bits of red hair. She knew if she didn't act quickly, she'd be beheaded in the lava lake. She spun back and forth.

"Can't you use your magic?" Fen asked.

"*No.*" His voice was a whisper but pounded in her brain. The finger swung madly in the pouch. "*My magic is bound in this place, until someone lifts me out. You are the first to actually touch me. That deserves congratulations.*"

She accidentally brushed his head against her arm and felt a burn there. She would have to be careful to hold it farther away from herself. It made it hard to balance.

Then an idea came to her.

Fen set her feet as solidly as she could. The stone was slowly sinking.

"What are you doing?" he asked as she drew her sword with her left hand. *"You will not be able to beat them hand-to-hand."*

"I'm saving myself."

She threw the sword directly at a guard. It was a somewhat awkward throw, but she'd aimed well. He moved too slowly to parry the blow and the blade sank into his chest. He fell backwards into the lava and as he vanished, she thought she saw him give a bit of a sigh.

Fen leapt through the opening, ducking as the other swords whistled over her head. She had to place her left hand on one of the stones—burning herself—but then managed to flip up so she landed on her feet.

"Impressive!" Mansren said. *"You are quick of mind and foot. Lovely, lovely, lovely! You've bought yourself only a few moments, though."*

The Queen's guards were pursuing. She ran. The vines on her soles had mostly died and the remainder couldn't grow fast enough to protect her. The bottoms of her feet were burning now. She threw herself onto the ledge. One Queen's guard, his flesh mostly formed, was only fifteen yards behind her.

She couldn't let go of Mansren's head to climb, so she drew back her arm and hefted him skyward. He landed on the stones far above her and rolled right to the edge of the pit.

"You are not showing me the proper respect." His words were followed by laughter. *"In my heart of hearts—well, if I had a*

heart—I hope you live. If death claims you, you can die easy knowing you have impressed me."

She'd never dreamed he'd be so talkative.

The angle of the wall made it nearly impossible to climb. She was trapped.

She glanced back to see that the nearest Queen's guard had skin now. He was moving with such speed that lava splashed across his legs. "By the command of Queen Servilia, you are sentenced to death," he shouted.

Fen needed something to grab on to. She could have stabbed the sword into the wall and leapt off it, but it was at the bottom of the fire lake. Her knife wouldn't penetrate the stone. She had nothing.

No, not nothing! She remembered. She reached into the pouch, pulled out Mansren's stone finger and slammed it against the wall. It sank easily into the stone and she couldn't pull it out. Without a backwards glance, she stepped onto the finger and jumped as high as she could.

The Queen's guard swung his sword and sliced just where her foot had been.

Fen found a ledge and held tight with her wooden hand. It pulled her up before the guard could swing again. He tried to climb on his own, but his lack of a complete set of muscles made it impossible.

Fen reached the top and collapsed next to Mansren's head.

"*You've left my finger behind.*"

"I can't go back to get it." She lifted his head to look in his amber eyes. "Are you truly Mansren?"

"*I would nod, but I have no neck. Yes, I'm the one called Mansren. And I am forever in your debt, mortal.*"

"Was it you I spoke to in Helwood?"

"*It was a manifestation of my will. Whatever was promised will be yours. I am made of words. I am my word. It is my bond.*"

"You promised to free my sister from Queen Servilia," she said.

"*It will be done. Have no doubt. What is your name?*"

"Fen."

"*A good name. A strong name. Well met, Fen. I am honoured to be in your debt.*"

She glanced down. The Queen's guards were climbing on each other's shoulders, forming a human ladder. It wouldn't take them long to ascend. She was certain the Queen already knew Mansren had been stolen.

Fen ran to the edge of Velchan's Forge.

"Marcus," she shouted. "Marcus!"

One of the dots below her moved, just visible in the moonlight.

"Yes." His shout was not much more than a distant whisper.

"Grab what's left of your cloak," she shouted. "And catch this! Don't hold it with bare hands."

"*I would prefer if you carried me,*" Mansren said.

"It's not possible," she answered. "I need both hands to climb down. I assume you won't break."

"I never break," he said.

Another shout came from below. But Marcus's words were lost to the wind.

"Good luck," she said as she held the head over the edge.

"*Good luck?*" Mansren sounded shocked. "*Is that a joke?*"

"No," she answered. Then she shouted, "Here he comes!"

And she dropped Mansren's head over the cliff.

CHAPTER TWENTY-FOUR

A LEAP
OF FAITH

FEN'S CLIMB DOWN THE FORGE WAS HAMPERED BY A series of leg cramps. Her arms had lost all their strength and it was almost impossible to grip with her burned hand. There were tears in her eyes from the smoke.

But again, her wooden hand saved her: it clutched. Gripped. Stayed steady. The wooden fingers pushed vines into the tiniest of cracks. Climbing felt even more natural with the hand. Everything did! She'd be dead now without it, she realized. Several times over.

Only when she was nearer the bottom did she see Marcus lingering below as if he were waiting to catch her. Mansren's head had been left on a stone, and Ithak knelt before it.

Marcus helped her down the last few feet, taking her wooden hand in his. "You look horrendous," he said.

"Well, *you* jump into a burning lava pit and fight twelve Queen's guards and see how you turn out!"

"I didn't mean to offend you." He gently touched her shoulder. "You did all of that? I am amazed."

The concern in his eyes indicated he was genuinely sorry, so she patted his hand. Then she inspected herself: there were scratch marks and burns along her feet and legs. Her skin was stained charcoal black. Her red hair, though darkened by soot and sweat, hadn't suffered any damage.

They went over to Mansren's head. It looked as if Ithak were praying to him. "*Ah, my liberator returns,*" Mansren said. "*You've made it farther than any other I've summoned.*"

"You summoned me?" Fen said. "That's not how I remember it."

"*I provided a path and you chose it. Now we should leave. The guards will throw themselves over the edge once they've climbed out of the pit. They are the least of our worries—there are much worse dangers on their way here.*"

Fen slipped her knapsack over her shoulder, and then reached out and clutched the top of Mansren's head, urging her fingers to grow slightly longer so she could get a tight grip.

"*It's not the most royal of ways to travel.*" Mansren's amber eyes glittered with humour. "*I'd prefer a litter with a fine selection of grapes. Be so kind as to point my head forward. We should now flee with great haste.*"

A sound like thunder boomed in the sky, followed by a loud cry. Fen jerked her head left and right, scanning the heavens, but she couldn't see where the noise had come from.

"*Of course, it may be that we are too late.*"

"What was that?" Marcus asked.

"*An old friend has arrived. Now run, my companions.*"

They raced down the path away from Velchan's Forge. Fen discovered it was not an easy task to descend the mountain with a head in one hand and her other hand covered in heat blisters. Marcus helped her over the more difficult sections.

The holes in her shoes meant her bare feet smacked painfully against the rocky ground. She ignored the pain from her heat blisters and was reminded that Ithak was the son of a shoemaker. If they'd had time, he could have fixed her boots. That thought brought a smile to her lips.

Mansren's head was light or heavy, changing moment by moment. But the presence of Mansren was more of a burden. It emanated from the head. Pressed against her thoughts. Pushed her forward.

"*That direction,*" Mansren said, motioning with his eyes. "*There's a better path there.*"

They reached a plateau and raced across it. Then they followed several mountain-goat paths Mansren found. At one point, Marcus offered his waterskin, and Fen had a long swig. Her stomach rumbled with hunger, but she ignored it. There was no sign of pursuit by the guardians of the forge.

"*The twelve have heavier armour,*" Mansren said. "*They are slower than us.*" He appeared to be having the same thoughts at the same time. *Could he read her mind?*

"*The Queen's minions will soon come at us from all directions. She has opened every gate, flooded every road with her carrion.*" Mansren gulped in a breath. Fen felt the air coming out the bottom of his head. "*Ah, the freshness. This is a nice break from burning in a lava pit. Perhaps I can wait another thousand years.*"

"We can't wait!" Fen said.

"*Then get me to the river. It's our best chance for escape.*"

Light was brightening the edges of the sky and the land they traversed became flatter, easier to run across. Marcus and Ithak were clearly visible now, and even more clearly, she saw how her clothing had been burned. Ithak had been unusually quiet since the appearance of Mansren, as though in awe. He hadn't spoken one word since she'd descended the forge.

A hound barked loudly enough for it to echo around them. The sound made her legs weaken. Another hound answered the first one's cry.

"*My lovely infernus hounds,*" Mansren said. "*I designed them for pursuit—an ironic shame they're pursuing me. Run at an even greater speed, my friends. If we escape, it'll be a tale they'll tell for ten thousand years.*" Fen ran without regard to her injuries, to the beating of her heart. She was racing so hard that a rushing, roaring sound filled her ears. Her blood pumping?

No. The sound was the waterfall they'd passed on the way up. The river that led to it glittered far below them in a chasm. Glowing shapes took up positions across the water. Queen's guards! She turned to see that other guards were galloping down the stony paths behind them—at least thirty of them. Sparks flew from where horseshoes struck stone. Corvuses clouded the sky.

But even closer was a large pack of infernus hounds, eyes glowing red, smoke curling out of their nostrils. The tone of their yips and barks made it clear they scented blood.

"*Run!*" Mansren shouted. "*I command thee! Run!*"

Mansren's words were in her muscles, forcing her ahead. Fen stretched her legs even longer, pushed harder. She wondered if he could take control of her—or all of them—at any moment. Not that she needed an extra push. The sound of the barking hounds was enough. Marcus matched her, stride for stride.

"What do we do when we get to the river?" Fen asked between breaths.

"*Save your breath! Let me do the thinking. It's all I've been doing for the last millennium.*"

She stumbled once, nearly dropping the head, and Marcus yanked her to her feet. The hounds were getting closer to their heels.

"*The greater the odds, the greater the story!*" Mansren said. Fen saw with horror that another pack of hounds blocked their path to the river—they'd perhaps been herding their prey. Marcus drew his sword on the run.

"*They are speedy! Servilia has grown more adept at shaping things. Press on!*"

They ran right into the pack of hounds. Marcus swung his sword, and howling and blood followed. Ithak had gone invisible but he occasionally shouted when their snapping teeth found him. Fen glanced behind and saw three hounds only a step away, their jaws open, their teeth impossibly long.

She swung Mansren and hit a hound who immediately fell dead. Then another filled the gap and clamped onto the back of her leg. Pain shot along her calf and she stumbled. Mansren's head was knocked from her hands. She screamed as her burned hand slid across rough rocks.

At once, she was surrounded by hounds. She knew they'd be at her before she could get to her feet. She reached for her sword.

It was gone! Left in the forge.

Marcus leapt and landed beside her, swinging his blade in a wide arc. Warm blood dropped on her like rain.

"Get up!" he shouted. "Get up!"

"*Rise!*" Mansren commanded. "*And carry me forward.*"

Mansren was only a few feet away. Two hounds that had tried to bite him were dead. She grabbed the head and rushed headlong toward the river, not daring to look behind her.

They came to the edge of the chasm and skidded to a halt. Below them was a hundred-foot drop into the swiftly moving river that led to the waterfall.

"Now what, my lord?" Ithak said. Fen couldn't see him but his voice was close.

"*The answer is before you,*" Mansren said.

"We'll die," Fen said. "Marcus will most certainly drown."

"*No,*" Mansren said. "*Hold hands. Do not let go. Trust me, friends. And you, Fen, keep a strong grip on me—it is life and death for all of you. Oh, and don't be afraid to breathe.*"

The Queen's guards across the river raised their crossbows and loosed a flock of bolts. Other bolts thudded down from behind.

Fen stuck out her left hand and Marcus took it. It hurt to squeeze, but she did so as tightly as possible. Marcus reached for Ithak's hand.

"*Now jump,*" Mansren said. "*Jump!*"

They did, the bolts hissing by as they leapt toward the river.

CHAPTER TWENTY-FIVE

A
NECESSARY EVIL

THE WATER WAS LIQUID ICE. EVERY MUSCLE IN HER body tightened, and it felt as if her heart would stop. They sank down, down, down—Marcus's weight pulling them farther and farther. Mansren's head, too, seemed to grow weightier. They were soon deep enough to avoid the crossbow bolts zipping through the water. The current slammed into them.

Fen realized they were tumbling toward the waterfall. A drop from those heights would most likely be their deaths. Marcus's hand remained wrapped around her wrist. She kept her eyes open. She'd always been a strong swimmer and was used to holding her breath.

Marcus was turning red. Ithak was visible only because bubbles outlined his body.

They hit a hard, rocky bottom but continued to be swept ahead like so much detritus.

Marcus was wide-eyed, clearly out of air. He opened his mouth to breathe and Fen wanted to shout *no!* But he gulped in water.

She expected him to begin choking, but instead he looked confused. He sucked in again and a large bubble came out of his nose. She heard laughter in her head—Mansren. She breathed in a gulp. No water came in, just air.

Don't let go of me, he'd said. *Remember to breathe.* As long as they were all holding hands and connected to Mansren, they could breathe the water!

The current was a thousand hands pushing them toward the waterfall. She tried to set her feet. Failed.

They tumbled over the edge. She held tight to Mansren and even tighter to Marcus. The falls were much higher than she'd thought and she tumbled downward, the lake coming closer and closer with such speed there was no time to shout a warning.

They hit the water hard and Marcus was ripped from her grip. She opened her eyes and saw a flash as he was drawn under, sinking like a weight had been tied to his leg. His armour flashed again and again, burning up the last of its magic to give him life. He grabbed at his chest and seemed to be pulling at his armour as if trying to rip it off. Ithak had vanished.

Fen kicked as hard as she could, driving herself toward Marcus and keeping a tight grip on Mansren. Before she'd gone more than a few yards, the current grabbed her and twirled her away.

She looked left and right, but the water was too dark, too deep. There was no way to even tell in which direction Marcus lay. She kicked and kicked until she finally surfaced.

Fen drew in a deep breath and her ears cleared. The falls roared.

"*I so hoped you'd be able to hold on to them,*" Mansren said. His voice was not soft, but his tone was.

"I tried."

"*It's not your fault. I should've foreseen the impact and lent you more strength. Ithak can swim. The Queen's guard cannot. I'm so sorry he will die. He was a very interesting guard. A vow-breaker. A good sign.*"

"He's my—my friend," she said. "We have to find him!"

"*There's no time.*" Mansren's voice had an edge of desperation. "*Swim as fast and as hard as you can under the water. You'll be able to breathe, just as before.*"

"We can't leave them!"

"*Lower your voice! We'll never find them—the lake is too large.*"

"I have to try."

"*No. You will not. I apologize for what I am about to do: swim away from here, I command thee.*"

The words stuck in her head and forced her to move. She dived down, her legs, her body betraying her—responding to that command. Only her wooden hand tried, for a short while, to fight against the orders, but even it stopped and began aiding her swimming motion. She kicked again and again until she was deeper and farther way.

Her body was no longer her own!

Fen sucked in a breath. She was still able to breathe under the water.

Are you cold? Mansren's voice asked in her head. He could somehow put himself in her thoughts. It made her feel sick. *I will warm you, Fen.*

A warmth emanated from his head through her arm and into her body. *You'll swim far. And fast. I will feed you too.*

The sensation of hunger she'd been ignoring grew quiet. And her muscles were stronger now. She thrust ahead a great distance with each stroke. She thought of Marcus and Ithak, hoping that somehow they had survived. Ithak would have the best chance. But every time she tried to picture a possible way for Marcus to live, she only saw an image of him sinking to the bottom and staying there.

You cared for the Queen's guard. It's never easy to lose a friend. To lose someone you love. But there are bigger things than love at work today.

His voice reverberated around every thought. It was worse than the dream the Queen sent every morning.

Get out of my head!
I cannot. We are one right now.
Then stop stealing my thoughts!
I am not stealing them. They are floating alongside mine. Our enemies are gaining on us. Again I apologize for this transgression. Go faster, I command thee.

She kicked harder, gaining more speed. Above her, the sky was brighter. They had moved out of the lake and were racing along the bottom of a river.

How is this possible?
It's easier with just you. The truth is it would have been a struggle to keep all three of you alive. But keeping one alive is a relatively simple thing. For now.

She didn't tire. At one point she tried to stop and couldn't.

Let me stop.
No. Not yet. Do not fight me, Fen. I am doing what is necessary. If we had attempted to find your friends, we would be caught. And all our hopes dashed.

She instinctively pictured herself throwing him the moment he gave her back control of her body. As far away as she could.

That would not be wise. If you abandon me, then your sister will die. Choking on her own entrails.

That image stuck in Fen's mind.

Don't say such things!
The truth is hard. I'll release you when you've done your part. I promise. I do not enjoy binding you any more than you enjoy being bound.

She continued to swim, trying not to think. In time it grew dark.

Have I been swimming a whole day?
Yes. We are far from the falls that we fell down. It would take you weeks to walk back. This is the Tarnis River, or at least it was called that many years ago. Perhaps she has changed its name. She always did like putting her mark on things.

Fen swam. And swam. It was like something out of the heroic stories her father had told her. Stories of men who climbed mountains to save their loved ones from dangerous beasts. Fought armies single-handedly. Went to the moon and brought back life-giving fruit from the cherry trees there.

They did not speak for a long while. Had the sun come and gone again?

The river is turning toward the ocean now. We have trav-elled far enough. I release you, Fen.

She was suddenly in control of her body. She stopped kicking and floated to the surface in the dark, and then she climbed up the banks of the river and onto soft soil.

"*We are safe for now,*" Mansren said. "*Her servants cannot have followed us this far. Rest.*"

She found a flat, grassy patch, pushed her way through low brush and leaned the head against a tree. She was bone-tired and yet her body didn't ache. Even after swimming all that distance. She lay down.

Sleep, child. He was in her head again. She had wanted to throw him, but now she was too tired and didn't know whether she would ever have the will to fight him again. *You have shone bright as a star today. Sleep, Fen. Sleep. Sleep.*

And despite her fears and the image of Marcus struggling under the water, Fen did sleep.

CHAPTER TWENTY-SIX

WALKING WITH MANSREN

FEN WOKE UP TO THE QUEEN'S FACE INSIDE HER MIND. The image had faded slightly and blurred. Her voice said: "*Arise, your Queen commands it. Be fruitful and obey my laws.*"

Then Fen heard deep laughter.

Mansren's head was in the same place she'd left it, nudged up against a tamarack tree. "*So she still uses that old trick. A thousand years of casting her image into all those minds. She is not the most creative of souls. Does her visitation inspire you?*"

"When I was a child, it did." Fen rubbed sleep from her eyes. "I played the Queen in the Queen of the Castle game. But then my father died. And I lost my hand and much more to her. Now her visits anger me."

"*They are an intrusion. Though her simple methods have worked for a millennium.*"

"Your voice," Fen said. "It's so loud. So hard to ignore."

"*Oh,*" he said. "*I am sorry. Yes, I forget which plane I am speaking on.* Is this better?"

"Yes. It . . . it doesn't rattle around in my skull."

"Good. I'll keep my tongue tempered, Fen. How do you feel today?"

Her body, surprisingly, did not ache after all of that climbing and swimming. Even the burn on her palm had been salved. There was only one real physical ache. "I'm so hungry, I'm not certain I can keep going. I need to eat."

"I cannot use the same trick as I did in the river. But I can summon food. Name something."

"Roast auroch."

"Too large. Too great a distance. Ho.w about this?" He blinked his eyes twice. Fen expected a table of food to appear, as it had in the forest fortress. She glanced around.

"What am I waiting for?" she asked.

"Patience."

There was a movement in the nearby grass. Followed by a twittering and screeching sound. The shrieks became louder, almost human-like. Fen gritted her teeth together and thought of covering her ears. A black squirrel darted out into the open. "Bones to break for marrow," Mansren said. "A heart. Liver. I assume you've eaten rodents before—yes, yes you have."

"It's in pain!"

"Silence," he whispered. The squirrel stopped squealing. Fen also had to fight to speak.

"But—but that's not hunting."

"You said you were hungry, so I provided. I would've brought you a rabbit, but there were none nearby. There are snakes in those rocks, if you'd prefer."

"The squirrel will do." She was so very hungry. "I wish we had a fire."

"*Closer*," he said. Fen found herself leaning toward him. The squirrel, seeming at war with itself, threw its body against Mansren's head and fell dead. Its hide caught fire. "Sorry! Perhaps a little too well done!"

Saliva gathered in Fen's mouth. She used her knife to skin it and slice off the edible parts. In a few minutes, all that remained were bones.

"Are you full?" Mansren asked. He sounded kind. "I could get you a pigeon."

"I am full enough."

"Then I urge you to continue our journey."

She stood and picked him up. "You won't control me?"

"I apologize again for that transgression. We are partners, you and I."

She walked, following his guidance. They had travelled such a long distance under water. When she looked back over her shoulder, there was no sign of the mountain range. And what of Ithak and Marcus? Ithak was a slippery sort; he could be alive and not captured. Marcus had to be dead. She tried not to picture his last moments of flailing under the water and drowning. Bubbles coming out of his lips.

"Again, I regret not being able to save your friends," Mansren said.

"Don't read my thoughts!"

"I'm sorry. It is like picking ripe fruit, but I will try to resist the urge. You should feel no guilt for losing your grip on them. We were falling from such a great height that the impact would inevitably have forced us apart."

She slightly tightened her hand on his head. "Yet I held on to you."

"Your wooden hand is impressively strong," he said. "If you want, I can take the bad feelings away. The regrets. Even the memories that scar you."

"Take away my memories?" She nearly dropped him.

"I'm only looking for a way to soothe your pain. I have healed your burn and your hunger. Why not let me soothe this too? As a gift."

She drew in a deep breath. Would it be wrong to not feel sadness every time she thought of Marcus or May? Or her mother? But would the urgency to save May vanish too? "No! Those are my memories. My feelings."

"I've upset you. I'm sorry for suggesting it. I'm not mortal. I suppose in your short lives, each thought, each emotion matters more deeply."

"They do." Without those memories, she would be nothing. "What will happen next?"

"You take one step and then another until we have arrived at Helwood."

"That's not what I meant." The real question had been forming in her mind since the moment she'd accepted this task at the throne tree. "I want to know your intentions."

"To become whole. My arms itch for me. My legs. My fingers. All itch to be alive again—even the finger you left in the mountain."

"We'd still be in the lava pit if I hadn't used it as a step."

"I forgive you," he said. She didn't sense any sarcasm.

"But how will you rescue my sister?"

"It will happen. As a creature of pure magic, I assure you— you can trust my word."

"Can I?" This head she held was the strangest thing she'd ever seen. She felt as if she were holding a world in her hands. Or a weapon. "*Can* I trust you?"

"You can trust my words. They are all I am made of." She wasn't certain what he meant by that. "Your sister will only be saved by knocking down the walls of Regentium and lancing Queen Servilia's heart. Not only will May be free, but there will be freedom for all men and women. No more Queen to bind you. No Queen's guards—all of them dead."

She swallowed. There had been no time to really understand what Mansren was capable of. "All of them?"

"The guards are bound to her. They *are* her. Though that one you befriended, Marcus, gives me hope the bonds can be broken. Perhaps they don't all have to die."

"Why does anyone have to die?"

He looked as if he would laugh, but instead his eyes grew sad. "That is a question that comes from childish innocence."

"It isn't childish. Can't you just kill the Queen and no one else?" She thought of how Servilia had ordered her mother's death. It would be good to see the Queen die.

"If I can find a way to do that, I will. That's a promise."

They came to a tall hill. The land before them was flat, with yellowish grass and short trees. The sky above was a gentle blue with only a few clouds. And there were no winged creatures in sight.

"Don't watch the sky, Fen. I'll sense any of Servilia's winged spies long before they arrive. Let me worry about the big details. It's so long since I've had a proper conversation. I do hope we can become friends."

She wasn't certain what to think. It was like talking with a god. It was not friendship.

"Let me know when you are hungry again," he said, sounding almost motherly. "Now, tell me your real name. Your secret name. Friends should know each other's names."

She went cold. Had he looked inside her head again? "How do you know I have a secret name?"

"Your people are strong willed. They would fight against her control."

"I—I don't know my name. It was never spoken. It's written down, though. I have the words but I can't read them."

"Show me," he said.

She opened her knapsack and retrieved the pieces of vellum from the secret compartment. She held them out for Mansren to read.

"It's written in Chin," he said.

"You know the writing?"

"Yes. It was the language of the Zhuang."

The name sounded almost familiar. She was certain she'd heard her father whisper it. Fen felt a swelling of pride on hearing the name, followed by a sense of loss. "Who were they?"

"They were you. You are them. A thousand years of writing down the names in secret. You *are* a determined people."

"What . . ." She cleared her throat. "What does the writing say?"

"Your family name is Nong. It's the first name you see."

"We had family names?" She stared at the writing, but it meant nothing.

"Yes, before the Queen erased them. They were just too complicated for her. She adores simplicity. But she also knows the power of names. If she takes away your full names, she takes away a part of what makes you Zhuang. She takes away rebellion." He stared at the vellum for a few moments. "Your mother was Nong Jin Lin, your sister Nong Mei Mei, your father Nong Xiao and you are Nong Fu Fen."

Fen drew a deep breath. It was her name. Her secret name! All of their names! Finally spoken aloud. She wanted to memorize them and shout them to the sun.

"So I wasn't named after a marsh? The other kids used to tease me about being a marshy fen."

Mansren guffawed. "No! It means rich scent. Perfect for someone who can grow leaves, isn't it?"

Rich scent? She wasn't certain that was much better than being compared to a marsh.

"Do you remember the Chin language?" he asked.

"There is only one language. Illish."

"No," he said. "Servilia has taken more from you than you can imagine. Your mother and your sister, yes. But once the Zhuang had their own kingdom. They had thousands of years of culture. The great temples in the Grandfathers' Mountains. Rich stories and histories, all written on scrolls. And they spoke and wrote Chin. In a thousand years, she has erased almost all of it. Once you were a great people. And now you are ghosts."

"We are not ghosts!" Her words carried across the savannah before them.

"If you'd stood in the White Palace of Xiao, whom your father is named after, you would agree with me. The walls of the palace contained the ground-up bones of every enemy who dared attack it. Imagine the majesty of the warriors firing their bows from horseback, striking their enemies down. You would well up with pride if you'd learned the bronze drum dance. A vast, rich history. All ashes. And the few who remain bend their backs to mine the red dust. Ghosts!"

With each word he'd said, she'd pictured people just like her and her fellow villagers. In palaces. On horseback. "Is what you say about my people true? They really had palaces? Dances?"

"I have no reason to lie. Here, take this gift." He blinked his eyes.

At first Fen didn't know what he meant. Then she noticed when she looked at the secret names, she could now read them.

I can read!

She went over the names again and again, and each time her heart felt a little fuller. Her back straighter. "I understand what the symbols mean." If she could say them loudly enough, they would reach the ears of her mother's spirit.

"The Chin characters are yours forever now. A simple gift from me. A sign of our friendship."

Fen nearly tripped she was so busy reading the pieces of vellum. She wanted to find a scroll of Chin words. A book! "They're wonderful!"

"You are interesting, Nong Fu Fen. I've seen many wild-magics. None are as attached to the earth as you are."

Hesitantly, she lowered the names and then placed them back in her knapsack. "What do you mean?"

"The earth reaches for you, reaches through you. Does your hand tire?"

Her arms were slightly tired. Her muscles. But the wooden hand clutched the skull and held tight. It could hold him forever. "No."

"Usually there is one ability. One strength. But you seem to have connection with the land and those things that grow in it."

"I don't feel strong." She glanced over her shoulder and noticed a dark, small spot winging toward them. "A corvus," she whispered.

"I've been aware of it for most of the morning."

"It will see us!"

"It has," Mansren said. "Don't let your hood down. Hold me between yourself and the corvus so it can't get a good look at me." She held him in front of her, using her body to keep him out of the corvus's line of sight. In time, she felt like it might be working. But then a distant voice crackled, "Caw. Crimson. Caw. Head. Come!"

"I'd hoped to send it away," Mansren said. "That failed. Just run, Fen, as fast as your legs will carry you. And if you know the names of any of the old gods, pray to the fleet-footed ones."

"I don't know their names!"

"Then just pray. It'll make you feel better."

She ran.

"Crimson run. Crimson flee. Brothers. Caw! Come to kill!" The corvus was getting closer with each cry. Another, darker shape appeared behind it.

"Ah, a winged rider has found us," Mansren said. "We won't outrun a paladin."

Fen glanced back and saw that the winged thing was much larger than a corvus.

"Run faster," Mansren whispered. "It will give me time to think."

Mansren sent strength to her legs. She ran so fast across the flat landscape it began to blur. She raced through a herd of antelope, which stood in place and watched her pass. No one had ever dashed on two legs so quickly.

Mansren sighed. "Ah, it is too late, child." There was regret in his voice. "I apologize. The equusa was designed for speed. Even with a fully armoured paladin on her back."

A shadow fell across them and Fen cranked her neck to look up. She got an impression of something large and heavy above her—it was as if a part of the heavens had broken off. The wind from the massive wings was so powerful it threw her to the ground. She tumbled and rolled then stood, still keeping her grip on Mansren.

CHAPTER TWENTY-SEVEN

THE
PALADIN

THE CREATURE—THE EQUUSA—WAS HORSE-LIKE, WITH huge black wings, and yet the long neck and head were feminine, the face well-proportioned and vaguely human, despite its horse ears. It landed softly only a few yards away.

The rider—a Queen's guard—was larger than any she'd seen, his armour the purest and brightest gold, reflecting the sun a thousand times. He pointed a crossbow at her.

"Remove your hood," he commanded.

Do so, Mansren said inside her head.

She lifted her hand slowly and pulled the hood back.

"In the name of the Queen, drop the head you're holding."

Listen to him!

She released Mansren and he rolled in front of her, so he was looking up at Fen. He began to chuckle.

"Am I the only one who found that command humorous?" Mansren asked. He said the next line in a gruff voice: "Drop the head you're holding!"

The Queen's guard didn't smile. The equusa settled its massive wings, creating a breeze that stirred Fen's hair. Mansren had called him a paladin. Fen remembered that it meant he was one of the most elite Queen's guards.

Is he looking at me or you? Mansren asked.

He's staring at you, Fen thought.

The paladin dismounted, slipping his crossbow into a holster, and then drew his sword. It burst into flames. As he neared, Fen saw he did not look like the Queen. His hair was red, yes, but he didn't have the same face as Marcus or the guard who'd cut off her hand. "Move away from the demon," he said.

Listen to him, Mansren commanded.

Fen took several steps back, nearly tumbling over in her haste. The paladin marched closer, stopped and turned Mansren's head with the sword so that it faced him.

"Ah, it's you, Marcellus!" Mansren sounded as if he were meeting him in a tavern. The name was familiar to Fen. "How many breaths have you taken in the last thousand years?"

The paladin kept his sword pointed at the head. "You were always talkative, Mansren."

"Even molten rock didn't silence my tongue. Being bodiless has humbled me, though I did have my own magnificent thoughts for entertainment. I've had a long time to consider my vengeance."

Marcellus paled slightly. "You are still as powerless as the day we cast you in the pit."

"Yes, that's true, Marcellus." The way he said his name sounded like a threat. Then suddenly Fen hit upon who this man was: he was the first among Queen's guards. He would sit at the right hand of the Queen. "You're still mortal and have lived long past your allotted years. Servilia continues to hold you in high esteem. I designed your armour. Remember that?"

"It has served me and my brothers well."

"A thousand years and not a scratch. You should thank me."

"I thank you." He sounded as if he meant this, but the point of his burning sword never wavered.

"I designed your mount and gave her wings. You still use so many of my creations. Has the Queen done anything new in a millennium?"

"She has brought peace to the land," Marcellus said. "More than you could do."

"Peace is easy when all your enemies are slaves. Or dead. Oh hello, Roseus."

The equusa whinnied.

"Don't talk to her!" Marcellus shoved the blade a little closer. "I don't trust your silver tongue."

"It's not as silver as Servilia's. Are you still her lover?"

The paladin lifted the sword and Fen waited for him to strike. He stabbed it next to Mansren's head. The flames set the grass on fire.

"Ah, I've pricked a sore spot." Mansren's eyes were glowing with glee. "Will you toss me back in the lake of fire?"

"I'll do what my Queen commands."

"Simple as always, Marcellus. And will you kill the girl?"

"Wildmagics must die. It's the law. I'll carry two heads with me."

Fen took another step back. She slowly moved her right hand up to guard herself. *Run!* one part of her mind was shouting. *Run!*

Wait, Mansren sent. *Be still.*

"So many wildmagics executed," Mansren said aloud. "Or driven to hide in Helwood. But the red dust mines are running

dry. It's hard times for Servilia. She must be a rather unpleas-
ant ruler."

"I grow tired of this discussion, Mansren."

"Forgive me. I am rusty at conversation." He cleared his
throat. "Well, the girl has been very valiant. It would be kind to
give her a quick death."

"That's my intention. I am not you."

"You do have a gift for stating the obvious. Thank you, Fen,
for your help. I hope your sister will be safe. Though with your
death, she'll die too."

"No," Fen said. "She can't die. She won't."

"The Queen is not the most compassionate soul," Mansren
added. "And she never forgives."

"I won't let that happen!" Fen pointed her wooden hand at
Marcellus.

"Stay still, child," the paladin commanded. "I'll be quick.
That's a promise."

"He was quick when he stabbed me with that very sword."
Mansren let out a chuckle. "Of course, my back was turned. And
I shattered into a thousand pieces."

Fen set her feet in the earth and willed the vines to shoot
out. A single tendril flew from her finger and wrapped around
the paladin's arm. He sliced it with his sword. "Plants," he said.
"That is your power? You grow plants?"

Mansren began to laugh again.

Fen knew if she turned to flee, he'd run her through. He
would remain wary of her as long as she faced him. "Please,
child," he said. "Stay still. This won't hurt."

A rustling noise grew in her ears. Marcellus jumped toward
her, purple cloak flapping in the air, and she threw herself back
and fell to the ground. He landed a few feet away. "Despite what

Mansren says, I do not enjoy killing your kind," he said, sounding almost gentle. "But it is necessary work. We must keep the balance. We must keep the peace." He lifted his sword.

Fen put up her hands to ward off the blow. She knew that the sword would cut easily through her flesh and bones.

"No. Don't," she whispered. The rustling had grown so loud her words were drowned out. The equusa whinnied a warning. Marcellus began to swing the blade but then turned his head, distracted by another motion.

A thousand motions.

There were black creatures scurrying over Fen's arms and legs. Their claws scratched at her face. They climbed the paladin—a mass of squirrels and mice and rats clung to his body, followed by snakes and lizards. He brushed several away with one hand and still managed to aim the sword at her.

Fen jumped out of the way and the blade stabbed the earth where she'd lain.

Marcellus screamed in rage, then pain, but he dropped his sword. The rats and other rodents were gouging out his eyes. He fell to the ground. Every part of him was covered. His next shout was muffled when something wriggled into his mouth.

Fen reached for his sword, worried he might still get up.

"Don't touch that," Mansren warned.

She grasped it with her wooden hand but, to her surprise, it burned her. She dropped the blade.

"That flame is designed to burn wildmagics," Mansren said.

She shook the pain away. Marcellus was fighting below that mass of creatures, trying to throw the tiny beasts off. But soon the quivering slowed and then it stopped.

Fen approached Mansren and lifted him up. "It's a horrible death for him," she said.

Mansren looked down without any sign of pity in his amber eyes. "He won't die. Eventually the animals will fill their stomachs and he'll regenerate. But we'll be long gone. Now, turn me toward Roseus." She did so. "Good equusa, Roseus," Mansren said softly. "You remember me, my child, don't you? I made you."

The equusa moved her head up and down. Fen was still taken by how human that face looked, if not for the V-shaped ears and soft hide. "Put out your hand, Fen. Roseus is a kind soul, despite her masters. She won't bite. And she loves apples and sugar cubes."

A moment later, Fen was touching the mane of a creature she'd only ever dreamed about. The Queen had ridden one of these when she descended from the sky and turned Mansren to stone. Maybe this very one.

"She is that very one," Mansren said, reading her mind. "Now, get on her. And please do so without dropping me."

ON DARK
WINGS

BEING IN THE SKY WAS NOT REAL. THAT WAS WHAT FEN felt as the wings of the equusa took them easily into the air. Several corvuses followed at a distance but soon were lost to the speed of the creature. This was a magically created beast who had lived for over a thousand years.

"Faster, faster," Mansren said. "We must go faster."

Fen wasn't certain whether the words were spoken to himself or to their mount. It was all she could do to hold on tightly with her left hand. The journey was not smooth. Each sweep of the wings made the creature go up and down, and up and down. The world below Fen became smaller. The trees, round circles. The horizon so far away it seemed to curve. They flew over a village with strange mud huts and a red pit beside it. Tiny people were looking up. At her.

I am Fen of the Skies! It made her feel like she was in a dream she'd had as a child. The sky was the place where only birds and magical gods flew.

And wildmagics.

"It's a wonderful feeling, isn't it?" Mansren said. "To take to the air. To sit astride this great beast." Roseus whinnied. "Sorry. This *majestic entity*."

The equusa was slick with sweat and gave off a sweet, familiar scent.

"She smells like roses!" Fen said.

"Yes, Servilia demanded a mount with a heavenly bouquet. So that's what I created. You have a brave heart, child. Most girls your age would be shaking with terror."

"It's wonderful!" she said, keeping a firm grip on the pommel. "I feel as if my heart might burst with joy and fear."

"What an interesting way to put it. At times you remind me of her."

"Of who?"

"Queen Servilia."

"Don't say that!" Fen nearly shouted the words. "I'm nothing like her."

"Don't take offence. She is a knife, and you are a, well . . . a wooden chopstick." He chuckled. "She was once a dusty villager like you. But Servilia knew what she wanted and pursued it relentlessly. Until she was Queen of the whole land. Fear did not stop her."

"I feel fear. Often."

"Yes. But it doesn't halt you from trying to save your sister. That's my point. Fear can be a shadow on your heart that prevents action. But you act despite it."

"I am not like her!" She said this so vehemently that her free hand shook, and along with it, Mansren. "I don't kill!"

"You killed Kang, the rice harvester."

She cranked his head around so they were staring eye to eye. "How do you know that?"

"Forgive me. I saw that memory in your head." He did look regretful.

"The vines killed Kang!"

He seemed to be trying to nod. "They are a part of you. Yes, it was accidental. But you also killed a corvus."

It was hard to meet his gaze, but she didn't flinch. "I had to survive."

"And so does the Queen. You only see the stony side Servilia presents to the queendom." He let out a soft, wistful sigh. "You'll find this hard to believe but she used to compose poetry for me. Me! And one day she dived off a cliff into the ocean to fetch a ring I'd thrown away in anger. She brought that ring back to me and promised her love. Forever."

"That sounds so . . . so heroic."

"No more heroic than climbing a mountain full of fire to save your sister."

Fen didn't know what to say to that. "If she really did dive into the ocean, then why don't we know that story?"

"Servilia would never admit she once loved me. It's so much easier to have you all hate Mansren." He licked his lips. "You are perhaps even stronger than her."

"How can that be?" Fen asked.

"She's not a wildmagic."

"But she can cast spells. Can create immortal Queen's guards. It's said she can float in the air. Or shoot fire from her hands. People say she's the greatest wildmagic in history."

"Yes, she can do all those things. But they don't come from within her. They come from the magic dust that every village mines and brings to her. She and her artificers have learned how to shape it. I taught her to concoct the elixir that would make her immortal. But take away her red diamond necklace, her red rings—all those baubles and the dust that made them—and she is as human as you or . . . well, you're not a good example. As human as most every other mortal who walks this land. As I said, she imagined royal immortality and she pursued it."

Am I like her? Fen wondered. Her mother had called her obstinate. Single-minded. If she saw a sunberry, she'd climb to it. When she wanted a glass butterfly for May, she stole it. When her sister was taken, she crossed salt mires, rivers and mountains to try to get her back. Fen would fight off hounds, corvuses and Queen's guards.

She wanted to hold May again. To hear her voice. To be certain she was safe.

How far will I go? She was certain once Mansren was whole, he would disrupt the queendom. Defeat the Queen. But Fen was uncertain what would be destroyed in that process. Was saving her sister worth that?

They travelled in silence for some time until she saw a white scar in the earth. It stretched for leagues toward the ocean. The familiar rotten smell burned in her nostrils. "That's another salt mire." She was glad they were only passing near the edge of it.

"Yes." Mansren looked down upon it somewhat glumly. "That was the city of Kashta. The Kush lived there. Their descendants still inhabit the grass-hut villages, of course. Servilia destroyed it, just as she did the other eight cities."

It did not look to be a stain as large as the Great Salt Mire, but it was still big. Something dawned on Fen. "But you—you were her partner. She wrote poems to you. You must have helped her."

"You're a quick one. Yes, I was by her side then. A general under her spell. I did believe we were bringing peace. The nine cities had fought so many endless wars. We had a way to stop the fighting. Forever."

Fen had another thought, and with it came anger. "Then you destroyed the Chin city. You slew my ancestors. Pulled down their temples."

"I regret that." He spoke slowly and carefully. "I believed we were making Irthra—forgive me, it's Illium now, isn't it?—better. Stronger. It was a sacrifice that had to be made to stop the wars."

"How could someone as smart as you be fooled?"

"I was younger then. A new—a new creature. I trusted her. I loved Servilia. I know you don't think me capable of love. But I was. And I believed her promises."

Fen imagined what the Chin city would have been like. He'd mentioned a white palace earlier. There would be markets. And thousands of people who looked like her, talked like her. All gone. "You murdered them."

"I did." There was a tremendous sadness in his voice. "It's too late to ask forgiveness. What I helped to do was unforgivable. But I ask for understanding. And—oh dear."

"What?"

"I don't want to alarm you but Marcellus's brothers are here."

"Where?" Fen turned her head. She saw only a smattering of white clouds. Then in the distance directly behind them were two black dots. Within moments they became shapes, wings moving. One shape grey. One white. Metal riders glinted in golden armour.

"They will have found Marcellus, of course," Mansren said. "If his tongue grew back, he would've warned them about my little rodent-summoning trick."

"Faster," Fen whispered into Roseus's ear. "Faster!"

It felt as if they were frozen in place. Yet their shadow was far below, crossing a river, a hillside, a field—all in an eye-blink. She strained to see ahead, trying to spot Helwood.

"How far are we?" she asked.

"Soon we'll spy the ancient woods," Mansren said. "Though the chances of making it there are growing slim."

"How can you be so calm?"

"When you've lived as long as I have, this is just a small moment in a long line of moments. I will not die and they cannot destroy me. If you are killed, then I'll fall to the earth and they'll build another prison. And I'll plan my release."

"So you have nothing to lose?"

"My sanity," he said. Fen glanced at him to see he wore a sardonic smile. "I fear the boredom of waiting. The new torments Servilia will surely invent. Something worse than burning in lava." He paused. "I, of course, would mourn the loss of our friendship."

The dark line of Helwood drew itself across the great distance. Fen sucked in a breath of joy. Of hope. With each wingsweep, it came clearer. A long black shadow of salvation. The paladins, though, were much closer now.

"It will be a terribly near thing," Mansren said.

"How do I make Roseus go faster?" She couldn't keep the desperation from her voice. "There must be a way!" It felt like sacrilege, but Fen kicked the equusa's sides and the creature neighed angrily. "Faster!"

"Don't kick her! She knows our urgency. She is the oldest of the equusa. And slightly slower."

Roseus whinnied again, such a human-sounding noise. But she flapped her wings even harder.

Mansren winked at Fen. "One just needs the right motivation. We may actually make it. I feel hope springing up in my heart. I am speaking metaphorically, of course."

A flaming bolt whizzed straight down beside them, hissing as it split the air. Fen turned and saw that the two paladins were still a great distance away. "How can they fire that far?" she asked.

He sighed. "Look up."

A paladin on a white equusa was diving from out of the sun.

A SOMEWHAT GENTLE HEART

Fen pulled the reins to the left and Roseus rolled out of the way of the descending paladin. His flaming sword missed Fen by the span of a finger, singeing her hair.

They plummeted toward the earth, and the equusa tried to right herself. It took all of Fen's strength to grip the reins with one hand while holding on to Mansren with the other. The ground was coming closer and closer, but at the last moment Roseus flung out her wings and swooped up and away from certain death.

Fen gathered her wits and her breath and then twisted to see the paladin right next to them, his mount's wings nearly knocking her from the saddle. He swung. The blade passed near her shoulder. She turned Roseus sharply, putting several yards between them and their enemy.

"Mansren, tell me what to do!" she shouted.

"Don't die!" This was followed by a laugh. She was tempted to drop him to the earth.

Maybe that was the answer! They wanted his head more than hers. She could release him and flee on Roseus. No, the paladin would just slay her and return for Mansren. It wasn't as if he could escape on his own. Though maybe he could summon an army of rats to carry him.

Then, as she watched the paladin swoop down to gain speed and loop up in front of them, the answer came to her. The paladin was now coming straight in their direction. His equusa had its wings tight against its body. The paladin clutched the blade in both hands—he could hold himself to the beast with just his knees. This time his swing would be true.

Fen hefted Mansren with all of her might. They were so close there was no time for the paladin to dodge. He raised his sword but it shattered on the hardness of Mansren's skull. The head knocked the paladin from the equusa and he clutched Mansren's head as he fell.

It was a long way down. He landed with a horrible *thump*. His mount dived after him, winging its way to its master.

"Take us to Mansren," Fen said. "Please." Roseus changed course and with a few swift movements landed next to the fallen paladin. He was on his back, writhing back and forth, but he couldn't get up. Mansren's head sat on top of his chest, as if it were pinning him to the earth. His mount was a few feet away, squealing and snorting, waving its wings, mad with fear.

Fen jumped from her mount, avoided the white equusa and skidded to a halt near the paladin. The stink of charred flesh brought back memories of her arm being cauterized, but she didn't shudder.

"Cast it from me," the paladin shouted between clenched teeth.

"This is a young paladin," Mansren said. He looked quite comfortable in that position. "No more than a hundred years old. Still wet behind the ears." Below Mansren, a halo of black spiderwebbed across the guard's armoured chest.

Fen stood still. The man was in such pain and she did feel pity despite the fact that, only moments before, he'd been trying to lop off her head.

"If you wait long enough," Mansren said lightly, "I might burn my way through him."

Fen edged up to the paladin and lifted Mansren's head. The guard's chest was all black, as though coals had been burning there. His armour was cracked, revealing charred skin beneath it. The guard couldn't get to his feet. His caved-in chest heaved, and he struggled to breathe. "I'll have your head," he rasped. "I'll have it."

"Not now you won't," Fen said. There was no outward sign that he was healing. Maybe Mansren's magic had somehow drained him of the Queen's blood.

"Kill him," Mansren said, as if he were asking her to pass the salt. "It's the only way to be certain he won't follow."

"No! I'm not a killer."

"We've already established that you are. You just have odd rules about whom you kill."

"For a god, or magic being," she spat, "or whatever you are—I find you to be truly exasperating. I'm not killing him."

She stepped back and the Queen's guard didn't make a move. He truly was broken. His equusa moved in and nudged at him.

Fen looked to the sky. The other riders were still a fair distance away, but they were gaining by the moment.

"I guess he'll live," Mansren said. "That was a clever gambit, though. I didn't expect to be used as a projectile. I've chosen well in a saviour."

"We have to leave," she said, climbing back onto Roseus. With a whinny, she took to the sky, wings wafting the long yellow grass. Soon they had gained their previous heights.

"You have a somewhat gentle heart," Mansren said. There was no sarcasm in his voice.

"My mother said to give others a chance to show their best nature," she answered.

"Wise words, for a human. But I had no mother. In my experience gentle hearts are, unfortunately, the first to die."

She thought of the many times she'd nearly died since she'd left Village Twenty-One. "The key is to know when not to be gentle."

"More wise words. I have much to learn from you, Fen." It sounded like he meant it.

She glanced over her shoulder. The paladins remained far enough away she felt no fear of them. Helwood was a black shape that was drawing closer.

"There is something this 'gentle heart' has been wondering," she said. It surprised her how confident she sounded. As if she weren't questioning one of the most powerful beings in the land. "What happens when I place your head back on your body?"

"I'll be whole again."

"Yes! I know that. But I want to know exactly what you'll do."

"I will manifest myself and my destiny."

"You're being muzzy—just playing with words. What will you do?" Again, she was amazed by how strong she sounded.

"I will save each and every one of you," he said. There was no joke in his voice this time. "Including your sister. I promise. As to the ways and means I use to accomplish that—Fen, you do have a gentle heart, despite what you've learned recently. Just leave the details to me. My heart is far from gentle."

Those last words were spoken almost as a whisper. They echoed in her head. If his heart wasn't gentle, what was he capable of doing?

CHAPTER THIRTY

MANSREN RISING

Fen kept a tight grip on the reins, turning her head this way and that, expecting any moment to see an enemy diving out of the sun. But Roseus maintained a steady speed and their pursuers did not catch up.

Helwood was now a giant black blanket spread out below them. She could not help but see it as a great mystery that had grown on the earth. The forest stretched for as far as she could see to the east and south. No wonder the Queen feared it. She couldn't put her stamp on it.

The last time Fen had been here, she wasn't alone: she thought of Marcus, perhaps the first Queen's guard to survive Helwood. No. He hadn't been a Queen's guard any longer. He was his own person. Had perhaps died his own person.

And Ithak. Was he rattling his way to Regentium in a cage? Or was he slowly stumbling back to Helwood alone?

Roseus swooped down and neared the canopy. Something moved below them. At first Fen thought it was a flock of dark-winged birds taking to the sky, but she was wrong—the leaves had opened up and the branches spread apart. It was as if the forest knew Mansren had arrived.

"Is Helwood a part of you?" she asked.

She expected Mansren to laugh. But he was silent for several moments before answering. "No. Helwood was one of the first living things on the land. And if I am entirely honest, I somewhat fear her deep roots. Her slow thoughts. Perhaps she has her own plans. And yet she accepts me. And, I can only assume, agrees with my goals."

The fact he feared Helwood piqued Fen's interest. She hadn't imagined he could fear anything. "Is she the oldest thing?"

"The mountains are older."

"But you're old too." She couldn't help feeling young and stupid for asking all these questions. But her mother had often said without questions there were no answers. "Where did you come from?"

This time she did get the laugh. "I'm not that much older than the Queen. One day I just *was*. So very long ago, I came into being. There was nothing special about it. I thought thoughts. I spoke words. I had formed in a black seam of magic dust. The only black seam ever found. I can see by the look on your face that you doubt me, but it's true. The first creature of pure magic. Now, my gentle saviour, take us down."

The canopy had opened wide enough that she saw Mansren's wooden fortress below them. The throne tree was still in the centre. There were many black shapes on the ground, but they were too distant to make out.

She guided Roseus out of the sun and downward. The

leaves and branches intertwined quickly above them, blocking the outside light, but glowing filaments floated in the air just as before. There was a sound louder than the wings of the equusa.

Shirkers! Their vocal cacophony set her teeth on edge. They had multiplied since her departure—there were perhaps a hundred now. Some were as small as her hand, others six or seven feet tall.

Roseus landed near the throne tree. The equusa neighed nervously as Fen stepped off. The shirkers circled them but kept their distance, perhaps frightened by the winged mount. Or by Mansren. Fen held Mansren's head above her like a lantern and several of the shirkers fell to their knees.

"Thank you, Roseus, for carrying us," Mansren said. The creature made a soft neighing noise and seemed to almost bow. "Fen will lug me the final few yards."

Fen's legs were shaky, her hips sore. She took a step and the shirkers parted. When she was a short distance from Roseus, the dark creatures were brave enough to come closer—staring up in awe at their master.

She began walking toward the tree but stopped when a shirker blocked her path and spoke in another language. Mansren paused for only a moment. "Yes, you may."

The shirker rubbed its hands. At the same moment, Roseus neighed in alarm and flapped her wings, the air forcing most of the shirkers back. Several stronger ones grabbed hold of her reins. The creatures were small but were heavy as stones.

"What are they doing?!" Fen asked.

"Roseus serves no further purpose. And my children are hungry. It's been a thousand years since they've fed on equusa flesh."

"They're going to eat her!" Fen shouted. "They can't!"

"They deserve this reward. They've been so patient and loyal."

Roseus flapped once, twice, nearly rising above the grabbing hands.

"Give her to me!" Fen swung Mansren's head around, nearly striking a shirker. "She's mine. My mount. Give her to me!"

"What would you do with an equusa?"

"I demand her. As part of the deal."

"The deal is set." His voice was firm. "I will save your sister. You should have asked for more, Fen, but you have a gentle heart. And you are a child. I'm sorry this causes you distress."

The shirkers swarmed over Roseus, pulling her down. She was able to knock several of them through the air with her wings and legs but soon they covered her, clinging with their sharp-nailed fingers. The equusa thumped into the ground, exhaling in her pain.

Fen raised Mansren's head, prepared to throw him.

"Our agreement will be broken if you don't carry me to my throne." His words were steady. "Your sister will die. You will die. But if you keep your promise, I'll keep mine. Roseus is already marked for death. Choose your fate now."

A rage shook in her muscles. With every part of her soul, her self, she wanted to cast him down. She stood that way for several heartbeats and then lowered her arm.

She turned away, wanting to block out the sound of Roseus's struggles. Fen had heard horses in pain before—one had broken its leg in the market and made a ragged, horrible, hard-breathing whine. It was the same noise Roseus was making now. The shirkers pulled, grunted and fought over her. And ululated their satisfaction as they consumed the equusa.

"A wise choice," Mansren said. "One must always pick the stronger side."

I had no choice! No. That wasn't true. She could have cast

Mansren down. But that would have meant the death of herself and her sister.

You remind me of her, he had said. Fen wondered if it was true. She stumbled toward the tree and up the staircase. *How powerful will he become?* He was growing heavier with each step. She had returned Mansren to his home. The centre of his power. The tree rumbled with his presence. *What am I unleashing?*

"You do not celebrate this glorious moment," Mansren said. "But history is turning on its axis today. And you are the fulcrum." She glanced back to where Roseus had been, but there was no sign of the equusa. Fen was close to vomiting. But she swallowed her anger and her fear and continued to climb.

The shirkers gathered around the tree. First one voice and then another began to sing until they became a chorus. They sounded like children. But there was an eerie harmony to their song. She had not expected to hear that.

"You'll be known as the girl who journeyed to the mountain, climbed an impossible height, walked across the fire, swam a thousand leagues, flew through the air and brought back the head of a god." Mansren said this without a hint of mockery. "It will be a story told for a hundred thousand years. Fen of the Wooden Hand. Fen who saved her sister."

"Will they tell the part where I let Roseus die?" She spat out the words. "And where I allowed you back into the world?"

"You are bitter now. But understand this: everything that is the Queen's must be burned to ashes. Even the equusa."

Fen came to the throne where his headless body waited.

"A sight for sore eyes," he said. "I almost cannot believe it. Bring me closer, little Fen. Closer."

There was a sense she was walking in a dream and the air was becoming thick around her.

"I long to breathe again," Mansren said.

She held the head above the statue for a moment. *Can I still stop this?* She pictured using her vines to throw him through the roof and her hand tingled in response. The shoots were ready to grow. To fight. But what would that do? The shirkers would find him. Or Mansren would burn through her hand.

The last time she'd been here, she'd seen May. Had touched her hand. She couldn't abandon her.

Fen placed his head with the smallest *thunk* on his stone body.

A vast silence descended over the shirkers. Mansren closed his eyes, a look of satisfaction on his face. Slowly that look turned to confusion. He opened one eye and then the other.

"Awake," he said. "Awake, body!"

But nothing happened. Fen took a step back. She could feel the tree trembling slightly below her feet.

"*AWAKEN!*" The shout nearly made her fall to her knees. A command so strong, it had to be obeyed. But his body remained stone. She felt a glimmering of relief. Perhaps he would not rise. The Queen was slowly dying, wasn't she? She would fall, maybe even be pushed off her perch by mortal hands . . . and somehow May could be rescued.

But if Mansren rose, she was certain nothing could defeat him.

She edged closer to the stairs. Mansren glared at her. "You've tainted me with that hand!" he hissed. "You've betrayed me! Just like she did."

"I—I didn't." Fen stared at her wooden hand. How could it affect Mansren?

"They'll tear your liver out," he whispered. The mass of shirkers whispered and hissed in response.

"*Liver! Liver! Liver!*" They were a sea of anger, broiling below her.

"I didn't do it. I didn't!"

He shut his eyes and was still. The shirkers fell silent.

"Ah, that's it," he said. "I was a fool to think a mortal could change me—a girl! It has just been too long since I've breathed. I need a breath to remind me. Come closer, Fen."

"W-why?"

"You will breathe a breath into my mouth."

"That's madness!" She covered her own mouth.

"No. It's life. I need your breath."

"I promised only to bring you here." She put up her hands. "Not to—to . . . do that."

"I could have my shirkers travel to the nearest village—to your village—and bring an infant to me. I would take her mortal breath and then toss her to them, to sate their hungers. I would, of course, have you watch."

"You wouldn't."

"*DON'T BE A FOOL!*" he shouted. Again, she nearly fell to her knees. "I have been in pain for a thousand years. Does one human's minuscule suffering compare to that?"

Fen inhaled deeply through her nostrils, calming herself. She set her feet. "There—there must be a new deal."

He smiled. "Perhaps you are not so soft."

"You'll save my sister as before. And keep Marcus safe."

"He's dead. So that will be easy."

She swallowed. "Then . . . my village too. And anyone who is not in the Queen's army."

"You ask too much! Ask for something smaller. Ask now!"

"My friends. Marcus. Ithak. You'll keep them safe. Along with my sister. And my village."

"Done." Fen heard satisfaction in his voice.

I should have asked for more.

"Yes, you should have," he echoed. "But lessons must be learned. Now come closer. I would prefer you did this of your own free will."

She found the strength to edge toward him. Once the Queen had kissed those lips. Over a thousand years ago.

"Closer." She took several small steps to stand right beside him. He opened his mouth. She closed her eyes and wrinkled her nose and tried to stop from retching. She managed to lean down. Their lips touched and she breathed into him.

In an instant her breath was being pulled out of her, unravelled as if he were gathering it from her lungs and along with it, her life. Her light. Her energy. She couldn't pull away. More and more of her essence came out until she felt empty. A shell.

Stop! she tried to say. She reached what felt like a final breath, exhaling everything that was her into him. All of it. *Stop! Stop!*

Then his stone chest moved, the vines snapping around him, and Fen fell, landing on her back. For several moments she was unable to draw a breath, her vision growing dark. She saw her mother's face. *Huzi*, she said. It was a word from the old tongue. *Breathe.* Then Fen found the strength, the memory of breath, and inhaled deeply.

She was only slightly aware of what was happening around her, so deep were her breaths. But at the edge of her vision, she thought she saw the statue of Mansren moving. She turned her head in that direction.

He was standing now, the vines snapping off him. His night-black body was fully flesh again. The oak creaked as if it was barely strong enough to hold him. He took a step, testing his legs. He opened and closed his hands.

Then he pointed toward the heavens. The canopy opened above them and a blazing bolt of bright-white light came out of his right hand, shooting skyward. A *boom* split the air. He stood like that for several seconds, the tree branches bent out of his way so all of that brightness glowed in the sky. She was forced to look away. Even the shirkers had averted their eyes.

The noise stopped. The brightness faded, though it remained burned in her vision. Mansren brushed his hands together. "That will serve notice to Servilia," he said. He looked down at Fen. "Breathless, aren't you? All of you worms shall be breathless before me."

We're not worms. She couldn't get enough air to say the words out loud.

Her next thought was: *what have I wrought?*

He pulled Fen to her feet and then gently lifted her chin, so she had to look directly up at him. His palm was so smooth, his fingers cool. His amber eyes glared into hers. "You are a curious girl, Fen of the Wooden Hand. Very curious. A Zhuang to the bone. Yes, I destroyed your emperor's city. Your people dared to not bow before Servilia and me. So I tore those palaces down and turned your people to dust, your land to salt. To nothing. Leaving the Great Salt Mire in its place. Your stubborn emperor, Xiao, would make no deal with me. So he was the last to die. The scattered refugees were all we left of your kind."

"You feel no regret for killing my people!" she whispered harshly.

He nodded, grinned and tapped her forehead with a finger. "No. I don't. And the killing is not done. You've made a grievous error. In our deal, you asked me to save your sister, your friends, your village. But not once did you request protection for yourself. A simple, foolish and fatal mistake."

He slid his hand down to her throat.

CHAPTER THIRTY-ONE

A SONG
OF POWER

MANSREN SQUEEZED. FEN GRABBED HIM WITH HER LEFT
hand but he was smiling, looking down at her as if she were an
insect. She clutched his arm with her wooden hand, the vines
growing and burning along his flesh as she did so, but even they
couldn't make him loosen his grip. His fingers sank deeper into
her neck. Once again her breath was gone.

"I am not ungenerous." He released his grip and she fell
to his feet. "Remember: in life-and-death negotiations, always
think of yourself first."

Her neck burned where his hand had touched her. She
sucked in a painful breath. *I've made a horrible mistake. I should
never have trusted him.*

"What sort of Mansren would I be if I didn't allow you to live
after your heroic journey? You returned me to myself, and I am
very grateful for your sacrifice. You must be hungry and thirsty.
You certainly are dirty. I shall fix that." He gestured and she was

lifted bodily from the tree and drifted downward. There was a sensation of her clothing vanishing and then water splashing every part of her, wetting her hair, momentarily blinding her. A moment later, heat and clothing were wrapped around her. When she landed softly on the ground, she was perfectly clean, wearing a magnificent red dress that shimmered brightly. A royal dress! Her hair was intricately braided behind her.

A table set with food appeared. The shirkers opened a circle around it.

"I have a Queen to kill," Mansren said. "Please eat, drink and rest." A bed with golden legs appeared against the wall of his fortress. Mansren turned away from her.

Fen looked down at her clothing. The dress was bright and smooth. She touched it. The fabric was so amazingly soft that no human hands could ever have done the stitching.

"I don't wear dresses." Her voice was ragged. "I'm a villager."

Mansren turned back to her and stared down, smirking. "Ungrateful child." He snapped his fingers and Fen was again in grey trousers and a green shirt and vest. Nothing fancy, but the thread was still smooth. Mansren again turned his back on her.

Most wildmagics could do one miraculous thing—such as shoot fire from their hands, float or, in her case, grow vines. But he had done several hundred magical things in the last few moments with only the smallest of gestures. And not even a hint of exertion.

The table was littered with grapes and cheese, steaming meats and pork buns. As before, there were several bowls of noodles just as her mother used to make them. Despite her conflicted feelings, Fen could not stop herself from eating. Each mouthful was alive with taste, but it hurt her throat when she swallowed, as if Mansren's hand were still gripping her. The meat was cooked to perfection and didn't cool. Every apple and mango had the smoothest of skins, with no sign of a bruise.

The shirkers watched her. They'd consumed Roseus in such a short period of time. Would they also want to consume her? She was magical. But they eventually turned away to stare toward their master.

Mansren was no longer in sight, though she assumed he was sitting on his throne.

She ate and ate, not certain if she would ever get full, drinking from various goblets of fruit water. She picked up an orange, running a wooden finger over the rough skin. It still surprised her how her new hand could feel things through the wood.

And what was even more surprising was that she could name things in her original language, since Mansren had gifted it to her. The Chin tongue had a name for everything—of course it did. But as she held the dish of noodles up and said, "*Miyantow*," she couldn't have felt more amazed. This was the food her mother had served her whole life, that every villager had eaten, and they had only been able to use the Illian language to describe it. It tasted better now that she could speak its proper name.

She picked up an apple and said, "*Pingoh.*"

The words were another type of magic. Her mouth was meant to speak Chin words, her mind to think them. She'd been waiting for them her whole life. The handprint of the monster who'd given her this gift still burned on her throat.

She shed a few tears thinking of her father. Her mother. How they would have loved to have spoken these words openly. "*Ai*," she said. "*Ai.*" *Love.*

She drank mango water. And sat in a wicker chair. The food was heavy in her stomach and she blinked several times. Had he put something in it to make her sleepy? But perhaps her body was overtired. Her mind too.

The shirkers gathered into groups, facing each other and humming—each finding a tune. Fen had learned to sing from her mother, had an understanding of pitch. They were holding notes for much longer than any human could. Fen couldn't understand a word. Perhaps they had a language older than Illish or Chin.

"One becomes one becomes one," Mansren said, from far above her. She didn't know whether he was speaking to her or to them.

A bolt of blue lightning flashed so brightly she was momentarily blinded and knocked from her chair. She staggered back, blinking. Her eyes watered. The table of food had disappeared.

Her vision came back to her. A group of shirkers had been obliterated by the bolt. Then she looked closer—no, they had become one, fused into a giant shirker standing above her, twenty feet tall. Turning its head back and forth and then looking across at Mansren. It glided around the throne tree without a sound. Something that large should have made the very earth shake when it walked.

The remaining shirkers continued to sing. Another lightning strike came, then another, again and again, and from each rose a giant. Further strikes split shirkers in two, and they became smaller versions of themselves. A third group fused into a winged creature with twelve arms and a multitude of eyes. It circled the tree and landed in the uppermost branches. Soon it was joined by other winged creatures. A bolt struck right in front of Fen. She felt its heat and threw herself backwards. She kept backing up until she was against the wall. She had ended up beside the bed he'd summoned for her, so she sat on the edge and huddled there as the strikes continued.

The singing grew louder with the transformations and additions to the shirker army. She opened her eyes only briefly before having to close them against the brightness of the flashes. But burned upon her vision was the image of creatures of all shapes—some of them had wings and long birdlike snouts, others were as small as rats, but all were made of shadow and of substance at the same time. They numbered a thousand at the very least.

She covered her eyes with her hands and, not being able to control herself, she wept. For what she was witnessing would surely wreak a terrible destruction on anything that stood in its way.

She wept.

And wept.

CHAPTER THIRTY-TWO

A MORAL
QUANDARY

SLUMBER CAME TO FEN. TOO MUCH HAD HAPPENED. TOO many long journeys. And she was certain there was a sleeping potion in the food. When she opened her eyes again, she had no idea how much time had passed. The walls of the wooden fortress were now a great distance from the throne tree. They had widened to accommodate this growing army. No, it was more than an army, she decided. It was a mass. A horde. A swarm.

Wooshu: the word came unbidden to her mind. *Numberless.*

The host of shirkers was completely silent now. She could only hear her heart beating. She rose from the bed, pushing back the sheets. Had Mansren tucked her in with a gesture of his hand? Just as her mother used to do. Fen shivered.

The multitude around her was dark as night, shadows arrayed by shape and size staring up at the throne tree, which was now a great distance from Fen. It looked small. She couldn't see Mansren.

She picked her way through the horde. The shirkers paid no attention to her. Were they individuals? Or all cut of the same cloth, with the same thoughts?

She noted that their chests moved ever so slightly. They breathed! They needed air, at least, if nothing else. None of them were armed, but she knew, after watching the shirker fight Marcus, that they could form their hands into weapons. And she imagined the long claws on their fingers could cut most metal.

She worked her way closer to the throne. Soon she was walking beside such giants that she only came up to their knees. Their shadowy skin had a gem-like smoothness. But the smallest shirkers frightened her the most. For they were all claws and teeth. So tiny. She thought of the rats that had attacked the paladin Marcellus and how impossible it was for even someone as powerful as him to fight them off.

She'd been walking for a long while but the throne tree seemed no closer. Had Mansren warped and twisted the very fabric of time and distance? No, the wall was far behind her now.

She walked. And walked. The army was endless. All of this had been created from a few shirkers. And she'd had some small part in its formation.

Eventually she got close enough to see Mansren. He was standing next to his throne and staring toward the north. He turned his head slightly and motioned with his hand, and suddenly she was lifted into the air and floated quickly up to him. It was a gut-churning sensation to be totally in his control. She landed gently by his side. He looked bigger, more substantial now.

"It has been a busy three days," he said.

"Three days!"

"Yes. You slept. There was so much to create." From this vantage point, the army was on all sides. "I've been dreaming about this for so long. Do you know the pain you felt when they burned your arm? That is what I felt during every moment in Velchan's Forge. It sizzles behind each thought. My Queen did that to me."

"Is what you said true?" she asked. "Did you once love her?"

He fell silent and pursed his lips. "Perhaps once I would have used a word like that. Words can bind people together. But over time a word can be broken. A body can be turned to stone and broken."

"So it is true?" Fen said.

"Yes. But any such emotions for her or her kind were immolated in that mountain."

She looked around at the army. How many eyes watched this exchange? They were still standing in perfect stillness. Waiting for his orders.

"She can't possibly defeat you," Fen said.

"She's much weaker than she was when she broke me. So much magic has been drawn from the ground. Her queendom will collapse like a rotten melon."

"What will you do after you win?"

"Are you feeling guilt, Nong Fu Fen?" She didn't like how he spoke her name. "It will be a world of much more order."

"But what will be left for me? For . . . for my people."

"When the Queen no longer breathes air, you will still be breathing it. So will your sister. Take comfort in that. Perhaps that comfort will last a lifetime and ease you through the coming . . . alterations."

A chill went through her.

"I do have a sorrow to pass to you." He put a hand on her

shoulder as if in consolation. "My eyes have looked everywhere. Your Queen's guard is dead."

She drew in a breath. Even though she'd seen him trapped at the bottom of the lake, one part of her mind wanted to believe he was alive. That he had somehow survived. "How can you be certain?"

"I took stock of all Illium. If he walked on this earth, I would have seen him."

"No," she said. "You have to be wrong." She found she still didn't believe it. Not yet in her heart.

"I am never wrong." He didn't say this with smugness.

"And Ithak too? Is he dead?"

"It appears that way. For I have not found him either." He lifted his hand from her shoulder and she felt lighter. "Their names will be praised by future generations for their small part in my release."

He poked the air in front of him and whispered something in another language. *A spell?* "The Queen sends her eyes flying my way and I jab them out. I am stuck with a moral quandary: it is wrong of me to wait and draw out the pain, is it not? But I've felt countless hours of torture. A millennium of moments. She gathers her armies. She makes her walls stronger. Her artificers are shaping their weapons, her forges working to build more swords, more armour. All that fruitless effort. Am I being cruel, Fen?"

Yes. You are cruel. "Yes," she whispered.

She expected anger, but he nodded. "You are correct. You are my niggling conscience. There is no sense in being needlessly cruel."

He pointed toward the north. As one, the shirker army brought their feet together and let out a shout. It was enough to shake the trees, the foundations of the world. The walls that surrounded them opened wide where he'd pointed. The army began to march forward into the forest in perfect unison. She wondered why Helwood let them live. Allowed them to march through her like this. Perhaps the great forest didn't care what happened beyond its borders.

"Would you like to follow?" Mansren asked. "I will provide a mount." He gestured at four large shirkers and they formed into a horse-like creature. It stood still, next to the tree. "Take it. It's your beast. I call it Snowball. I will now lead my army." He floated down from the trees and walked among his shirkers. "You may not want to watch the war," he said over his shoulder. "But you should witness the ending of the Queen."

Witness? Fen didn't move from the throne as the army marched along. Did she want to see what Mansren had planned? It was becoming harder and harder to imagine any sort of good coming out of this. She stood, indecisive. It took many hours until the shirkers had all passed the tree.

Then, finally, Fen drew a deep breath. *Be as strong as a horse. Be as brave as a tiger.* It was a proverb her mother would whisper whenever Fen had difficulty with doing a task one-handed. In fact, she'd said it just before Fen's hand had been cut off. Fen went down the steps. Snowball waited; its eight long legs lowered and she climbed onto its back. She found its flesh cold. There was no saddle. There were no reins.

"Go," she whispered. "Follow."

It did. She trailed after Mansren's army.

CHAPTER THIRTY-THREE

A GLINT
OF SILVER

RIDING SNOWBALL WAS NOT LIKE RIDING A HORSE.
There was an impeccable fluidity to the creature's gait. The
eight legs always kept the body on the same level as it skimmed
across the ground. It reminded Fen of the smoothness of the
equusa when she had spread her wings and glided through the
air. Tears formed in Fen's eyes at the memory.

It took very little time to leave the forest. Not a tree or a
leaf seemed to be damaged, but once they were in the open,
Fen saw that the ground had been turned black by the mass of
shirkers. The army was spread out across the horizon. Mostly
it was a formless mob in the distance, but the largest of the
shirkers—the giants—were clearly in the lead, stones in a sea of
darkness. The Queen must know by now this army was marching toward her.

Fen stared down at the ground they were crossing. A light
layer of ash had settled on every blade of grass.

What if I go the other way? She could cross the ocean to whatever lands lay there—maybe this creature could walk on water. She could flee anywhere—away—to avoid seeing how this would end.

No. Mei Mei was in a dungeon in Regentium. Even just thinking her sister's true name—the name her mother and father would've spoken aloud—gave Fen strength. "Nong Mei Mei," she whispered. Fen would have to ride straight ahead to have any chance of seeing her.

Hours passed. At times Fen fell asleep on the back of the beast only to awaken a few minutes later, her eyes wild, surprised to still be in this world, with these monsters continuing to march in front of her. She gradually gained on her massive quarry.

When she looked behind her, Helwood had vanished into the distance, and a flattened and dark swath was left for as far as she could see.

She heard cracking in the distance and she wondered if it was trees falling before the army. But she couldn't see the beginning of it.

Then, quite suddenly, the shirkers all came to a stop.

Fen squinted and saw a tiny glint of silver in all that black. "Faster!" Snowball made its eight legs blur, catching the army, stepping over the smaller shirkers and skirting around the larger ones. Finally she could see Mansren standing in an open field. His army had given him several steps' worth of space. His back was to her, and he was talking to someone. He blocked her view as she rode up but Fen heard a woman's voice. *"Do not come any farther. You will break on the mighty walls of Regentium."*

Fen had listened to that voice every waking morning of her life.

"I will not break," Mansren said. "And I will never be bound again. Not by you, Servilia, and not by anyone."

Fen rode up and was surprised to find that one figure was standing and holding back the entire army. Giant shirkers loomed on either side of him but he took no notice—he was glaring up at Mansren. The guard had no weapon. His armour was mostly broken or had been torn off. His face was that of a Queen's guard but so familiar—

Marcus!

His features were a rictus of anger. He looked half-burned. Half-mad. His hair was mostly black now, but with a tinge of red.

He was alive. Alive! There was blood on his chest, and it took a moment to slow her thoughts down and realize it was dried. He was wearing ripped trousers and a tunic.

"*Keep back, Mansren.*" The Queen's words came out of Marcus's mouth. Just the sound of her voice made Fen tighten her fingers into fists. "*You'll be torn asunder. Your head will be cut from your shoulders.*"

"You've done that once, my dear." Mansren's voice was smooth and calm. "There is nothing left for you to do but die. I've had some time to consider the uselessness of mercy."

"*You will be the one to die.*"

"You are growing repetitive. Prepare yourself, Queen of nothing. You betrayed me, knowing that one day you would pay for that betrayal. Well, it is time to claim what is owed me."

Marcus let out a scream and rushed toward Mansren, fists up. He struck him again and again, his hands making a *thud thud thud* on Mansren's chest. Mansren stared down at him, bemused. Then Mansren flicked him away and Marcus flew through the air and skidded across the ground. He did not get up.

In a heartbeat, Fen was off the back of Snowball and running to him. She rushed past Mansren, pushed the shirkers out of the way and kneeled beside Marcus, lifting his head from the black dust left by the shirkers' tramping feet.

"Ah, Fen, you are reunited with your friend," Mansren said. "My spies did not see him. But they were looking for a Queen's guard. And he no longer appears to be one. The Queen has sent many messengers to speak with me. All have died long before reaching me. But not this one. I did not harm him. That was my promise to you. And speaking of promises . . ." He leaned down and touched Marcus on the shoulder. Marcus jittered and shook, his eyelids fluttering open. His eyes were turned back in his skull.

"Stop it! Stop it!" Fen shouted. "What are you doing?"

"I'm not harming him," Mansren said. The last of the armour clinked to the ground, like pieces of paper sliding off Marcus. Foam appeared on his lips. "I am fulfilling my promise. I'm taking the Queen out of him. No longer will he yearn for her orders. Her presence. Her love." The red hair on Marcus's head grew dark. And curly. Mansren took his hand away.

Marcus was still for several moments. Then he coughed hard, opened his eyes and blinked. "Ah, Fen. I can't believe it's you." He reached out a hand and touched her face but didn't seem to have the strength to hold it there. "It's wonderful to see you! I—I thought you were dead."

"I believed the same of you." She ran her hand through his hair.

"It was a close thing." He coughed again. "I'm sorry about that shouting. I wasn't myself."

She laughed, almost a belly laugh. A rush of relief, of joy was spreading through her. It really was Marcus!

Mansren joined her with his own guttural laugh. It made Fen stop cold. "There is pleasure in seeing youth reunited," Mansren said. "And seeing the aged return too. Show yourself, Ithak."

Ithak appeared only a few feet away from Mansren. He was looking up, his eyes wide, and he clearly trembled. Though Fen wasn't certain whether it was with fear or anticipation.

"Ithak is honoured to be in your presence, my lord," Ithak said.

"I know. Soon, my servant, you shall reap your rewards."

Ithak bowed. "Thank you. Ithak always remains at your service."

"Your part is done. Please join your friends and watch the glory unfold." Mansren made a motion and the shirker army began to move quietly past the prone figures. He turned to join his army, which was already moving into the distance, so great was their speed. His legs blurring, he soon disappeared.

"Marcus, Marcus," Fen said. She grabbed his hand, holding it tightly in her wooden one. His fingers were ice-cold. "How is it that you are alive?"

"That is a story and a half," he said. "Can you help me up?"

She pulled him to his feet.

"Oh, it was quite the sight." Ithak rubbed his hands together. "Our little guard drowning a full fathom down. Held at the bottom by the weight of his armour. He tore most of it off, piece by piece, and swam for the surface. Nearly as naked as the day of his birth. A shame he wasn't strong enough to go the full distance. He began to sink again. So very sad."

"You helped me, Ithak," Marcus said. "I won't forget that."

"Ithak was short of air. Befuddled, that is all. Ithak paddled down to him and pushed him up. Marcus swims with all the skill of a dead badger."

"You surprise me, Ithak," Fen said. "I'm beginning to believe you care."

"Insults! Lies!" he hissed. Then he winked. "Ithak did kindly lug him to shore. And we hid from the guards. They were after you, of course. They knew you were gone and did not care about a little drowned Queen's guard and a valiant, invisible wild-magic."

"But how did you get here?" Fen asked. "It's an impossible distance."

"Ithak and I walked, avoiding patrols," Marcus said. She still couldn't get over how dark his hair had become.

"You skipped the part where Ithak stole clothing for you," Ithak said. "Ithak grew tired of you being naked."

"Uh, yes, there was that." Marcus rubbed his forehead. He seemed to be blushing.

"I had to leave you. I would have stayed and tried to help. But Mansren forced me to swim away."

Marcus touched her shoulder. "It's all right. We knew you'd be going toward Helwood, Fen. If you were alive, that is. We also knew we had a long journey ahead of us."

"He was mopey at times," Ithak piped up. "Fen this and Fen that."

Marcus gave Ithak a light punch. She wondered at how close they seemed to have become since she'd last seen them.

"When the flash of bright light burned the sky," Ithak said, "we knew you had made it to Helwood and that Mansren had become, well . . . Mansren."

"Yes. He has become himself." Fen wanted to add, *He's become something horrible.*

"There was only one quick way to return," Marcus explained. "So Ithak, brave little Ithak, stole a vial of Queen's blood from one of my brothers and we found the nearest section of Queen's Road. I drank the blood and we travelled here."

"He carried Ithak." Ithak hugged himself. "Like a baby. In his arms. Ithak slept most of the way."

"You ran?" Fen couldn't hide the shock in her voice.

"It is possible," Marcus said. "We went by so many fallen corvuses. Dead Queen's guards and mangled soldiers. Then the Queen, she—she found me. And got inside me again. It's such a terrible feeling. I became her eyes."

"And mouth," Ithak added. "A foul mouth, Ithak must say."

Marcus touched his skull. "I never want to hear her voice again."

Fen thought of how Mansren had been in her head, had forced her to swim. She wanted to explain that she understood.

"I have so much to tell you," Fen said. "I'm so happy to see you. Both of you. Come with me." She took both their hands and was surprised Ithak didn't pull away.

Snowball waited behind her. The creature bent its double-jointed legs and she stepped on, bringing Marcus and Ithak with her. They sat on the beast's sleek, wide back.

"Go," Fen said. "With great speed."

Snowball ran across the earth, trying to gain on Mansren's army.

"It is so wonderful to be reunited," Ithak said. And Fen thought he actually meant it until he added, "You two will block any arrows from hitting me."

CHAPTER THIRTY-FOUR

TO BEAR WITNESS

THEY RACED THROUGH A PASTY BLACK DUST. THERE WAS no indication that any tree or blade of grass or flower had ever been on it. Or any living animal either.

"Faster," she said, and Snowball responded by summoning more speed out of those eight legs.

"What do you hope to do?" Marcus asked.

"Only to be present. To witness. I created this."

"Created?" Ithak laughed. "It was inevitable. Mansren guided each step you took since the moment you left your village."

"I made choices," she said.

"So you believe," Ithak shot back.

"We made choices." Marcus touched his chest. "I chose to take off my armour. I chose to break my vow to the Queen."

"It was inevitable," Ithak said, though he didn't sound as certain. "All of it."

The sun rose higher in the sky. Mansren's army was a roiling black wave sweeping ahead of them. Fen felt as if perhaps the legion was travelling with even greater speed. Snowball took them to the top of a hill and Fen looked down.

There was a village in the distance. Several red flags waved from a central square. The village had been built next to a stream, a tall mill on one bank. Fen squinted, certain she could see villagers running from their homes. They were tiny figures.

"What place is that?" she asked.

"Village Eight," Ithak said. "Wheat-growers and cow-milkers. We are very close to Regentium."

"Will Mansren go around it?" Marcus asked.

"But how could an army that large go around?" she said.

"They went around us."

The shirkers swarmed toward the village. People were fleeing desperately now, pushing their livestock ahead. Donkeys. Oxen. Sheep. Then the black wave splashed up against the village and the buildings on the outskirts fell, then the next row and the next row of huts. The mill collapsed, burst into flames and was trampled beneath the feet of the shirkers. Within only a few breaths, the village was gone. The people who fled were soon falling under the tread of the army. In moments, they, too, were gone.

"They're dead," Fen said. "All of them."

"That whole village," Marcus said. "It's as if it never existed."

"One can't just move an army out of the way," Ithak said.

"But he killed them," Fen said. "They weren't even armed."

Ithak shrugged. "One cannot stop progress."

"You truly don't feel for them?" Fen asked. It had taken all her will to stop from screaming this aloud. She must have said it more forcefully than she'd thought, for Ithak looked a little paler.

"Ithak . . . Ithak didn't expect this. Ithak thought only of the Queen falling. Of her getting out of his head."

"As did I," Fen said. "But these people"—she spread her hands at the ash around them—"they were alive just a few minutes ago. Mothers. Fathers. Sisters. I killed them."

"You didn't kill them," Marcus said.

"Choices I made brought about their deaths."

"You didn't know." Ithak's voice actually sounded soft. "None of us, even Ithak, knew how powerful Mansren would become."

"But if we'd waited," Fen said, "the Queen would have fallen on her own."

"People have been waiting for a thousand years," Ithak said. "Would you want to wait for another thousand?"

"I have to stop this," Fen said. "Somehow convince Mansren this total destruction is wrong."

"There's no halting it now," Ithak said. "We should just be happy we are on the winning side."

They rode silently. Most of the day passed. And not once did the army stop marching toward Regentium.

CHAPTER THIRTY-FIVE

THE BATTLE OF REGENTIUM

A RICH, WONDROUS SCENT DRIFTED THROUGH THE AIR. Fen looked ahead to see great fields of flowers in the distance— dahlias, tulips, anemones and others whose names she didn't know. "It's true," she said. "The stories are true!"

"The fields of flowers," Marcus said. "Yes, they're real."

"They never rot. Never die," Ithak said. "Even in the dead of winter, the snow melts around them. I'd rather be back in the Great Salt Mire. This is the stink of magic for no purpose but to please the Queen."

Despite that, Fen wondered at the beauty of it. Leagues of flowers. The army was marching through them and turning them black.

Then tall crimson spires appeared on the horizon. Fen wasn't certain if the red walls and emerald towers were a mirage. The tallest of the towers was a bright red—the Queen's tower. Below that tower would be the dungeon holding Mei Mei.

"That's Regentium?" Fen asked.

"It is," Marcus said. "It feels as if a hundred years have passed since I rode through those gates."

"I've never seen the city," she said.

"Of course you haven't." Ithak pointed ahead. "You're a villager. But every drop of sweat and blood of your ancestors, and of the ancestors of all villagers, went toward those walls and buildings. For a thousand years."

The city was the most beautiful of all jewels. It was said that no battering ram could ever make her walls crack. Every archer of the Queen was lined up along the parapets. And behind the gates, Fen was certain, the Queen's guards were waiting. Seven thousand strong. Impressive almost beyond belief, if not for the more impressive mass of shirkers moving toward them.

She felt only pity and fear for all who lay within the walls. There were corvuses in the air above the city, but any that strayed beyond the confines fell from the sky as if stricken by an invisible bolt.

Mansren's army encircled Regentium. The ranks that had seemed endless were thinned to complete the circle. They stood well out of arrow range.

Snowball brought the three of them closer.

"Do you think he will lay siege?" Fen asked. "And wait for them to starve?"

"No need," Ithak said. "Ithak is certain he will just break his way in."

As they approached the rear of the army, Fen patted Snowball's back and said, "Halt." Their mount drew up. "We shouldn't get too close," she explained. She had lost sight of Mansren.

The occasional shout from within the walls of Regentium

would drift their way, but whether it was in defiance or fear, Fen could not tell. Finally one of the Queen's catapults released a flaming ball of fire through the air, which struck within the mass of Mansren's army. Not a single shirker moved or cried out. They were consumed in the flame, but soon it was snuffed out, the smoke vanished and more shirkers moved in to fill that spot. Ten and then twenty flaming stones arced through the air, smacking full into Mansren's army. The shirkers stood silently.

"They're extremely disciplined," Marcus said. Mansren's army had no such siege weapons. In time the flaming attacks stopped.

A circle opened up in the shirkers, revealing that Mansren was standing on a small hill. His arms were crossed and he clearly wanted the guards and the Queen to see him there.

As if in answer, an equusa flew over the walls, its paladin holding a golden spear. Once they had gone several wingbeats, the paladin drew back his arm to throw. The spear flew in an arc directly at Mansren. It had been aimed perfectly but it dissipated into smoke only a few feet away from its target. Mansren hadn't even gestured.

Mansren pointed at the paladin and both rider and horse burst into flames. By the time they hit the earth, they were nothing more than burning clumps of flesh.

A trumpet sounded behind the walls. Then another joined in. The gates opened and the Queen's Guard came riding out in formation, the sun catching their silver armour, their banners flapping. Row upon row of guards stormed out onto the plain. Then the gates closed. Fen saw Marcus tighten his fists, as though he might want to be riding with them. "I grew up with the sound of the trumpets." There was longing in his voice. "They have marked my blood."

A trumpet made three long notes and the guards drew into formation.

Mansren's army did not respond in any fashion.

Then as the trumpet began to play a quick tune, the lances were lowered, their sharp edges shining. The Queen's Guard had lined up into an arrowhead shape.

"That's all of them," Marcus said. "The seven thousand."

"Or what remains of them," Ithak added.

Another three notes were played. They sounded almost jaunty. The Queen's Guard charged toward the line of the enemy, aiming straight at Mansren. Marcellus led them—Fen spotted his golden armour.

"I know that man," Fen said.

"Yes," Marcus said. "He is the best of all of us."

The guards were soon at full gallop, creating a thunderous sound. They crossed the short distance with great speed. They seemed as if they would cut right through the shirker ranks.

When the Queen's Guard struck the enemy lines, the shirkers did not scatter so much as fold over, and the regiment began to cut through them as if they were made of paper. Their lances skewered shirkers, who then dissipated into smoke. Occasionally a Queen's guard would fall, struck by a blow. Or a horse would be tripped up by shirker hands. But another guard would fill the open spot. The armoured men penetrated farther and farther into Mansren's army.

The action was all such a distance away that it seemed unreal, yet Fen knew men were dying. They would be breathing out their last breath thinking not of their mothers, of course, but of their brothers. Or of the Queen. Fen had both loved and hated these guards for so many years now—one of those Queen's guards in that charge had taken her hand from her. Another had taken her mother. But all she felt was sadness. And guilt. Maybe there were others like Marcus.

She grabbed his hand.

A glint of gold indicated Marcellus's position. He was swinging his flaming blade, felling the shirkers left and right. He met taller and taller foes as the Queen's guards penetrated into the ranks. It looked like he was chopping down black trees.

All of the Queen's guards were now deep within the mass of Mansren's army. And those shirkers who had been trampled, who had looked to be dead, rose up, enclosing their enemy.

"They've encircled them," Marcus said. Guards were dying more frequently now, and their numbers became fewer and fewer so that soon they could no longer move forward against the taller shirkers.

The giants were swinging down arms shaped like hammers, crushing men with blow after blow. The Queen's Guard formed into a circle inside the enemy army. The circle grew smaller by the moment.

The guards were fighting so bravely. She gripped Marcus's hand even tighter. Soon there were twenty, then ten, and then for a moment Marcellus himself stood there surrounded by the shirkers and swinging in all directions.

The giants backed away and Mansren waded through the ranks and stood before Marcellus. The words they exchanged were too distant to hear, but after a moment Marcellus raised his sword to strike and his shout travelled that distance: "For the Queen!"

Mansren brought his hand down, cutting Marcellus in two. Each side became ashes as it hit the ground.

Mansren bent down and lifted up the paladin's flaming sword. He threw it and the blade flew a great distance to stick into the walls of the city.

The shirkers began to sing.

CHAPTER THIRTY-SIX

A WORLD WITH YOU AS MASTER

FEN AT FIRST WANTED TO COVER HER EARS. BUT THE
sound was so beautiful. Each note sung perfectly. A song as loud
and powerful as the army. The hairs on the back of her neck
began to rise with each crescendo.

Then as they sang this song of such clarity, the tallest of
the shirkers moved forward through the ranks toward the walls.
Soldiers on the parapets loosed arrows in great abundance and
they punctured the creatures, sticking to them. Some giant shirkers fell and disappeared as if a warm rain had dissolved them,
but the majority marched forward with the song surrounding
them. Perhaps even empowering them. Catapults launched fire-
balls that ploughed into these giants. But they did not slow until
they came before the very walls.

The giants began to bang on the red fortifications that had
stood for a thousand years. Walls invested with magic dust to
withstand the strongest siege engine.

Whoomp. Whoomp. Whoomp. Each blow made Fen's heart skip a beat. Cracks began to form in the wall. Then crevices appeared. And finally a long section crumbled to the ground, taking with it all the soldiers standing on the parapets.

Mansren's army followed like a wave through that opening. Within moments, the gates opened and the shirkers spread into the city like a sickness.

Mansren walked through the gates. The walls had turned black and were crumbling, falling apart here and there.

"We have to follow," Fen said.

At her command, Snowball took them forward.

"How can this all be falling so easily?" Marcus asked.

"Mansren is just too powerful," Ithak said. "It's like watching a giant step on a bug."

They rode through the gate. How thick it had been. Fen had expected to see battles, great fights, but there was only a layer of ash on the streets. She didn't spot one soldier or citizen. The merchant who'd asked for Queen's justice all those years ago when she'd stolen the butterfly was likely dead, or soon would be. So would any other citizens of Regentium.

"Did you have brothers, Ithak?" she asked.

"One. Younger by five years. He is likely long dead."

"If he had children, then they will be dying today too," she said.

"Perhaps." He went silent.

The shirkers were moving closer and closer to the centre of the city. The markets were empty. Large stone houses stood, but there was not a servant or an animal to be seen. They were walking through piles of dust.

"Faster!" Fen commanded. Snowball skittered over rubble, stepped over shirkers. Soon it became clear the battle was not over. Soldiers were fighting and fleeing ahead of them on the streets. But when any shirker darted close enough to touch a soldier, the man would turn to ashes.

Fen, Marcus and Ithak were now riding within the ranks of the army. They stayed far enough back not to be caught up in the fighting.

At the centre of Regentium was the great market, and at the centre of that stood the Red Tower, the tallest building in all of Illium. It was so tall that Fen had to stretch her neck to see the very top.

She knew the Red Artificers worked inside that tower. And below it, as deep as the tower was tall, would be the dungeons. Soldiers and townspeople were crowded in front of the tower, edging closer and closer to each other as they were surrounded by the invading army.

"Let them go!" Fen shouted when she neared Mansren. He was standing with his hands on his hips. "The battle is won."

"I do not need a conscience, Fen," Mansren said. "Avert your eyes to what will unfold."

She couldn't stop herself from continuing on: "Spare the townspeople's lives, at the very least. They have done nothing to you."

He rolled his eyes. "If it will keep you quiet!" He gestured and the shirkers stepped aside to open a clear space in their ranks. The townspeople stared. Then one young man ran through safely. He was followed by a woman carrying her child. Then the remaining citizens fled through the opening.

A small group of ragged Queen's guards, some missing limbs but not bleeding, stood with their swords in hand. They looked very young to Fen.

"Those are greenlings," Marcus said. "They haven't finished their training. So they weren't in the final charge."

Mansren strode ahead and the defenders stepped back. "Bring out the Queen," he said. His voice boomed loudly enough to shake the tower. "Come out, Servilia. Or should I knock your tower down?"

There was a long silence. The shirkers held completely still. The rest of the city had grown equally quiet, a city that only an hour earlier had been teeming with activity.

Mansren stepped even closer to the tower, now alone between the two sides. He raised his arms as if already celebrating his victory. "She makes me wait!" he shouted. He did seem to be smiling. "Even after all these years, she makes me wait."

The front gate opened and a woman, much smaller than Fen had imagined she'd be, strode out. She seemed no more than thirty years old. Her face was so familiar—Fen had seen it every morning for most of her life. Queen Servilia's back was straight. The Queen's Guard opened a path for her and even the shirkers backed away.

She halted only an arm's length from Mansren. "So you have come all this way, through all the years, for your vengeance." Her voice was clear and steady. "I suppose you expect me to tremble before you?"

"I would prefer that," he said. But in her presence, even he seemed somewhat subdued. Not as tall. Not as powerful. "You have kept well," he said. "Your face is just as I remember it."

"As is yours," she said.

"You attempted to melt it. Alas, that did not work."

"I was only protecting my interests, Mansren," she said. Fen wanted to hate her. This woman had severed her hand. And yet there was such bravery in her. It made it difficult to remember all the reasons to hate the Queen. She faced Mansren without a trace of fear.

But her bravery was only equalled by her evil. Servilia had worked her father to death in her mines, killed her mother and captured her sister, who was, Fen hoped, alive below that tower at this very moment.

"You have won," Servilia continued. "Congratulations, you've taken everything away from me. You are the greatest power to ever have existed. Is that what you want to hear, Mansren? It's not the truth."

"You never spoke the truth," Mansren replied. "Not once. You broke your oath to me. To rule together as one."

"I broke it easily. For I knew one day it would come to a war between us. I at least had a thousand and ten years of being Queen on my own terms."

"I would have built a city a hundred times the size and opulence of Regentium. We would have reigned for ten thousand years together."

"Your need to talk constantly would have driven me mad!" she shouted.

A silence followed. Then, oddly, both of them laughed. But Mansren's eyes were hard, his jaw clenched.

"Will you just do what you have come to do?" Queen Servilia spat. "A world with you as master, it is not worth living in."

Then she took a step back, lowered her hand and shot out a green blast that made Mansren stagger. The flames went into his chest and drove him into the line of shirkers, scattering several of them. Fen noted that the Queen's diamond necklace was glowing, as though she were drawing power from it.

Mansren set his feet, took a step forward and made a sweeping motion. The flames went out.

Queen Servilia shrugged. "I had to try. I didn't think turning you to stone would work again."

"I give you your one thousand and ten years back." He stepped up to her and touched her forehead. Ever so gently. For a moment, nothing happened. Then her skin began to wizen, to dry, so that perhaps the thousand years were all added to her at once. Fen could scarcely believe her eyes as Servilia rapidly aged, becoming only flesh, then bones, and then dust at Mansren's feet. A wind picked up the dust and she was blown away.

Fen took a deep breath. Was that all it took to rid the world of the Queen? After over a thousand years? Mansren's power was truly staggering.

Mansren stood looking at the space where the Queen had stood only moments earlier. His hands had formed fists, and she wondered if, finally getting his revenge, he was perhaps disappointed.

And if he was disappointed, what would his promises mean?

There was only one way to know. Mei Mei was waiting. Fen slipped off Snowball and pushed through the shirkers until she stood next to Mansren.

"What of my sister?" Fen asked.

"My conscience returns," he said. She thought there was a tear in his eye. "Go. Find her. I'll leave the tower standing for now."

She and Marcus went through the doors of the Red Tower and wandered empty halls until they finally found a stairwell that led downward. There were more stairs than she had seen in her lifetime, circling ever deeper toward the dungeon. Eventually the stairs became rugged stone and the way grew darker. There were prisoners reaching through metal bars. Others dead in chains. The guards had obviously fled.

She kept running until she came to a level where the cells were smaller. Cages, really. This was where Servilia kept the children she held hostage. Fen heard sniffing. Even weeping. But mostly the prisoners were silent, staring at her with big eyes as if they didn't believe she was real. She found a familiar area—the section she'd seen from the throne tree. The pile of rags was still inside the cell, not moving. Fen lifted a set of keys from the guard station. It took her several tries before she found the one that opened the door. She handed the ring of keys to Marcus. "Release the other children," she said. "And the prisoners above us."

Marcus nodded and left.

Fen drew in a breath. The smell was horrid. She thought of the distance she had travelled: fleeing her village to Helwood, travelling to the Forge and back, and now ending up here. Finally, here.

"Mei Mei," Fen said. Her sister's real name. That was the one she would use. There was no response. "It's me, Fen. It's your sister. I've come for you."

The rags moved. The child was so dirty it was hard to discern her from the cell itself. But Fen saw eyes that stared with fear. A thin, pale face. *It's not her!* This girl didn't look familiar at all. She was certain it was her cell. Was Mei Mei dead?

Then the child half-crawled into the light. Her face was thinner but it was now familiar. Mei Mei! She looked older. Her sister stepped onto the dirty straw. Fen wrapped her up in her arms.

"Mei Mei," she repeated.

May returned the hug, weakly. Fen scooped her up and was amazed at how easy she was to carry. She had grown lighter. "The Queen is dead," Fen said. "You are safe, dear sister. Safe."

"Are you truly here?" May asked. "Is this real?"

"Yes, it is." Fen carried her up the stairs and Marcus joined her partway up. Other prisoners bumped past them as they fled to freedom.

"Is Mom outside?" May asked.

Fen bit her lip. Had the Queen hurt May's mind? Or was she hallucinating? "Don't worry about that right now. You are safe. Safe." There would be time to explain everything. She brought May through the long hall and into the sunlight.

There were no more Queen's guards and no signs of any struggle. That, Fen found truly frightening.

"So you have found her." Mansren was standing near the door, the shirkers gazing lovingly toward him. "Our pact is done. You have served me well, Nong Fu Fen."

"And what will you do now?" she asked.

"There is a judging tone to your voice, Fen. I don't like it."

"I deserve to know." Her voice was steady. She saw, out of the corner of her eye, that Marcus had moved closer to her. He had his hand on his sword hilt.

"You want to understand what you wrought, do you?" He gestured in a circle. "I will raze this city. It is a symbol of her. Then I will build my own city and name it Mansentium." He grinned, showing his red teeth. "Actually, that would be a stupid name. There is plenty of time to find the right one. A new name for Illium, too, of course. I will destroy her roads and build my own. All roads will lead here, so that every mortal can easily crawl to me with their supplications."

Fen hugged May closer. "You would turn us all into slaves?"

"Do you call the horse you trained a slave? The oxen? Or the sheep you slaughter?"

"We are more than sheep," she said.

"You are not. And I know I will soon grow bored. I will raise even vaster armies and cross the oceans and conquer the lands there. That should entertain me for millenniums to come."

"So we are only here to entertain you?" she asked.

"This conversation is growing tiresome. I have some affection for you since you carried me out of the forge, but I no longer have patience. You have your sister. Your Queen's guard. Return to your village and live your life."

"You promised you wouldn't harm Marcus or May or Ithak." There was a growing sensation in her hand as she spoke, gentle but insistent. As if it were reminding her that it was there.

"And I will not harm them. I always keep my promises."

"And does that hold true no matter what happens in the future?" There was a fire in her blood. No, something stronger than fire. As though her body were feeling the life she had. A life he had not created. A life that belonged to her.

"Fen . . ." Marcus said. And she wondered if he guessed her intentions.

"That's a curious question. I am my word. So the answer is yes."

She handed May to Marcus, and he took her easily, but May held on to her sister, pulling on her shoulder.

"No, Fen, no," May whispered. "No. No."

It was hard to do, but Fen stepped away from her sister and broke her grip. She was face to face with Mansren now. "I have to stop you, Mansren," Fen said, though her voice was tired.

"You've gone mad, child. Remember, I made no promise to spare your life." He smirked.

She planted each foot in the dust. No, deeper: below the road. Into the soil itself. Her arm, the wooden hand, was alive and was willing, and she raised it. Mansren still had that smirk on his face. Perhaps she could wipe it off.

"Don't be a martyr," he warned. "In my world, they will all be ground to dust."

She grabbed his arm with her wooden hand. How she loved

that new hand. How powerful it was. How much a part of her it had become. She felt the strength of her magic reach down into the ground, into her depths, and pull and push and burst forth from her through that hand. As if the very roots were reaching to the deepest parts of the earth. Perhaps even to the forest of Helwood itself.

Mansren tried to pull his arm away but failed. "How can this be? Release me. Now."

Her hand was growing, the leaves and vines shooting up his arm, across his chest. He turned his head, his eyes flaming, bringing to bear his magic on her. The branches snapped and burned and flames ran along her flesh, but Fen gritted her teeth. For the wood was growing faster and faster. Bark encasing him, wrapping around him as she rooted deeper and deeper into the earth. The trees outside the city, the fields, the rice, the ancient old ones of Helwood, each of them found her. Sent their growing energy. Their patience. She willed that energy, that growth out of her. Out of the ground and into him, around him. Encasing him.

Imprisoning him.

"Stop," he commanded, but she thought she heard a desperate tone. "Desist, child!" The vines grew into his mouth. And she was aware of his shirkers coming closer, but the branches shot out, forcing them back. Soon Mansren was bound to this spot, rooted and completely overgrown. Would it be enough? She thought of Mei Mei, of Marcus, living in a world without Mansren. Of all the people who would be free. As long as Mansren was bound.

To be certain they were safe, Fen decided she had to give over her life, her spirit, everything that was her. Anchor herself deep into the ground like roots holding him there. Roots that would forever grow each time he struggled, each time he tried to escape. Her life was ebbing out of her through her hand and trapping him. The light dimmed as the branches thickened around them both. Mansren stopped struggling, though she sensed his anger underneath that wood. But she was bigger than that anger. Older. More patient.

And still the branches grew.

"No!"

It was not Mansren's voice. It took her a moment to recognize it. Her thoughts were getting slower, more tree-like. But it was Marcus who had shouted.

He was swinging his sword. At her? At the branches? It didn't matter, it was too late.

Too late.

Her death was near. For whatever was working through her was more than her mortal body could contain. She gave herself over to it. Gave herself up.

The sacrifice was worth it. Her sister would be safe. Marcus would be safe. Every mortal would be safe.

Then she felt a familiar pain. A childhood pain, in her right arm.

The pain of a part of her being cut free.

CHAPTER THIRTY-SEVEN

ALL IN
A NAME

THE SUNLIGHT CAME THROUGH THE OPEN WINDOW ON the second floor of the inn. This particular window had never seen direct sunlight before, but since there were no longer walls to block it, the sun inched across the room and lit a bed. Slowly, the light made a young woman's eyelids move. She stirred. Moaned. Said something in a language that no one else in the room understood.

"Fen," a girl said. "Fen. Are you awake?"

Fen opened her eyes. Brought her hand up to block the light but failed. It took her several moments to understand there was no hand on that arm. Only bandages. And it hurt. It hurt so much. She lowered the stump, lifted her left hand and cupped it above her eyes. This time she succeeded in stopping the sun from blinding her.

Mei Mei stood beside the bed. Her face looked thinner than Fen remembered. Her hair needed a good trimming and several good washings. She was dressed in trousers and a thick sweater.

Standing behind her was a tall white-skinned man in grey clothing. She didn't recognize the stranger and assumed he was from Regentium. He had the symbol of a pestle on his shoulder—so she knew he was some sort of physician.

"She is awake," the man said. "And responding well. She will live." Then he turned to her. "You have saved us."

Another shadow moved into the light, and it took several moments for her to recognize Marcus. He was wearing a brown cloak and his hair looked much darker. It needed a wash, too, she decided. His blade was still on his belt, his hand resting on it.

"What happened?" she asked. She raised her right arm to look at it.

"I'm sorry for the injury I caused," Marcus said.

"You cut it off?" She had a vague memory of that moment. Of seeing his blade out of the corner of her eye. Or was that a memory from a long time ago?

"I could not let you go," he said. "You mean too much to me."

Fen found the strength to smile at this comment and then said, "But if you did it, then is Mansren . . . Is he free?"

Marcus shook his head. "Your hand still holds Mansren. Still grows green."

She felt an ache. That sense of power—of connection and completeness—that her wooden hand had given her was gone. She pulled a lock of her hair forward to discover it was turning dark. Her natural colour.

"She will not go septic," the physician said. "Her arm looks as if it will heal well. The wood, the wildmagic, won't return."

She knew instantly he was correct. There was no sense of

the vines, of the green power that had been part of her for so long. It was all gone now. Along with whatever magic came with it. She was . . . she was just Fen. She had given up one of the greatest gifts of her life. She wanted to stretch out her mind and make her hand grow, as it had before.

But then she looked at Mei Mei. Her sister was watching her quietly. Had the prison changed her? Fen reached out her left hand.

"Take me to the window, little sister," she said.

Mei Mei came to her and pulled her up, and with Marcus's help, Fen got out of bed. She leaned on his shoulder and they led her to the window.

The great walls were gone. "What remained of the battlements fell down overnight," Marcus said. "The tower too. And the forge of the Red Artificers. The Queen's Guard's barracks. All gone. Even the shirkers vanished."

In the courtyard below was a huge collection of rubble. In one clear section stood a wooden statue. There were branches pointing every which way and growing toward the heavens.

It was Mansren. Fen felt him raging in his wooden cage. Alive. But bound forever, she hoped. As long as that tree kept growing.

A small man was on his knees before the tree that was Mansren.

"It's Ithak," Marcus said. "He hasn't moved since yesterday."

"I hope he'll forgive me one day," she said.

She looked out the window to the south. She could see a long way. Much of the city was rubble. But beyond it in the distance, the land was green. She would take the time to travel and talk to the people of the other villages. There would be Zhuang and Berbers and Kush . . . she didn't know all the names. She would discover them. Maybe if Ithak did forgive her, he would show her where that librarian had lived. They could find the old knowledge again.

The Chin language stirred in her brain. A language she should soon start to teach. There would be time for that too. And time to travel home to rebuild her family hut. And to make a paper dragon and, along with Mei Mei, to burn it in memory of their mother. It was a tradition she had taught Fen. A tradition Fen would keep alive.

She glanced at her arm and thought, *I am Fen of the One Hand again*. But immediately she knew she was wrong. That wasn't her name anymore. That wasn't who she was.

You are more than Fen. Her mother had told her that a thousand times.

"I am Nong Fu Fen," she said aloud. Her name echoed in the room. The sound carried out the window as though a bell had been tolled.

ACKNOWLEDGEMENTS

CREATING A WORLD OUT OF NOTHING IS SO MUCH EASIER when one has help. I'd like to thank Suzanne Sutherland, Derek Mah and Marty Chan for helping me find the story's magic. I also want to thank the Saskatchewan Arts Board for its kind support.